A LIGHT
IN THE
WINDOW

BOOKS BY MARION KUMMEROW

Not Without My Sister

To all the brave people standing up for justice and humanity

CHAPTER 1

Margarete was preparing dinner when the air raid warning went off. She turned off the stove and hurried down the staircase heading for the basement, when her employer pushed past her.

"These bloody English bombers!" he shouted and shoved Margarete aside. She stumbled, but he was so intent on saving himself he didn't falter once in his steps. His wife was ahead of him, rushing down the stairs and screaming for their daughter to hurry.

Once she managed to get up again, she grabbed on to the stair railing and had made it down to the first floor when the world around her exploded. Something hit her head, and she lifted her arms to protect herself from the searing pain, even as she stumbled and fell to the floor.

Debilitating pain.

Blackness.

Some time later, Margarete came to. She opened her heavy lids, trying to remember what had happened. There was dust and rubble everywhere. The sirens were still screaming. She moved her head and a searing pain shot through it. Raising a hand to her temple, she pulled it away, terrified at the bright red stain of blood on her fingertips.

Dust from the debris made it hard to breathe and she coughed, sending throbbing pain through her head and neck each time.

Oh yes, something hit me. Slowly she took stock of her position, relieved when she could move her legs and arms. One arm hurt like hell, making her hand almost useless, but otherwise she seemed unharmed.

Looking above, she slowly drew her knees up and pushed herself into a sitting position with her good arm. The dust slowly settled and she got a clearer look at where she was—trapped beneath part of the staircase. Apparently it had broken into two halves and formed something of a small cave, which she now tried to crawl out of.

Margarete spent long moments pushing with her feet to move the collapsed building materials enough to gain her freedom. Every movement sent twinges to her head, but she kept struggling.

Once out of her cave, she gasped at the picture of utter destruction around her. The entire building had collapsed, the roof tiles scattered around like pebbles. It was eerily silent. She crawled over a collapsed wall, swallowing convulsively when she saw the dead bodies of her employers Herr and Frau Huber lying a mere ten feet from the entrance to the basement.

Giving the corpses a wide berth, she crawled toward the opening in the wall to leave this ruin, when she suddenly stared into their daughter's lifeless eyes. That awful girl had tormented her with anti-Jewish slurs and hostile acts ever since Margarete had started to work for her parents. Now she was dead. Her corpse was blocking the only access to the outside, and Margarete paused for a moment to gather up her courage.

Despite the awful situation, she couldn't help but think the world would be a much better place without Annegret Huber. Just as she determined to climb over the corpse, the sound of a whining child captured her attention. She turned her head to look for the source of the noise. A young boy, around six years of age, was crying and pushing at the boards which pinned his leg in place. She'd seen the son of the gardener around the house before, numerous times, but she wasn't inclined to help anyone but herself. Especially not a Nazi boy.

Margarete had crawled halfway over the pile of debris toward Annegret's body when her conscience stopped her. *Damn*! She looked back at the whining child. Terror and pain were etched on his face. Sighing, she made her way over to him and began removing the boards that had trapped his leg. None of this was his fault; he was only a child.

As she removed the last board, she heard the sounds of the rescue team coming. "In here. We're alive," she called out as loudly as she could manage.

"Can you make it out of the building?" a voice shouted right back.

"I think so," she answered, cradling her injured arm against her stomach. It was throbbing fiercely after she'd been forced to use both hands to remove the last board. She closed her eyes for a moment and breathed, before she was able to point at the pile of debris with Annegret's body and asked the young boy, "Can you climb with me over that?"

He nodded, still sobbing, with his face covered in dirt and the tracks of his tears. Margarete flashed him a crooked smile and nodded. "Good. Let's go then."

They carefully made their way over the broken timbers that had once supported the roof, the little boy holding on to her skirt while following closely behind her. Annegret's face stared at her, her body covered by a layer of dust and her legs twisted unnaturally. The thought of climbing over the girl's dead body made Margarete want to vomit, but it was the only way out. As horrible as it was, she and the young boy would have to make their way up and across the lifeless body, or risk becoming two more casualties of this war.

She pulled and pushed the boy, telling him to keep his eyes on the exit and not think about anything else. Trying to follow her own advice, she crawled over the dead girl, when she saw something peeking out of her jacket pocket. A piece of paper.

"Go ahead. The rescue team is waiting for you. Make sure they look at your leg."

"What about you?" he asked, darting a glance at Annegret's face in horror. "Is she…?"

"I'll check her out, then I'll be right behind you. Go on now." She waited until he was moving toward the exit once again, and then she reached for the paper. It was Annegret's identification card. Curious, she read what it said: Annegret Huber, born June 28, 1921 in Berlin. Two years younger than Margarete. Long light brown hair and hazel eyes, just like herself.

She tucked the identification card into her pocket, before she climbed over the dead body. The boy had stopped to wait for her instead of moving on.

"Where's the girl?" he asked and glanced at her with frightened eyes.

"I couldn't help her. She was already dead. Let's get out of here."

But he refused to move and stared at her wide-eyed. "Why are you so nice to me? You are a Jew." He pointed at her and Margarete looked down to see the yellow star sewn onto her jacket. The feel of the identification card still at her fingertips, she realized this was her chance to survive. Tell the rescue team she was her employer's daughter. But for the ruse to work, she had to get rid of the yellow star.

She pulled the jacket with the abhorred mark from her shoulders and stuttered, "It… it was a stupid game. This *Judenstern* belongs to the dead girl. She was our maid."

Shocked by her own boldness, she stood there in awe, until the boy poked her. "You should get your own jacket then, or nobody will believe you."

Whether he understood she was about to lie her way out of this or not, he'd just given her a great idea. "You're right. Wait here for a minute. I'll grab my jacket and purse."

Back at Annegret's corpse she pulled the girl's jacket and purse from where they lay half buried beneath her body, placed her own papers into Annegret's pocket and finally pinned the yellow star to the sleeve of Annegret's blouse.

Now she is Margarete Rosenbaum and I'm Annegret Huber. God, please forgive me.

CHAPTER 2

December 1941 Paris, France

Wilhelm Huber stared at the ringing telephone with disdain. It was two minutes to five and he had no intention in getting tangled up in extra work that would delay his quitting time. Especially not tonight, when he'd finally sourced tickets for the coveted new nightclub performance at the Moulin Rouge. Since attending one of the shows that featured can-can dances and raucous songs had been included on a must-see list for German soldiers on a recreational visit to Paris, it had become almost impossible to make reservations.

Ignoring the phone, he neatly piled the last correspondence from the large stack he'd been working on and then leaned back in his chair with a sigh, wishing the insistent caller would hang up. For a moment Wilhelm considered picking up the receiver, but the chiming of a church bell saved him. Five o'clock. Public office hours were over and the caller would just have to try again in the morning.

He got up to put the correspondence in the card-index cabinet, locked it, put the key into the drawer of his desk, locked that one as well and tucked this key into his trouser pocket. Before he walked through the door, he glanced one last time around the office, making sure everything was immaculate, before he left the drab place with a spring in his step.

"Have a pleasant weekend," he told the French worker in the anteroom, before he half-heartedly saluted the Hitler portrait on the way out.

When he stepped into the street, buzzing with bicycles and pedestrians, he inhaled the city's distinct smell. Others might complain, because they preferred a battle post where they could garner medals and promotions, but for him Paris was a dream come true. The moment he'd first stepped off the train about a year ago, he'd fallen in love with the French capital with its rich supplies of wine, good food and beautiful women.

Apart from all the conveniences it offered, the biggest perk of staying in Paris was the fact that he'd finally gotten away from the stern supervision of his ambitious father. Not to mention his mother, whose uppermost goal was to get him married off and who thus presented him with an incessant line of suitable, albeit boring, women. How much more fun it was to be the cock of the walk amidst marvelous French girls, many of whom seemed eager to please their new masters in every way possible.

The debaucherous nightlife suited him much better than the boring day job in the orderly room of the SS headquarters, and if it had been up to him, he'd have gone without all the military stuff and lived like "God in France" as the German proverb said. But, unfortunately, one thing didn't come without the other.

Walking the short distance to his apartment in the center of Paris, he pondered the one thing that wasn't perfect in his life: his financial situation. The vibrant city offered someone like him everything he could ever wish for, but such luxury came with expenses his salary as SS-Oberscharführer couldn't provide for. He'd have to talk to his father again about another additional allowance. Despite his father's disdain for Wilhelm's extravagant lifestyle, he'd come around with the money. He always did.

Wilhelm greeted the concierge, Madame Badeaux, who seemed to lurk all day in her caretaker office, only to leap at her tenants with an indecent number of nosy questions. At least she wasn't hostile or unfriendly like the one in his last building. He indulged her with some small talk, before excusing himself and rushing up the stairs to his one-bedroom apartment on the third floor, taking three steps at once. He could have taken the elevator, but made it a habit not to since he wanted to stay in shape.

The representative architecture of the Art Nouveau—as the French liked to call the *Jugendstil*—with its stucco ornaments, beautifully carved banister and colorful wall paintings had definitely seen better times.

But with the war going on and their reckless opposition to the German government, French people had neglected their cultural heritage. If only they would see how much better life could be if they worked with their new rulers instead of against them.

He opened the door to his apartment, and walked into the only bedroom, his freshly pressed dress uniform hanging behind the door. At least the laundry woman worked to perfection. He had been lucky to find her, since an impeccable look was of utmost importance. Just as he was buttoning up his tunic, the telephone in his living room rang and he walked over to answer it.

"Wilhelm Huber," he said with a gaze into the giltwood mirror decorated with hydrangeas and lilies that was hanging above the matching cabinet with the telephone. He stood two inches taller than the rest of the family, and the blond hair, greenish-brown eyes, and a sharp nose wielded a magnetic power over women, who usually threw themselves at his feet. Even the small red birthmark beneath his left eye couldn't deter from his good looks, but helped give him a mysterious, brooding appearance. This was enhanced even more by the uniform, which gave him an authoritative touch that only added to his appeal to the opposite sex.

It certainly wasn't the lack of willing potential wives that kept him a bachelor, which was another point where he didn't see eye to eye with his family. They all seemed to think that at the age of twenty-four it was way past time to get married and beget children for the Führer. The begetting wasn't the part he opposed, though, he thought with a smile on his face. He planned on 'working hard' for his Fatherland tonight after the show in the Moulin Rouge.

"Wilhelm, thank God I finally reached you," came a mildly distraught female voice he recognized immediately.

He inwardly groaned and looked at his wristwatch. He'd have to cut her right off, or risk being late for the show. His sister-in-law, Erika, had an annoying habit of drawing out even the simplest message into a lengthy story about all and sundry.

"Erika. I was just on my way out to meet with my boss." He hoped this would be enough of a hint for her to make it short.

Instead of the flippant reply he expected, she said, "I've been calling you at the office, but it seemed you had already left."

So, she had been the incessant caller. His curiosity was piqued. "I was in a work meeting most of the day."

"There was an accident."

"What kind of accident?" The fact that she was calling, and not Reiner, automatically led him to assume something must have happened to his over-achieving older brother who was their father's favorite son, following in his footsteps as he built a stellar career in the SS.

"There was intense bombing last night in Berlin…"

The phone line crackled and Wilhelm barely held onto his patience. "Erika, can you get to the point, please?"

"If you would stop interrupting me," she said indignantly.

"Sorry." He gritted his teeth, knowing from experience that interrupting her would only cause her to lose her train of thought and draw out the conversation even longer, until she finally came to the point. "You were telling me about the bombing last night in Berlin." He rolled his eyes at his own reflection in the mirror, hoping that Erika would tell him whatever the news was before his French mistress, Florence, arrived to go to the show at the Moulin Rouge.

"Yes." Erika paused and he pictured his brother's slender brunette wife, wearing her hair braided pretzel-style over her ears, picking an imaginary dust grain from her drab ankle-length skirt. He had no idea what Reiner saw in her, although sometimes appearances deceived, and maybe she was a firecracker in bed. He had to suppress a loud laugh at the thought of dull Erika riding his brother in ecstasy. It made him think of the plans he had for Florence and him later that night.

"Look, there's no easy way to say this... the bombing... you know how these vile Englishmen are focusing their attacks on residential areas, while our own Luftwaffe only ever attack military targets in London? I mean, what kind of people are the English? First, they won't even consider joining forces with Hitler, when he so graciously offered it to them, and now—"

Another glance at his wristwatch and his patience snapped. "Erika. Please get to the point. I can't keep my boss waiting."

"Since when are you so eager to work overtime?"

Her words offended, especially because they were true. It was only thanks to his father's position and influence that he'd been accepted into the SS, despite his lack of ambition and zeal. In marked contrast to Reiner, who was the textbook example of an ambitious, snappy and obedient SS man, traits that had just recently gained him the promotion to SS-Obersturmführer, the equivalent of a first lieutenant in the Wehrmacht, while Wilhelm was stuck at the rank of technical sergeant.

"I'm always eager to serve my country. Did you want to tell me anything of importance?"

"Well, you clearly don't want it any other way. Your parents are dead," she snapped.

He cocked his head, grimacing at the mirror. What a silly woman, did she really think she could scare him? "Look, Erika, now's not a good time for morbid jokes."

"It's the truth."

"What is the truth?"

"Your parents are both dead. The Englishmen—"

His hand tightened around the receiver and he leaned against the wall, his legs trembling all of a sudden. "No."

"Yes."

"It can't be."

"It is."

"But how?"

"I tried to tell you before you interrupted me several times…" Erika droned on and on about the bombing and their house apparently collapsing, people scrambling outside, rescue teams digging up the injured and dead, but he didn't even listen. He had a clear vision of what must have happened, since he'd witnessed enough bombardments with his own eyes. When his trembling legs wouldn't support the weight of his body any longer, he slowly sank to the floor, grasping the phone receiver like a lifeline.

It was true, he hadn't seen eye to eye with his parents on many issues, and had thanked God every single day for his deployment to Paris, far from their supervision, but that didn't mean he wanted them dead. They were his parents, for crying out loud!

"How dare they?" he screamed into the phone, not sure whom he blamed more for their demise: the English bombers, Hitler who'd started this war, or his parents themselves for being too complacent to leave Berlin for the comparative safety of their country house in Plau am See, about two hours north of the city.

"… I'm sure our Führer will revenge your father's death and send those nasty Englishmen a message."

"He will?" Wilhelm's brain had stopped thinking coherent thoughts, such was the unexpected grief mixed with anger washing over him.

"Poor Reiner is devastated. He's already begun taking over your father's responsibilities," Erika said.

"No doubt he's got his eye on Father's position." It wouldn't be above Reiner to seize the opportunity with both hands and put himself ahead for the race in the promotion carousel that would inevitably follow.

"How dare you say that? Everything he does is for the good of our family. Your good, too."

He didn't want to fight with her, since the horrible news had drained all energy from him. Therefore he kept quiet, trying to process what had happened. Then a worrisome thought entered his mind.

"What about Annegret?" His twenty-year-old sister had lived with their parents, spoiled rotten by his father.

"I'm sure she's fine." Erika's voice sounded much too chirpy.

"What do you mean, you're sure?"

"They haven't found her body, and since the bombing happened just before dinner time yesterday, she would have been out and about. You know how she is." The condemnation was loud and clear. Annegret craved life. She often frequented nightclubs and, despite her mother's attempts to make a good German mother and wife of her, she engaged in very unladylike behaviors, smoking being the most harmless one. But since Father had never been able to refuse his daughter anything, she did as she pleased.

"By the time you're here, she'll have shown up."

"I'm where?" Wilhelm had difficulty following.

"In Berlin, of course. Reichsführer Himmler has arranged for a state funeral to honor your father's sacrifice for our Great Fatherland."

"I can't just up and leave. I have work to do."

Erika gave an exasperated sigh. "That's the very reason I'm calling you. To give you enough time to arrange for your travels. The funeral will be a week from today and it wouldn't look good if you were absent."

He had been looking forward to spending the holiday season in Paris, immersed in the buzzing nightlife, eating and drinking too much, with one or more beautiful women hanging from his arm. The parties thrown by SS and Wehrmacht officers were legendary. But with the death of both his parents, who wanted to party anyway? He could as well travel to Berlin and meet old friends.

"I'll see to everything." He disconnected the call, staring blankly at the wall. How fast life could change. In the blink of an eye, he'd become an orphan although... a mollifying thought rose in his mind. Inheriting his share of Father's vast fortunes would rid him of all monetary problems once and for all. At least something good would come out of this tragedy. He lapsed into memories and flinched when the doorbell rang.

Sighing, he stood up and opened the door. At any other time, the sight of Florence's perky bosom, indecently flaunted by the low neckline of her evening gown, would have stirred his loins, but today he only gave her a tired smile and said, "We can't go."

Her beautiful brown eyes filled with disappointment and he shrugged turning around to let her see herself out. But then he thought better of it, retrieved the two Moulin Rouge tickets from his breast pocket and held them out to her. "Go with a friend of yours."

She quickly took the offered tickets, dutifully pressed her curvaceous body against his as a way to say thanks and then disappeared as quickly as she had arrived. His heart became even more weary. While he'd never pretended to be in love with her, he wouldn't have minded the company of a compassionate soul right now.

CHAPTER 3

Leipzig, Germany

Margarete Rosenbaum nervously picked at the woolen jacket she was wearing. It was the finest thing she'd ever owned, although strictly speaking it wasn't hers. It belonged to the dead girl she was impersonating.

Annegret wouldn't be nervous, she told herself. Holding her head high and giving that haughty look she'd seen so often on Annegret's face, she pushed through the doors of the university library and stopped in her tracks, gasping.

The Bibliotheca Albertina, as the Leipzig University Library was called in honor of King Albert of Saxony, was already impressive on the outside, but the majestic entrance hall took her breath away. The floor was laid with dark brown parquet contrasting beautifully with the cream walls and white columns. To both sides of the hallway, glass doors led to separate rooms, while in the middle a sweeping staircase led up to the second floor that was completely surrounded by a gallery.

Margarete had never seen such beautiful architecture and it reminded her faintly of pictures of Greek temples. It was amazing that in Hitler's Germany there were still buildings with such innocent beauty. Remembering why she was here, she walked straight into the office behind the first door to the left.

"How can I help you?" the elderly woman with graying hair tied into a bun at the nape of her head, asked.

"I'm Annegret Huber. I'm supposed to work here."

She and Heidi both knew it was a big risk, but they needed to register Annegret to receive ration cards for her, and when doing so, she thought she may as well go to the labor office and ask for a job. Since Margarete had never learned anything other than being a housemaid, there hadn't been many choices. But the woman at the labor office had been sympathetic and offered her the job as assistant librarian.

"Oh wonderful, you're the girl the employment office has sent us. I can't tell you how badly we need help."

Margarete was used to hard work, since she had toiled for two years like a slave in the Huber household. She involuntarily put up her arm to cover the yellow star on her chest, when she remembered she wasn't a Jew anymore. At least not outwardly. She was now a Nazi brat named Annegret Huber, a girl who'd never worked a single minute of her life.

She would have to find a balance between believably impersonating spoilt Annegret and the need to keep the job at the library, since Aunt Heidi—who risked her own life by letting Margarete live with her—couldn't provide for two people with her modest salary working in a grocery shop. Margarete hoped being away from Berlin, in a new city where nobody knew Annegret—or her—would help in this endeavor.

"I've never worked in a library before," Margarete said.

"Well, we'll get you up to speed in no time at all. I'm Frau Merz by the way." The woman reached out her hand and it took Margarete a few seconds to process what she wanted. As a Jew she wasn't allowed to shake hands with Aryans.

"Thank you so much, I'll do my best," Margarete said as she took the proffered hand. It was a peculiar feeling to be appreciated.

Normally the best she could hope for was people ignoring her, but more often than not, she received derision and insult. Passers-by hurled insults, hateful glances and even dirt or stones at her. She bit on her lip, calling herself to order. If anyone suspected the truth of her identity, she'd be arrested and shipped away to some place of unspeakable horrors.

Frau Merz put a sign that read "Back in 5 minutes" on the reception desk and then led Margarete through the breathtaking entrance hall to one of the reading rooms that was lined with paintings of grim-looking old men, presumably scholars who'd taught at the University of Leipzig since its inauguration in 1409. A few dozen students were sitting in the reading room, their desks loaded with high stacks of books.

She barely had time to take in the sight, because Frau Merz was walking fast through the room until she reached another door that said, "Employees Only."

She opened it and they walked down into the basement that was directly beneath the reading room and probably of the same size. But instead of a huge empty space with desks for students, this room was filled with hundreds of shelves, each of them overflowing with books. Piles of books were stacked on the floor, leaving just enough room for a lithe person to slip through.

"You like our book depository?" The love and pride of a true librarian shone in Frau Merz's eyes.

"It is… overwhelming." To tell the truth, Margarete had never seen that many books in one place. She remembered her time as a little girl, barely able to read, when she'd first visited a library with her mother. Later, when she'd started secondary school she had frequently spent entire afternoons soaking up the wonders of being among that many books. But that had been many years ago, before the Nazis had forbidden the Jews to use public libraries. Automatically she raised her hand once more to finger the hated yellow star on her chest, until she realized again it wasn't there. She had left that identity behind in the rubble of the destroyed house in Berlin.

"We just received a truckload of books from two Jewish owners." Frau Merz's voice didn't betray any emotion. "Your first task will be to sort them into our system and divide them into three piles: the valuable *volkstümliche* books that will later be put onto the shelves, while books on the index card here have to be set aside for destruction, and any subversive or demoralizing literature must be segregated into a locked area, where only politically reliable people are allowed to peruse them for scientific purposes."

Margarete looked at her with wide eyes. She'd never once thought the Nazis disdain for literature that didn't conform to their ideology would extend to scientific libraries like this one, and required the actual destruction of books. She almost felt sorry for the poor volumes who'd soon end up on the pyre, their pages burning in the raging fire, their content irrecoverably lost.

"If you have problems classifying one of the books, you can always ask me." Frau Merz pressed a huge catalog into her hand. "Write down any and all books in here. And," she paused for a moment, scrutinizing Margarete, "I know the temptation is huge, but you mustn't under any circumstances look inside the banned books. They are banned for a reason and a young girl like you, who is not yet solidified in her mental development, might be swayed by the lies they spew and take them at face value."

"Thank you, Frau Merz. I would certainly never read any of those abominable things." Margarete did her best to keep a straight face. She'd always read above her age and many of her favorite books from before the Nazis came to power had been put on the blacklist. What horrible things was a reader to learn from a book condemning war, like *All Quiet on the Western Front* by Erich Maria Remarque? Certainly nothing that was worse than the actual war Hitler had started, or the internal war against an entire part of the German people: the Jews.

"Which our Führer was wise enough to forbid." With these words, Frau Merz walked up the stairs, leaving Margarete alone in the basement. Alone with thousands of books.

Since working as a maid for the Huber family she hadn't touched a book, except for dusting them off. Herr Huber had always insisted that subhumans like her were better off working than getting ideas above their station. She wouldn't have had time to read anyway, because Frau Huber worked her to the bone. Margarete woke at five in the morning to prepare breakfast for her masters, before she spent the day washing floors, scrubbing laundry, doing the dishes, grocery shopping, sweeping, cooking and whatever else was needed until late at night after the family had gone to bed. Then she fell exhausted on the shabby mattress in the walk-in storage cupboard behind the kitchen she called her room.

Much as she disliked the Hubers, she was most wary of their twenty-year-old daughter. Beautiful, energetic and fun-loving Annegret could be the sweetest girl around friends, or when charming her father to indulge her every wish. But she also had a dark side, one she showed only to Margarete, who was just two years older than her, at every chance she got. That despicable girl had not only internalized Hitler's racial ideology, but had added her own streak of cruelty to it with her hateful slurs, like only last week when she had *accidentally* tripped over the bucket of water while Margarete was on her knees mopping the floor.

"Useless trash, look what you did! Wallowing in filth like a pig." Then she'd walked through the puddle and through every room in the house with her dirty shoes, returning with that vile grin on the face Margarete hated so much. "That'll teach you to dawdle. I'll tell my father to replace you with someone who actually works."

And now I'm her. The vilest girl on earth. Margarete shuddered, and quickly started sorting the books, since she didn't want to give Frau Merz any reason to complain.

"Fräulein Huber, have you taken a break for lunch yet?" Frau Merz suddenly stood beside her, giving an appreciative glance at the stacks of books. "You have sorted these, already?"

"Yes. And that small pile over there are books that were neither in the catalog nor on the list of banned books. I didn't want to disturb you with questions every time, so I collected them. I hope that was alright?"

"I'm amazed. Seems like the work office got it right this time. You can't imagine the kind of girls they've been sending me. Silly, spoiled girls, unwilling to work."

Margarete thought it better not to reply.

"You can take your lunch break right now and we'll go through them later. Come, I'll show you the kitchen."

Once there, Margarete retrieved the *Henkelmann*, the lunch box Aunt Heidi had packed for her that morning. The metal thermos box consisted of two containers stacked on top of each other: the lower one contained soup and the upper one two slices of bread, which was more than she'd usually eaten in a day in the Hubers' household. While the family ate well, she was supposed to live on the leftovers scraped off their plates.

Her stomach rumbled and she sat down to dunk the hard bread into the soup, before spooning the liquid into her mouth. Before the war, Aunt Heidi would never have allowed such uncouth behavior, but since her Jewish husband—Margarete's uncle—had been arrested for subversion, she had to pay the rent all by herself. She barely scraped by and never wasted a single morsel of food, so yesterday's hard bread crusts were softened in the soup. At least Margarete's salary as assistant librarian would help alleviate the monetary situation, even if she'd brought a whole slew of other problems into her beloved aunt's home.

In the afternoon, Frau Merz told her to take a break from sorting the books and learn how to work at the book lending counter. "We have a small inventory of publicly available books for the students, but for most books they need to come here, ask for the author or title and you will go to the inventory room to get it for them. If a book is listed as *geheim* or *gesperrt*, then this book is segregated and the person will have to show you their university identification and sign a list with their name, position, and for which scientific purpose they are in need to read that… piece of writing." Frau Merz seemed truly repulsed at the notion someone could actually open and read the books deemed harmful by the Nazi regime.

Margarete nodded.

"Unfortunately, there are sometimes elements who try to get their hands on these harmful writings without a just cause. As I said before, the temptation is big and young people can be so easily swayed. You must first take their name and address, and then tell them the book is currently not available."

"What happens to them?" Margarete asked.

"Nothing. We just keep that list and give it to the National Library, where the Gestapo has a dedicated office that keeps an eye on the inventory and its lawful usage."

Margarete swallowed hard. The list would go straight to the Gestapo, and Frau Merz believed nothing would happen to those people? If they were lucky, they'd get away with a simple interrogation and a warning that the next time wouldn't be so pleasant—at least that's what Herr Huber always said when boasting to his friends about how the SS used the Gestapo to get rid of people without dirtying their own hands.

A shudder rushed down her spine at the implications of her actions. She might just send one poor lad into the Gestapo's claws. Even though the real Annegret would dance with glee if she were still alive and got the opportunity to rat out undesirable elements of society, Margarete simply couldn't do what was expected of her.

That night she returned home to her aunt with a heavy heart.

"How was your day, Margarete?" Heidi asked.

"Good." There was no reason to involve Heidi in this.

But over dinner, a delicious potato casserole with carrots, Margarete picked at her food despite being hungry.

"It doesn't look like everything's just fine."

Margarete gave a heavy sigh. "It's not. At first the new job was great. I spent most of the day in the basement sorting books into good, undesirable and outright dangerous." She cocked her head, seeking her aunt's gaze. "Just like they sort us humans into good, undesirable and dangerous."

Heidi's hand came to lay on hers and she felt the warmth, the love, but also the desperation. Her aunt was a chatty, friendly woman of forty-five years. As a young girl she'd fallen in love with an equally young boy and they got married in 1915, three months before he'd been sent off to the Great War, from where he'd never returned.

Heidi had been devastated by the loss of her first love, and hadn't found love again until more than a decade later when she'd met Ernst, the younger brother of Margarete's father. Heidi's family had been dead set against her marrying a Jew, even an assimilated one, but at the age of thirty, she hadn't given two hoots about her family's permission and had gone ahead and married Ernst.

Faint memories of their wedding popped into Margarete's head. The beautiful bride, the cheerful atmosphere, and her own princess-like dress as she walked down the aisle, strewing flowers for the bridal couple.

Ernst and Heidi had been the happiest couple Margarete had known, but unfortunately they'd never been blessed with children of their own. Despite the fact that many couples who waited until a later age struggled to conceive, malicious gossip among Heidi's family and so-called friends had it that it was her divine punishment for marrying outside her race and later taken it as proof for the rightfulness of the Nuremberg Laws when they were introduced.

Of course, back then, Margarete hadn't known about any of that and she'd enjoyed her frequent visits to Aunt Heidi and Uncle Ernst to the fullest. It had always been such fun to be with them and, for once, Margarete didn't have to share the attention with her three older siblings.

"It's only books, dear," Heidi said, resting her warm blue eyes on Margarete.

"But it's not! They expect me to write down everyone who asks for one of the forbidden books and at the end of the week this list is given to the Gestapo for further use."

Heidi paled, no doubt thinking about her beloved husband, but her voice was steady as she talked again. "The Albertina is a scientific library, so surely everyone asking for these books will have a viable reason to read them, and nothing will happen to them. It'll just be a formality."

Margarete shook her head. "A formality that will surely lead to problems for some people on the list. And it will be me who delivered them to the henchman."

"You can't talk like that. Anyone with a bit of common sense knows not to ask for a forbidden book without a valid reason."

"And what if they don't?"

"Then they must have been sleeping for the past eight years. You and I, we can't overthrow this system."

"But I don't want to be a part of it either!" Margarete got up and left her half-eaten portion on the table. Heidi should have it. Unfortunately the apartment was too small to give her aunt a wide berth. Margarete didn't even have a room to herself, but slept on the sofa in the living room. Agitated, she grabbed her coat—Heidi's coat actually, because Margarete had arrived at her aunt's house with nothing more than the clothes on her back—and went outside into the cold December night.

Walking briskly in the city darkened by the blackout, she didn't feel the icy wind burning her face and tugging at her clothes. She didn't even feel her legs becoming numb from the cold, nor the tears of rage running down her face. Faking being a Nazi girl was more horrible than she could have ever imagined. At least as the Jewish maid in the Huber household, nobody had expected anything of her other than submission and deference, certainly not to step up and denounce fellow citizens.

Despite the sorrow weighing heavily on her heart, she couldn't help but notice how peaceful Leipzig seemed to be. She passed several policemen and SS patrols, but none of them so much as glimpsed in her direction. For the first time in years, she felt safe walking in the streets and didn't have to hunch her head between her shoulders in an attempt to become invisible. No passers-by hurled insults at her, and one woman even cast her a smile and said: "Good evening."

Slowly, the rage settled down, and she came to realize that her own freedom and safety came at a price. She still struggled with the implications, but vowed that she would find a way to keep up appearances while not actively harming other people. For now, she returned to Aunt Heidi's place with the knowledge that she would go back to the library the next day, or else she might raise suspicions and endanger not only her own life, but also her aunt's. Heidi was already in a precarious situation herself, having married a Jew, and she'd even gone so far as to shedding his name, Rosenbaum, for her less conspicuous maiden name Berger.

CHAPTER 4

That had to have been the worst train ride Wilhelm had ever experienced. For financial reasons he'd opted to travel second-class and had regretted this decision from the moment the train had pulled out of the train station Gare de l'Est.

He gritted his teeth as someone shoved into his side once more. The train was bursting at the seams with boisterous soldiers going home for Christmas, as well as the odd civilian squeezed in amongst them. He'd given up his seat about an hour ago for a young mother with two small children and taken a flip-up seat in the gangway, where he, along with many others, was an obstacle to the movement of ever-more passengers, constantly having to jump up to let people with oversized luggage pass. A veritable trip from hell. If Reiner weren't so stingy, he would have given him an advance on his inheritance and sent him a first-class ticket to Berlin.

It had been difficult enough to convince his superior to give him leave so shortly before the holidays. Wilhelm unconsciously sat straighter, remembering the conversation with SS-Obersturmführer Bicke the morning after Erika's phone call.

He'd walked inside the huge corner office that was so much nicer than his own drab room overlooking the main street from a single window, and had patiently waited, after saluting with the required enthusiasm and a ramrod straight spine, eyes focused on Hitler's portrait on the wall behind the man sitting at the desk.

"Oberscharführer. What do you want?"

"Herr Obersturmführer, I'm most distraught having to inform you that my father, Standartenführer Wolfgang Huber, has perished along with my mother in a vicious attack by British bombers."

Bicke looked up from his papers. "I'm sorry to hear this, your father was one of the most respected men in the Reich."

"Yes, he was a true hero." Wilhelm added a trace of pride to his voice, in an effort to show that he saw his parents' death not as a personal tragedy but as a heroic sacrifice for the Führer. Grief-stricken mothers had been arrested for lamenting the death of their fallen sons: he wouldn't make the same mistake. A good German never showed weakness, especially not in the eye of adversity. "Reichsführer Himmler is of the same opinion and has arranged a state funeral for my father. As the second son, my presence is, if not insisted upon, highly encouraged."

"Hmm." Bicke took up a gold-plated fountain pen and played with it. "You are aware that we're short-staffed as it is?"

"Yes, Herr Obersturmführer." Half of the staff would be on furlough for Christmas and New Year.

"I understand your need to honor your father, but this is a very inconvenient time to request furlough. How am I supposed to run the Paris headquarters without staff? The French are only too willing to exploit every little weakness we show, and I wouldn't put it past the resistance to launch a major operation if they believe we won't be able to react promptly."

While Wilhelm had looked forward to spending the holiday season in the vibrant city of Paris, he'd nevertheless made it look like a sacrifice he'd been willing to make for the sake of his superior—all with a possible promotion early next year in mind. This was a slight setback to his plan of endearing himself to Bicke, but he'd already thought of a solution that would serve them both.

"May I make a suggestion?" Wilhelm asked.

"Go ahead."

"The funeral isn't until next week, but if I could leave tomorrow, that would give me time to arrange everything and then return well before Christmas and pick up the slack for those leaving on furlough." Wilhelm closely observed his superior's facial expression and added for good measure, "Of course I'd be available during the holidays as well, if needed, to make up for any work that might have been neglected during my absence."

Bicke nodded very slowly. "Very well. If that is the case, I'll sign your papers. Two weeks starting today, not a single minute longer." He screwed open the precious fountain pen in his hand, took a furlough form from one of the drawers in his desk, filled and signed it right away. "Here you go."

"Thank you so much, Herr Obersturmführer. You can count on me." With another fervent "Heil Hitler" and a masterful clicking of his heels, Wilhelm left the office with his travel permit in hand. He didn't actually relish going home, but the least he could do to honor his parents was to be present when they were buried.

A jostle to his thigh brought him back to the present. The train had stopped in Strasbourg and SS border patrols entered to check on everyone's documents. After a glance at his uniform, they gave his ID and travel documents only a perfunctory glance.

"Coming home for Christmas, Herr Oberscharführer?" one of the lads asked him.

"Yes," he said graciously, since there was no need to enlighten the corporal about his personal issues.

"How's life in Paris?"

"Not sunshine and roses. The French Résistance is quite unreasonable in their opposition to the German master race, but we're showing them every day how traitors are treated."

"Well done," the young corporal answered. "Although... have you heard that the Americans have entered the war?"

Wilhelm believed he heard a note of anxiety in the younger man's voice, although the lad was trained too well to actually voice any concern over war matters. No doubt was permitted that Germany would come out of it victorious and stronger than ever before.

"Of course I heard it, since it's been all over the radio. Paris is not the end of the world and we stay on top of the news." He inserted the slightest touch of indignation into his voice. How could any SS man worth his salt not know that after the Japanese attack at Pearl Harbor, the US had immediately declared war against them. "It won't affect us, though. The US is a corrupt, decadent nation, weakened by its large population of Jews, negroes, and whatnot. The Japanese will annihilate them."

The other man's eyes widened. "Herr Oberscharführer, I'm afraid you haven't heard the newest development, no doubt because you've been traveling all day. Hitler declared war upon America too, only one hour ago, at three p.m."

"Serves those corrupt cowboys right, if you ask me. Well, if the Japanese don't finish them off, then we will, once and for all. *Sieg Heil!*" Wilhelm saluted, but truth be told, he had a very queasy feeling in his stomach. He wasn't privy to the Führer's thought process and would never suggest that he knew better, but the military top brass often didn't see eye to eye with Hitler and grumbled silently at some of his reckless decisions. Despite their decadence, the Americans were still an enemy to be wary of, since they made up in numbers what they lacked in courage and determination.

Several hours later, the train pulled into Berlin Westkreuz station and masses of people disembarked. Wilhelm impatiently waited his turn and when it came, he stepped down onto the platform and inhaled a deep breath of air for what felt like the first time in hours.

He'd only brought along a small suitcase and it didn't take him more than a few minutes to cross the station, go through the security controls—his uniform giving him free access to pass without having to wait in the queue—and then he stood in front of the station and looked at the city he'd grown up in.

Erika had warned him his parents' house was reduced to rubble and he would have to stay with them, but of course Reiner was too busy to pick him up from the station and Erika didn't know how to drive, so he had to use the suburban train like any average citizen. As if the fifteen-hour train ride hadn't been hardship enough.

Wilhelm sighed and descended into the bowels of the station to cross over to the S-Bahn headed to Wannsee where Reiner lived like a king in a detached house on the shore of the Wannsee. God only knew where he'd got all his money. Wilhelm had suspected for years that their father had been funneling wealth into Reiner's hands, sidelining the needs of his other two children.

In Annegret's case this was understandable, since she still lived with her parents and had no living expenses to account for. But leaving Wilhelm out high and dry was inconsiderate to say the least. Just because Father supposedly wanted to teach him lessons about making do with his salary and living within his means. Wilhelm scoffed. Money was there to be spent, and he wasn't unreasonable in his lifestyle. He certainly didn't splash out on a big house with huge gardens like Reiner did. Instead he lived in his requisitioned one-bedroom apartment in Paris, which given he didn't even pay for it, was inexpensive in the extreme.

The suburban train traveled along the Kronprinzessinenweg, the formerly majestic boulevard in the west of Berlin. What he saw was astonishing damage to the buildings lining the track, some of them still smoldering in the aftermath of last night's bombings. The further he got, the sparser construction was and some greenery popped up here and there.

It was a refreshing change to the gray-on-gray that dominated the area around Westkreuz. On a whim he decided to get off at the station nearest to his parents' house and walked the short distance that had once been so familiar.

But today nothing looked the same. The entire block had been razed to the ground and nothing but charcoaled ruins stood against the white winter sky, giving the area an eerie feel. He shuddered and turned up the collar of his greatcoat, but it couldn't ease his shivers, because the cold in his bones wasn't caused by the freezing temperatures. The last hundred yards or so he found himself running and he arrived at the formerly proud building with a racing heart.

Blood rushing in his ears, he didn't hear a sound except for his own hammering pulse as he stopped in his tracks, his mouth hanging agape. Frantically he looked around, searching for a clue, not actually believing what he saw. He retraced his steps to the last standing building he found and walked back to the place where he'd lived for many years, not recognizing the place anymore.

In fact, there wasn't a place. Not even a ruin. It was a huge nothing spreading in front of him, where the impressive *Gründerzeit* mansion from the last century had stood before. Wilhelm fought against nausea as he walked across the lawn with bricks scattered like pebbles. Here his parents had died.

He thought of his mother, strict and uptight like a good Prussian woman, but nevertheless kind-hearted toward her children. Suddenly the smell of freshly baked apple pie wafted into his nose and transported him back to his tenth birthday, when he'd fallen from the tree and twisted his ankle, not to speak of ripping his trousers.

His father had made him run a mile on the hurt ankle to teach him that a German boy didn't whine or succumb to pain. After the ordeal, his mother, in a rare show of affection, had wrapped him into her arms and given him a slice of her heavenly apple pie with a generous dollop of cream on top. *May God rest her soul!* A strange yearning to put his head onto her lap and cry his eyes out overcame him. But his mother was dead, caught beneath the tumbling construction, after yet another vicious attack the cowardly Englishman.

He cursed. Hitler had been nothing but kind to the English, offering to let them join his Thousand-Year Reich as peers, and how had they paid back his generosity? By randomly killing innocent German civilians. What kind of awful barbarians were they?

A young boy, around six years of age, came running down the street, following a ball. Wilhelm stopped the ball with one foot and kicked it up into his hand, feeling the soft leather and the weight. In his youth he'd loved to play soccer like so many other boys.

"Here you go." He threw the ball and after a short pause, added, "That's quite the damage here."

The boy nodded with an important expression on his face, apparently in awe of the SS uniform. "Yes, Herr Scharführer, the building took a direct hit." He pushed out his chest and went on his toes. "I was in there when it happened."

"You were?" Wilhelm looked between the boy and the rubble, doubtful that anyone could have gotten out of there alive.

"Certainly. Me and a young woman were the only ones to get out alive."

"Do you know her name?"

"No, but she lived here. She helped me, because my leg was stuck beneath a board. See." The boy pulled up his trouser leg to reveal an angry red wound that was scabbed over.

"You are very brave."

The boy smiled with pride. "When I'm grown up, I want to be SS like you. They're the best."

"You'll have to train hard, but I'm sure someone who managed to get out of this heap of rubble will make it."

"Oh… but it didn't look that bad after the bombing," the boy said with a dismissive gesture. "The rest of it crumbled just yesterday. I can tell you; it was quite the show. Whoom!"

Wilhelm had to smile at the boy's enthusiasm and searched his pockets for a gift, but came up empty. "Thanks for the information."

He returned to the suburban train station and waited for the next S-Bahn that would bring him all the way down to where his brother lived in one of the nicest neighborhoods on the Wannsee.

Half an hour later he was knocking on the front door of a detached house surrounded by a big garden and with a view of the lake. The door opened and his brother appeared. Reiner was a burly man with slightly more flesh on his bones than was good-looking. He had the same blond hair and green-brown eyes as Wilhelm, but they suited him less well and his face looked bloated from eating and drinking too much.

"Wilhelm," Reiner greeted him with an outstretched hand. Wilhelm's family had never been one to show affection and the only person his father had ever hugged in public was Annegret, and only when she was still a child.

"Reiner." Wilhelm shook his brother's hand, wondering how their relationship would go from here, now that the connecting links between them were dead.

Two little girls were peeking around the corner and Wilhelm stopped and squatted down so that he was at their eye level. "Hello, Adolphine and Germania."

The two children quickly hid behind Reiner's legs, and he stood back up. "They don't appear to remember who I am."

"They're just being shy because they haven't seen you for a while," Reiner explained. "Did you go by Mother and Father's place?"

Wilhelm nodded. "There wasn't much left of it."

"No, there wasn't." Reiner turned to his children and waved them forward. "Adolphine. Germania. Be good hostesses and say hello to Uncle Wilhelm."

The two children obeyed reluctantly, offering a *Hitlergruß*. They stood ramrod straight, their eyes straight ahead, right arm raised in perfect manner like two little soldiers. It looked cute, but at the same time frightening to see two kindergarteners who could barely walk straight in such a martial pose.

Out of courtesy for his brother, he returned the greeting, and then watched as the girls scampered off.

"Don't you think they are a bit young for this?" Wilhelm asked as soon as they were out of sight.

"If you had children yourself you would know that one can never start too early with the education to turn them into good German citizens."

Wilhelm deliberately ignored the stinger in his direction and asked, "Where's Erika?"

"She has gone upstairs to rest. I imagine she'll be down any moment, now that you have finally arrived."

Even as he spoke, the two girls returned with their mother in tow. A heavily pregnant Erika.

"Good to see you, Erika. When is the baby due?"

"Less than a month. It might even arrive on Christmas Eve. Wouldn't that be a wonderful present for our Führer?" Erika beamed and patted her immense belly. "We are hoping this time it's a boy."

"I'm sure Hitler will be pleased with this addition to the Aryan race." Before anyone could launch into a lengthy monologue about racial advantages, Wilhelm glanced around the entrance hall and asked, "Is Annegret here?"

"Not at the moment. Let me take your coat and get you inside first, you must be freezing," Reiner said, before he turned to his wife and ordered her to make a cup of coffee for his brother. Erika scurried to the kitchen, while the two men strolled into Reiner's office next to the entrance hall, to smoke a cigarette.

Exhaling deeply, Wilhelm asked again, "So, Anne is living with you?"

Reiner took another drag from his cigarette before answering and Wilhelm observed a nervous tick in his right eyelid. Something was wrong.

"Himmler has assigned an aide of his to take care of the funeral preparations, since Erika is so far along she can barely cope with her duties in the house and with the children."

It was quite obvious Reiner didn't want to talk about their sister, so Wilhelm decided to let it slide for the moment. "That is so very thoughtful of him."

"Yes, he's a truly kind and caring person."

"Why don't you get a maid to help with the chores, now that Erika will soon have three children to take care of?"

"Do I look like Croesus to you? Not everyone squanders money the way you do."

Wilhelm bit his tongue, since he didn't want to get into a fight with Reiner during the first hour or this would become a very long visit. "What about that maid our parents had? Margarete, wasn't it? As far as I remember, they didn't even need to pay her a salary."

"She was a Jew, for God's sake. Do you honestly expect me to bring that kind of vermin into my house to poison my children? I really have no idea why Father put up with her. He should have sent her to the camps months ago."

A horrible suspicion formed in Wilhelm's head. "Do you think our father... had an affair with her?"

"Hell no," Reiner scoffed. "He was a man with principles. He'd never have shagged a Jewess. Although... that girl, she was quite the looker. I often observed her in the bathroom when I was visiting."

"You did what?"

"Come on, don't play holier than thou. You know about the hole in the door."

"But that was when we were kids pulling pranks on each other." Wilhelm had difficulties hiding the shock that a grown-up married man would feel the need to spy on an unsuspecting young woman undressing in the bathroom.

"She had the same expression you have now, when I waited for her as she came out of the room." Reiner licked his lips. "God, I loved the terrified look on her face when I made my move. It does add an extra thrill to it, don't you think?"

"You did what?"

"Don't tell me you never showed a woman that her rightful place is beneath your sweating body? Are you a virgin, little brother?" Reiner laughed out loud.

Wilhelm had slept with too many women to keep track, but he'd never once forced himself onto one. Every single one of his bedmates had been there by her own decision. While he didn't delude himself into believing the women who shared his bed did it out of love, it always was for mutual benefit and oftentimes even their pleasure.

"But… she was a Jewess," he muttered.

"While I completely agree that we must rid the Reich and the world of every last one of this scum, I pursue a more practical approach than our father and believe the young and pretty ones can earn their keep while they're still alive."

"I… I had no idea…" Wilhelm murmured, completely shocked by the revelations. Having grown up in a strict Prussian household, he'd never even entertained the idea of willingly inflicting pain on someone, not even a Jew or other undesirable.

"No need to worry, I took great care not to get her pregnant, since that sort of harlot wouldn't be trusted to keep her mouth shut."

Wilhelm felt nauseous. The Jews were subhuman filth, responsible for all the problems and hardships Germany had to contend with. How could Reiner… Even the thought of being intimate with a member of that race made him want to vomit. He knew he should report his brother, because *Rassenschande* was a serious crime, and even SS officers would be punished for having sexual relations with a Jewess. But without evidence nobody would believe his word over Reiner's. Except, if he could somehow coax the girl into…

"Where is she now?"

"In hell, where she belongs. Her corpse was found in the ruins. At least the English bombers got one thing right."

Well, there went his plan to blackmail his brother with a juicy revelation. Just at this moment Erika entered with two cups of coffee and some *Weihnachtsplätzchen* she had baked for the Christmas season on a tray.

"It's only *Ersatzkaffee*," she apologized while setting the cups onto the coffee table in Reiner's office.

Wilhelm felt the need to say something nice to his cuckolded sister-in-law. "Hmm… those cookies smell delicious."

She flushed slightly and puffed a wisp of hair from her forehead as she walked to Reiner's side and bent down to add milk to his coffee, before she stirred it and handed him the cup.

"My Erika is a wonderful housewife. Her cookies are legendary, and all the wives in her women's circle come to her for recipes and advice." He patted her behind while she stood at his side, seemingly waiting for something. "That will be all, sweetie, you can prepare dinner now."

"Thank you, darling," Erika said and left the office.

"She's just perfect, isn't she?" Reiner gushed about his wife. "And once the baby has arrived, she'll be as beautiful and lithe as before. I mean, the whole thing with begetting children for the Führer is well and fine, but being stuck with a wife resembling a hippo really isn't much fun."

Wilhelm preferred not to answer, since he'd had enough taste-less revelations for one day. He bit into a truly heavenly tasting cut-out cookie in the form of a Christmas tree and decided to compliment Erika on her baking skills as soon as he got a chance.

Washing down the crumbs with *Ersatzkaffee* he said, "So, what's going on with Annegret? I assumed she'd be staying with you."

Reiner set down his cup with a sigh. "She's missing."

Wilhelm frowned. "Missing?"

"Yes, she wasn't among the dead they dragged from the ruins, but neither could I find her in any of Berlin's hospitals, and, believe me, I have had my aide search all of them."

"Maybe she wasn't at home during the bombing?"

"That's the problem… we don't know. But if she wasn't, why wouldn't she come to see us? She knows where I live." Reiner lit another cigarette and blew smoke rings into the air. "It's not like she has anywhere else to go."

"You're right, that's very strange." Wilhelm thought hard. "What if she went to the country house?"

"I already phoned the housekeeper but she would have informed me the minute Anne arrived anyway."

"Why didn't you tell me?"

"What would you have done? Have you already forgotten that you were in Paris?"

Wilhelm shrugged. He couldn't have done anything, but it would still have been nice to know about Anne's vanishing. Honestly, she was probably pulling a prank on them and would show up again when she decided it was in her best interest and not a moment sooner.

At least he hoped so. Four years younger than him, and six years to Reiner, she'd known all her life how to use her status to her own advantage and get her brothers punished for her own wrongdoings.

Yes, she must be oblivious to the fact that everyone was searching frantically for her and would show up the next morning like nothing ever happened. Just like she'd done the day she turned sixteen and had spent the night gallivanting around town with a friend. Mother had been out of her mind with worry and Father had moved heaven and earth to search for his precious apple of the eye, when she'd returned the next evening, drunk as a sailor.

He clung to that notion, because if he admitted the truth, he was worried to death about his sister. They might have had their difficult moments, but he still loved her and wouldn't want anything to happen to her and, even if Reiner would never admit this, Wilhelm knew he felt the same way.

CHAPTER 5

Margarete smiled as she handed over the books the student had asked for. "Good luck with your assignment."

"Thank you," the young woman said, pulling on her gloves and wrapping her scarf around her head as she moved toward the door.

The freezing winter air rushed through the open door and Margarete shivered in her seat. It was a slow day, since most students and teachers were preparing for the winter break that would start a week from now. She got up to shelve the returned books and started when a man in his fifties sidled up to her.

"Excuse me, Fräulein, I didn't mean to startle you."

"No, no, it's alright. What can I do for you?" She suppressed her ingrained fear of strangers and gave him a friendly smile.

"Where do I find the chemistry section?"

"Over there." She pointed him in the right direction and leaned against the nearest bookshelf, trembling with fear. Since she'd turned twelve, her mother had impressed on her to steer away from anyone in a uniform, to make herself as invisible as possible and to never talk to a stranger, no matter how friendly they seemed. Drawing attention to yourself while being a Jew never led to anything good, even before they'd been forced to wear that dreadful yellow star, singling them out as Enemies of the Reich and making them fair game for anyone looking for a fight.

But she wasn't a Jew anymore. Margarete Rosenbaum had 'died' about a week ago from a direct hit to the building where she'd lived and served as maid to the Huber family. She'd been in the kitchen, cooking dinner when the air raid warning had gone off. As a dutiful German who'd been taught all her life that there must be order above anything else, she turned off the stove, hung her apron on the nail behind the kitchen door and pulled on her threadbare jacket with the yellow star sewn onto its chest, since she wasn't allowed to leave the house without it.

Like every other citizen, even the Aryans, she kept her identification papers with her at all times, in the pocket of her only jacket. Herr and Frau Huber pushed past her, making her stumble and fall. They never even slowed down to help her up, and why should they? She was only a Jew. A subhuman destined to be worked to death. She knew Herr Huber himself had signed the order to have her deported to some labor camp by the end of the week.

Anyone else might believe these camps weren't half bad, but she knew better. She'd often overheard the Standartenführer as he'd entertained guests or talked on the phone. She knew that none of the deported people were ever supposed to return. Squeezed of their last drop of blood, they were to toil day and night until they simply dropped to the ground to never get up again. *Vernichtung durch Arbeit*, extermination through labor, they called it and it served a double purpose: keep the German war machinery afloat and get rid of the enemies of the Reich. Margarete's gut twisted as she relived the anxiety during the air raid at the Hubers' place.

The faces of Herr and Frau Huber came to her mind. She couldn't feel sorrow for them. Herr Huber himself had been responsible for the death of tens of thousands of Jews and other undesirables, he had deserved to die. As had his wife. Frau Huber might not have been actively involved in the sinister actions of her husband, but she'd shown Margarete nothing but disdain during her two years serving the family. Not a single kind word, or even a gesture of caring like loaning her a warm coat when she had to go grocery shopping in snow and ice.

"Fräulein, are you alright?" a deep voice asked.

Margarete blinked a few times. The rubble disappeared, and instead rows and rows of bookshelves emerged. She looked into the angular face of a man in his fifties with completely white hair.

"Yes, I just… it must be because I skipped breakfast this morning," she quickly invented an excuse. "I'm fine now." She smoothed down her skirt. "How can I help you?"

"I'm looking for a book about the Weimar Republic."

Alarm bells rang in her head. Every book that painted the Weimar Republic in a positive light—or glorified it, as the Nazis called it—was on the list of restricted books.

"I'm afraid those are only available after requesting them on one of our forms. I'll need your teaching credentials and the exact reason why you need this book for your scientific work."

"I'm a teacher of literature," he said.

"You'll still have to fill in the form. Let me get one."

"No, no, that won't be necessary then." He suddenly seemed to be in an awful hurry.

"But I'll still have to take your name and address…" she started saying, but he had already turned on his heel and rushed off. Almost automatically she went after him, but stopped the chase a few steps later. If she caught up with him, she would have to take his name and record it on that awful list, adding a remark that he'd behaved suspiciously.

She'd rather let him slip away.

Frau Merz appeared in front of her out of nowhere. "What did he want?"

"Who?" Margarete's heart was racing faster than a horse in full gallop.

"The man you were just talking to."

"Oh him? Nothing." Frau Merz's probing stare made her stomach do flip-flops and she added, "I was feeling a little nauseous suddenly and had to lean against the bookcase to steady myself. He noticed and asked me if everything was fine. I'm sorry, it won't happen again."

Frau Merz stared at her some seconds longer before she said, "So far I have been pleased with your meticulous work, but if there's an unseemly reason for your sick feeling, I'm afraid I must let you go."

When the meaning of Frau Merz's words penetrated her brain, Margarete flushed furiously. "Oh no, Frau Merz, I'm a decent woman! How can you even...? I would never..."

The older woman nodded. "Our Führer welcomes any and all children into his people, even those born out of wedlock. But as a public institution, we need to rise above all moral suspicion."

"And I certainly do!" Margarete made an indignant expression and turned around, hiding her fury. But it wasn't just the outrageous insult Frau Merz had hurled at her that made her blood boil. She seethed at the woman's hypocrisy. How could she say the Führer welcomed any children, when at the same time Jewish offspring were treated worse than animals. and she'd even overheard Herr Huber joking about drowning newborns in water barrels like the vermin they were?

A violent shudder ripped through her body and she had to use all her willpower to keep on walking straight, determined not to show another sign of alleged morning sickness.

When she walked home in the afternoon, she welcomed the sleet settling on her coat, her hat and gloves. Small snowflakes that immediately turned into water when they landed on a surface. That's how she felt: as though she was disintegrating.

Aunt Heidi wasn't home yet, so Margarete took to peeling potatoes for their dinner. She'd thought her biggest wish was to survive, but now she wasn't so sure anymore. If her safety meant risking other people's lives, she didn't want that.

"Hello, Margarete, how was your day?" Aunt Heidi swept into the kitchen with a bag full of groceries. "Look what I got. Now that we have a ration card for you as well, food won't be so scarce anymore."

Margarete couldn't even bring herself to feel joy over this news and continued chopping. "Good."

"What's wrong? Has something happened at the library?"

"Not really." Margarete told her aunt about the incident with the restricted book, but without mentioning that Frau Merz had suspected her of being in the family way. "I feel so bad."

"But you didn't put his name on the list, now, did you?"

"No." Margarete sighed. "But what if he had insisted on getting the book?"

"Maybe he was an academic with a valid reason?"

"Auntie, he wasn't. I could see it by the frightened look in his eyes when I asked for his university identification."

"Then he's learned something and will know better in the future," Heidi said, putting the peeled and chopped vegetables into a pot of boiling water.

"And the next person who comes in?"

"Then you'll do exactly what you were asked to do. Nothing less. Nothing more."

"But the Gestapo…"

"… Have their hands full with more important stuff than a random person who wants to read a forbidden book. Probably nothing would even come of it."

Margarete looked at Heidi, hoping she was right. "You really think so?"

"I do."

Margarete was quiet for a long while, before she murmured, "I don't know how much longer I can do this. Annegret was such an awful person… and a die-hard Nazi… I just don't know how much longer I can go on pretending to be her." Truth be told that wasn't her only misgiving about the current situation. She'd jumped at the first and best opportunity for survival and had come to the only person she knew would help her: her favorite aunt. But now that she'd been here for a week, she realized that her very existence put Heidi more at risk with every day that passed. But she couldn't tell her aunt this.

"You can do anything you put your mind to," Heidi said, patting her on the shoulder. "Set the table, I'll finish cooking dinner."

After setting the table for two, Margarete walked into the sitting room and grabbed the small amulet she'd hidden in the sofa upholstery. Her parents had given it to her at her secret Bat Mitzvah. It was the only reminder she had of them, a beautiful round silver pendant on a silver chain. It showed a Tree of Life, made of beautiful silver strings representing the branches, atop a shimmering blue-green opal-like background. She held it between her hands, thinking about her family and the happy days when she was just a child. Before Hitler came into power, all those many, many years ago.

The pendant was innocent enough, but she still didn't dare to wear it for fear someone might turn it over and recognize the Hebrew inscription "Mazel Tov." Back in 1935 her parents hadn't believed the situation would become as bad as it was now, or they would never have given her such a compromising piece of jewelry. And now they'd all been deported. Every single one of them, even the wives of her brothers with their small children.

"Dinner is ready," her aunt called from the kitchen.

"Coming." Margarete tucked the amulet back down between the pillows. As much as she wanted to wear it around her neck to feel the strengthening presence of her parents at all times, she wouldn't even do so in the safety of Heidi's home. Not because she feared Heidi would see it, but because there could be a knock on the door anytime and a curious neighbor, the police, or some other person might get a glimpse of it.

Annegret surely would never have worn anything with Hebrew letters on it, not even if it was the latest high fashion. No, it was better to keep the amulet hidden away and only delve into its energy in the safety of Aunt Heidi's apartment.

CHAPTER 6

After supper, Wilhelm was sitting on the floor with one of his nieces on either side of his crossed legs. They had warmed to him since his arrival, and had invited him to their makeshift tea party. He'd jokingly asked if they didn't want to maybe build something with blocks, or play with cars, but that had only gotten him a stern look from his oldest niece and a warning frown from Erika.

"Wilhelm, they're girls. They don't have cars and blocks," she'd chided him.

"Can you play with us, too?" Adolphine asked her mother.

"No, sweetie, I have to wash the dishes and iron your father's uniform."

"And Papa?" the girl asked again.

"Your father has important work to do, he can't waste his time playing with dolls. Isn't it enough to have Uncle Wilhelm join your tea party?"

Wilhelm saw the girls' faces fall before they dutifully gathered up their toy tea set and their dolls. He sent a glare towards his brother and then muttered, "You might have taken a few minutes and joined us."

Reiner scowled at him. "I don't have time for playing. We are at war, or have you forgotten?"

Wilhelm tried not to let his brother rile him up. "I haven't forgotten."

"Uncle, come on." Germania pulled on his hand.

"I'm coming, poppet. Go upstairs to your room with your sister and set up, I shall be there shortly."

"How are things going on the Russian front?" Wilhelm asked his brother.

"You know that I'm not allowed to divulge classified information."

"Oh, come on. I'm not some random civilian. I'm a member of the SS, just like you."

"Not like me, you're several ranks lower." Reiner loved to rub his superior rank in Wilhelm's face.

"Well, I guess there's nothing you know anyways, since you're not directly involved." Wilhelm knew exactly how to play his brother and observed with joy how Reiner's expression changed.

"That is where you are mistaken, my dear brother. I'm privy to an amount of classified material you can only dream of. I even have direct access to Reinhard Heydrich and Reichsführer Himmler."

Then it was true: Reiner was already working behind the scenes on his next promotion. Their father's job had to be filled and that would likely open up a string of promotions leading up to his position.

"I heard the Wehrmacht is retreating," Wilhelm probed.

Reiner took the bait. "Losers and weaklings. The Wehrmacht's claiming the weather is too cold and they are regrouping. Regrouping, my ass! They are running from the enemy and I have no idea why Hitler is allowing it. Where have the German traits of courage, determination and steadfastness gone? Poof, like Cinderella at midnight. They were only a dozen miles from the center of Moscow, and let the stinking Russian winter defeat them. I tell you what, if the SS were running Operation Barbarossa, we would have raised the swastika over the Kremlin weeks ago."

Wilhelm knew that the situation in the east was bad, but he hadn't imagined it was *that* bad. In Paris, they had only received positive news of an impending occupation of Moscow, the coveted Russian capital. "Is it that the Russians are better equipped to fight in these arctic temperatures?" Wilhelm surmised.

Reiner gave a short bark. "It's supremely annoying. It's so cold, the fuel in our vehicles and aircraft is freezing, while the Ivans somehow keep their machinery working. I'm sure they must have made a pact with the devil."

"Perhaps they're using vodka instead," Wilhelm joked.

"Uncle Wilhelm, are you coming?" Adolphine asked from the hallway.

"Right now. It seems I am needed at a tea party," Wilhelm said and walked upstairs where the two girls were waiting for him. Just as he reached the landing, Reiner called after him.

"I'll be meeting a few important people in the morning. You should attend, since it would do you good to rub some shoulders, now that you don't have Father's help anymore to further your career."

Wilhelm actually had no intention whatsoever in participating in the promotion carousel, as a new job would only entail more work, more bootlicking and less time for the beauties of Paris. But he put a good face on and replied, "Certainly. I'll be there. At what time?"

"Eight."

Of course, the overzealous top brass had to meet at a time when any sane person was still asleep, more so during furlough. He much preferred the French *savoir vivre*, where people rarely did business before nine in the morning.

The tea party was plenty of fun and he enjoyed the carefree time with his nieces, until Erika arrived and put them to bed.

The next morning, Wilhelm got up early, shaved and combed his hair back with Brylcreem, before he put on comfortable pants and a pullover to meet the family over breakfast.

Reiner looked up from his newspaper when he entered the dining room, and stared at him in blank disbelief. "What on earth is this?"

"What?"

"Your attire."

"I'm on furlough. I thought—"

"An SS officer never leaves his house in civvies. You're a disgrace."

Wilhelm groaned. "You and your exaggerated correctness."

"I won't put myself up for ridicule by bringing a French *clochard* to the meeting. Either you dress properly or you stay here."

Erika stepped out of the kitchen with a cup of hot coffee and a plate for Wilhelm. "Here you go."

"Thank you, Erika."

"Wife, please go upstairs and press Wilhelm's uniform. I want him to look presentable for the meeting."

"No… Please… Erika, I don't want to impose on you, you have more than enough on your hands as it is."

"What nonsense, Erika is proud to serve the Reich every way she can, even if it's something as unimportant as pressing your uniform. Aren't you, darling?"

"Yes, Reiner. I wouldn't want Wilhelm to look anything but perfect," she said and scurried upstairs to take care of Wilhelm's uniform. For some reason he didn't like the idea of her snooping around in his room, which was entirely irrational, because it was actually her room, and he had nothing to hide inside his small suitcase. Not to mention that he was used to having strangers clean, dust, wash and press his belongings.

"Don't you think you should treat Erika with a bit more respect? She's your wife, not your servant."

"She's also a good German woman and thus her most joyous task is to care for her family, which currently includes you as well. So, don't lose your calm and let her do what she does best."

Wilhelm swallowed down a remark, since it would only get them into a fight over the role of women.

Half an hour later they left the house and got into Reiner's staff car, whose driver had been waiting in front of the house for them.

"Who will be at this meeting?" Wilhelm asked.

"You'll see. Heydrich, Himmler, some subordinates, and support staff... You should feel right at home."

Wilhelm pretended not to notice the dig. His brother didn't understand why he was content to work as a glorified secretary, when he could potentially have a much more important and authoritative position. But then again, Reiner had never understood Wilhelm.

He remembered the day his father had first sent them to the Hitlerjugend. While Reiner had immediately stepped up to volunteer as a leader, Wilhelm had spent his time thinking about ways to get through the exercises with the least amount of effort. His true love had never been war games, but art. In another life with another father, he might have become an arts dealer or arts collector. Maybe now with his impending inheritance he could become an important patron, collecting the best pieces and showcasing them in special exhibitions under the patronage of the Führer, a fervent art lover himself.

They arrived at the office building at Berlin's prestigious boulevard Unter den Linden. He followed Reiner inside, nodding to a few of the older officers who had known his father.

A fresh-faced young man in SS uniform approached him and Reiner. "I'm so very sorry for your loss. Your father was an admired man. His sacrifice won't remain unpunished."

"Thank you. We're all still very much in shock, but we will use this awful attack to spur us on and take revenge on the enemy. Sieg Heil!" Reiner snapped into the *Hitlergruß* and Wilhelm and the young man followed suit. Wilhelm barely stopped himself from rolling his eyes at Reiner's theatrical reply. Why couldn't he behave like a normal person, just once in his life?

"It must be such a relief that at least your sister escaped that heap of rubble unharmed."

Wilhelm choked and broke into a coughing fit. "Our sister? Annegret? Are you sure?"

"Yes, I was personally there on site, helping process survivors and watching out for subversive elements that like to use the chaos after a bombing for sinister motives. After checking her papers, I was the one who organized the immediate travel permit and train ticket to Leipzig for her." The young man must have noticed Reiner's deadly stare, because he seemed to shrink a few inches and added, "Naturally I ensured she was driven to the station and safely put onto her train. It was the least I could do for your late father. He was an example for all of us."

Reiner growled. "Leipzig, you say. Would you know for how long she planned to stay there?"

The young man looked unsure, apparently wishing he'd never talked to the Huber brothers.

"She has called us twice, but every time the line was too crackly to understand a single word," Wilhelm lied. Whatever Annegret was up to, it wasn't anyone's business except for her family's. He had to nip any possible rumors in the bud.

"*Meine Herren*, I'm terribly sorry, she didn't say. All she said was that she was going to stay with your mother's friend." The young SS man quickly bid his goodbyes and left the room as if the devil incarnate was after him.

"At least we know she's alive," Wilhelm said.

"And apparently well, which takes a worry off my shoulders, because she's still my sister," Reiner admitted. "Although she should have called us, because she would know how worried we were about her disappearance."

"Right. We need to get into contact with her and find out why she ran away. Maybe she needs our help?"

Reiner gave an absentminded nod, apparently pondering how to find their sister.

"Do you know anyone in Leipzig?" Wilhelm asked.

"Not me. And I'm sure our mother didn't have friends there. As far as I know she never even went there."

"That's strange. So why on earth would Anne choose to go there?"

"She's erratic like that." Reiner lit himself a cigar. "I sure have more important problems to attend to than to search for my twenty-year-old missing sister."

"I wonder whether she's alright. Why did she make something up like that and why hasn't she phoned to let you know she's alright," Wilhelm mused, holding his own cigarette up for Reiner to light.

"The girl is nothing but trouble. Instead of indulging her every whim, Father should have beaten the whimsical ideas out of her head. At least that's what I will do if Germania or Adolphine ever get funny ideas." Annegret had been an insubordinate youth, always testing her parents, spending nights out in cabarets where no decent woman wanted to be seen, smoking and cursing, much to the chagrin of her mother.

"Maybe Anne was shell-shocked and needed to get away from Berlin and the bombings?"

Reiner scoffed. "Our sister? That girl doesn't have an emotional bone in her body. I tell you; she wasn't distressed, she's trying to hide something."

"Or someone. A boyfriend maybe?" Wilhelm said, dragging on his cigarette.

"I would know about a suitor."

"Not if it's the kind she didn't want to tell our parents about."

"Bloody hell! I swear, if I ever find out that is true I'll give her the spanking our father hasn't."

The day dragged out on meeting important people, making final arrangements for the funeral, enjoying lunch in one of the finest restaurants in Berlin, and then more meetings. Reiner seemed adamant to introduce Wilhelm to all the decision-makers to further his career, and Wilhelm couldn't help but wonder why. He'd never given two hoots about his achievements before—except for mocking the lack thereof. Maybe it came with his new role as head of the family that obliged him to seek the best position for everyone, or maybe he simply felt he needed a blood-related ally now that Father was gone.

Late in the afternoon Reiner decided enough mingling had been done and said, "Let's get out of here."

"Nothing I'd love more."

"I'll just tell Erika," Reiner said and picked up the phone to dial a number. "Hello, darling... No, unfortunately not... We'll grab a quick bite and continue to work... I can't say for sure how long... No, don't wait up for me... Sweet dreams." He hung up, giving Wilhelm a salacious grin. "And now the fun part begins."

"Didn't you just say we have to continue to work?" Wilhelm tried to swallow his disappointment, since he longed to get away from all the stuck-up pricks, enjoy a hearty meal, plenty of alcohol and then lose himself in the warm arms of a woman.

"We'll do our duty and have fun doing it, if you know what I mean."

Wilhelm didn't. At least he thought that couldn't be what Reiner was suggesting, since his brother was a married man. Several other men entered Reiner's office and it was quickly decided to have dinner at one of the less respectable variety halls.

Wilhelm inwardly groaned, not because he didn't enjoy the company of scantily clad women personally, but because he somehow felt guilty on Erika's behalf. That woman was about to give birth to her third child and, all the while, her husband was enjoying the bachelor life. Which was the very reason why Wilhelm had resisted all his mother's efforts to match him up. He simply wasn't the guy for just one woman but couldn't fathom infidelity to someone he'd made vows to. He was way better off with a housekeeper and changing mistresses, than a wife of his own.

The driver parked in front of the vaudeville house and asked, "Shall I wait?"

"No, that won't be necessary. We'll take a cab when we're done. You can take the evening off, but wait for me in front of my home at seven tomorrow morning."

"Certainly, Herr Obersturmführer." The driver walked around the car to open the door for Reiner, while Wilhelm impatiently opened his own door and jumped out. If they were going to participate in Berlin's nightlife, he might as well enjoy it, although he doubted it would measure up to Paris.

Inside the lights were dimmed, and even this early in the evening, the air was heavy with tobacco smoke. The place was packed with men in uniform and the odd woman wearing a gaudy feather boa. As he'd expected, the revue show was nothing to write home about. It was loud and garish, the dancers readily exhibiting their attributes. Talent, though, hadn't seemed to play a role during the audition process, but long, slender, well-formed legs certainly had. Although, judging by the leers, the audience had come to see the legs and not much else.

Once the show was over, the girls bowed to the applause and then turned around, flapping their barely-there skirts way up over their lovely bottoms. Cheers broke out, as one girl after another left the stage and paraded through the audience, most of whom seemed eager to snatch a closer look or feel.

Wilhelm, though, wasn't impressed. The revue had all the elements of a veritable show in the Moulin Rouge, but none of its class. It was nothing but a poor imitation of French elegance, talent and style. He had been but a boy during the Roaring Twenties, when Berlin was a metropolis, a city of fun, talent, lust and decadence, and truly great stars like Marlene Dietrich had performed here.

As he turned around to his companions, each of them had a girl sitting on their laps, schmoozing up to them, except for himself. He shrugged and grabbed his greatcoat. "See you fellas later."

"You leaving already?" Reiner asked, between kissing the bosom of the platinum blonde dancer.

"Yes. I'll be visiting a friend. Don't wait for me." Suddenly Wilhelm was in a hurry to leave this place. Extramarital affairs were a frequent occurrence and as long as they weren't made public, nobody scoffed at them. On the contrary, since young and hereditarily healthy SS men were encouraged to spread their "gifts" far and wide to beget children in and out of wedlock, who could blame the married officers for wanting to serve their country in the same way? Maybe Erika wouldn't even mind anyway, since she was probably too far along to please her husband for some weeks to come.

Wilhelm hailed a cab outside the vaudeville hall and got it to drive him to the apartment of an old friend of his, who he knew would receive him with open arms. Ellen, an up-and-coming actress—whom the press were already calling "the new Dietrich"—and he went all the way back to their childhood and had been best friends ever since. They had shared many passionate nights, but neither of them had ever demanded exclusivity from the other one, not least because she cut both ways.

CHAPTER 7

On Friday, Margarete arrived at the library to discover that Frau Merz had stumbled down a ladder and sprained her ankle. Since such a minor injury wouldn't deter a good German like her from doing her duty, she had it wrapped and elevated on a step stool as she sat at the main checkout desk.

Later that afternoon Frau Merz beckoned her over. "My dear, it's Friday and I need a small favor."

"Of course," Margarete immediately agreed. "Do you need something for your ankle?"

Frau Merz waved her hand and gave a small laugh. "No, nothing like that. But usually on a Friday, I deliver the list of people seeking to consult one of the restricted books to the Gestapo headquarters—"

"I thought you said they came here?" Margarete interrupted her, fear gripping her chest, before she reminded herself that Annegret had regularly rubbed shoulders with Nazi officials, including the Gestapo, and so she had nothing to fear from them.

"No, no… We deliver the list to their office at the *Deutsche Bücherei*. They are much too busy to run such menial errands."

Margarete wanted to protest that for the people whose names were on that list, the task was going to be anything but menial. While most of them would be professors with legitimate reasons, some might not. For them it could be life-altering, and not in a good way. "I see."

"I need you to take the list down there for me. It won't be hard to find. Take the number seventeen tram and get off directly in front of the National Library. The Gestapo office is on the fifth floor. You just tell the receptionist that you've come to bring the list from the university library and she'll let you go upstairs."

Must I? Margarete screamed inside. But, knowing that she had no choice, she donned her coat, hat and gloves, took the list from Frau Merz and tucked it away in her handbag. She debated about losing the list on her way to the *Deutsche Bücherei*, but that would only draw undue attention to herself. Her fake identity as Annegret Huber was sketchy at best. Only two years apart in age, they both had wavy light brown hair that stopped just below their shoulders, and hazel eyes rimmed by dark lashes. They were approximately the same height, and Margarete could easily adopt Annegret's shrill voice.

But despite the similarities, they still looked quite different and anyone who had known Annegret wouldn't be fooled for even a second. That's why she had to keep a low profile and keep out of sight of the officials as much as possible. Huber was a common enough last name, but God help her if anyone suspected that she wasn't some random Annegret Huber, but SS-Standartenführer Wolfgang Huber's daughter.

She was banking on the fact that both his sons would be too busy to go looking for their missing sister. In fact, with any luck, they would believe she had also died in the bombing and that her body had been buried beneath too much rubble to retrieve.

Wilhelm was far away in Paris anyway and she hadn't even seen him in at least a year, while the despicable Reiner had never once inquired about his sister during his visits to his parents' place. Those calls had usually taken place when only his father was at home, about to leave for whatever important business.

Margarete had soon understood this hadn't been a coincidence, but was carefully orchestrated to catch her alone so he could attempt to force himself onto her. She shuddered at the memory of him touching her in the most inappropriate places and quickly turned her focus back to the present.

As her station came up, she jumped off the tram and walked the hundred yards to the entrance of the *Deutsche Bücherei*, a very impressive sandstone-colored building. On both ends of the huge structure were oriels of glass windows. It reminded her of a fairy-tale princess's palace, except that the building hosted incredible amounts of books—with the Gestapo masters deciding who was allowed to read which book.

Her stomach was tied into knots as she approached the grand staircase leading to the three black portals adorned with golden inlays. The portal was topped by the busts of Bismarck, Gutenberg and Goethe, and the inscription *"Freie Statt für freies Wort, freier Forschung sichrer Port, reiner Wahrheit Schutz und Hort,"* spoken by the Saxonian minister Graf Vtizthum von Eckstädt on occasion of first stone laying. A free place for free words, and haven for free research and plain truth. Margarete grimaced. The library had long ceased to be that place.

With her heart hammering against her ribs, she walked up the stairs and through the impressive portals that had demanded awe since the library's inauguration.

She stopped at the reception desk and said with all the courage she could muster, "Excuse me, Fräulein. I'm substituting for Frau Merz from the university library and need to give this list to the Gestapo." She secretly hoped the woman would take the list from her and let her go, but no such luck.

"See that staircase over there? Go all the way up and then to the left."

Margarete nodded, fear rendering her almost immobile. Somehow, she managed to drag her feet over to the staircase, pushed the heavy doors open and climbed up. With every step she took her legs became more leaden, and fear squeezed her chest so tightly, she could barely breathe.

Ever since the Nuremberg Laws of 1935 she'd been giving a wide berth to any and all government officials. Not only the dreaded Brownshirts and the SS, but every kind of police or civil servant. The Gestapo was even worse, its reputation preceding the organization and Margarete had never heard a single good word about them.

Not even Herr Huber, who certainly wasn't afraid of the Gestapo thugs, had seemed to like the organization. Annegret though, wouldn't be afraid… Margarete took a deep breath and immersed herself into the role of a Nazi brat who had nothing to fear. Upon her arrival on the uppermost landing, she turned left, pushed open the swing door and stepped onto a brilliant white floor, adorned with stucco ornaments. Large red flags with the swastika in the middle hung from the parapets and the obligatory portrait of Hitler hung prominently on the wall.

She stopped in front of the first door with the sign *Sekretariat* and knocked.

"*Herein*," a male voice asked her to come in.

She needed all her courage to turn the door knob and step inside the lion's den. As soon as she closed the door behind her, she felt like a caged animal about to be slaughtered and all the courage she'd so carefully built while climbing the stairs evaporated.

A handsome young man wearing the gray SS uniform, but with police-pattern shoulder boards was seated behind the desk. He eyed her and then asked, "What's your business, Fräulein?"

Despite the fact that he was neither unfriendly nor rude, Margarete couldn't get out a single word. "I…" She struggled to get the list from her handbag. "I have a list… it's right here…" She glanced at the young SS officer and gave him a wry smile. "Sorry, it's stuck."

"Maybe if you removed your glove?" the man suggested, eyeing her with a neutral expression on his face.

Margarete could feel her face getting hot. She nodded and pulled her right glove off. She easily retrieved the list and handed it over to the young man, immediately replacing her glove.

"And this is?"

"The... list of people... who..." Margarete swallowed, if she didn't get a grip on herself really soon, he'd suspect something. Channeling fearless Annegret, she finally said. "I'm sorry, I'm a bit out of breath from rushing up the stairs."

He smiled.

"This is the list of people who have requested restricted books from the university library. Frau Merz, the head librarian, has sprained her ankle, or she would have brought it herself," Margarete explained.

"And you are?"

"Uhm... I'm Annegret Huber."

"Annegret? That's a beautiful name for a beautiful woman."

Margarete hid her surprise and forced herself to look at him in a friendly way. "I... I should probably get back to the library... you must be very busy..."

"It was nice to meet you, Fräulein Huber. Maybe our paths will cross again?"

She put on a pleased, yet shy, face and forced her voice to be even as she replied, "Maybe." Then she walked sedately out of his office, down the hallway and out the door onto the staircase. As she reached it, the urge to flee down the steps became almost unbearable, but she continued her slow measured walk all the way back to the tram station, determined not to let anyone see how much the encounter had shaken her.

She had expected scrutiny, disdain, even harsh orders to be barked at her, but never in her life had she imagined meeting a handsome and flirtatious Gestapo officer. As flattering as it was, and as friendly as he seemed to be—the fact that he was interested in her personally increased her risk of being exposed. No, she had to keep a low profile and stay away from the authorities as far as possible.

By the time she arrived at the university library, Frau Merz was already preparing to close up.

"Let me help you," Margarete said and rushed to the older woman who was hobbling along, carrying a stack of books in her arms.

"Thank you. This ankle really is hindering my work," Frau Merz said with a strained voice, but then pulled herself together and said in a chirpy tone, "but I won't complain about this little sacrifice, since others have done so much more for Führer and Fatherland."

"Um-hm." Margarete hoped her answer could be interpreted as agreement.

"I'll have all weekend to prop up my leg and on Monday I'll be as good as new."

"Get well soon." Margarete left the library and returned to her aunt's place. She managed to hold onto her emotions until she was inside the apartment, but the minute the door closed, she burst into big, ugly sobs.

"Margarete! What's wrong?" her aunt tried to comfort her.

"I just can't... I can't do this... please... I need to find another job."

"Unfortunately, that's not so easy. You'll need the permission of the labor office if you want to quit your job, and what reason would you give them?"

"That I can't go to the Gestapo's office every week?" she sobbed.

"You have been summoned to the Gestapo?" Heidi's face turned whiter than the snow falling outside.

"No… But… the list… *Deutsche Bücherei*… flirting…"

"Margarete, stop. You're making no sense at all."

Margarete tried to calm herself, but the sobs simply wouldn't stop. Never had she thought her rash decision to become someone else would have so many consequences. In fact, she hadn't thought at all when she'd been crawling across the rubble with the young boy by her side. The second the idea had crossed her mind; she'd acted upon it.

"You go ahead," she had urged the boy and then turned around to crawl back to Annegret's corpse. She had seen her identification card sticking out of her jacket pocket. Annegret was only two years older than Margarete herself, born on June 28, 1921 in Berlin. While the two of them didn't exactly resemble each other, the photograph was several years old and showed an ordinary girl with long, wavy brown hair and hazel eyes. She scanned the papers and smiled. No special marks. It would do to get her out of Berlin and into safety. On second thoughts she pinned the yellow star on Annegret's blouse and thrust her own papers into her skirt pocket, before she took off into her new life.

It was only when she emerged from the rubble and the rescue team assailed her with questions that she realized it wouldn't be a walk in the park. It was more than just papers. She'd have to actually become Annegret to stay safe. And now she had to talk, walk, think and act like the very person she'd hated most in this world.

"Are you even listening to me?" Aunt Heidi asked.

"I'm sorry, no."

"I said you have to lay low and sing small. You can't risk anyone connecting the dots and informing the authorities that you're impersonating someone."

Margarete nodded. "I know that. But… Frau Merz has sprained her ankle so I had to deliver the darned list to the

Gestapo office and there was this young officer. I think… he has designs on me. He called me beautiful, suggested that our paths might cross again."

"Oh dear. What did you say?"

"What was I supposed to say? I pretended to be flattered, but shy. Maybe that was wrong, but I couldn't think of any other way to get out of it." Margarete reached for her hanky and blew her nose. "Can't you get me fake papers?"

"I wouldn't know where to ask for them in the first place, and if you inquire with the wrong people, it won't end well. I'm already watched because of whom I married, and it's a big enough risk having anyone stay with me, even an Aryan like Annegret. No, we'll have to go through with your story and hope everything will turn out well." Heidi gave her a long hug and patted her cheek. "Besides, real papers are so much better than forged ones."

CHAPTER 8

Wilhelm lit a cigarette and passed it to Ellen, before lighting another one for himself. It was early in the morning and he really should get up and return to his brother's house.

"What are your plans for today?" Ellen asked him.

"Oh, nothing much. Visiting old friends, some Christmas shopping. We can have dinner if you want?"

She moved her head on his shoulder. "I already have plans for tonight, but what about tomorrow for dinner and more?"

"How could I refuse such a tempting invitation?" He chuckled and traced her soft shoulder with his hand, careful not to scatter ashes on her skin.

"Tell me about Paris. Is it as amazing as people say?"

"It is." His hand wandered across her chest, before he took another drag on his cigarette. "I love Paris. It's everything Berlin used to be in the twenties and much more. The food, the wine, everything is better there."

"Even the sex?" she asked with a naughty gleam in her clear blue eyes.

"Yes and no. The women are very pliant… But…" He stubbed the ashes into the ashtray on the nightstand. "It could be so much better if the French in general weren't so unfriendly. It seems their famous hospitality is nothing but a fairy tale. It's beyond me to understand why they aren't more accommodating. They should be happy that we've come to show them how an efficient government works, while letting them keep all their good things. But instead, many of them defy us every step of the way. Even those who work for us don't do it with honest enthusiasm, but more out of... I don't know... necessity?"

Ellen laughed her throaty laugh that made her entire stomach rumble. "Is that so strange?"

"Of course. Wouldn't you be grateful if someone came to show you the ropes of becoming a truly great nation? And wouldn't you grasp every opportunity to learn from those better than you are? Wouldn't you be proud to have the opportunity to be part of the greatest nation of all?"

"Well, maybe they just need more time to adapt to the new way of doing things?"

Wilhelm ran a hand through his hair, dropping some ash onto the bright white bedsheet in the process. Ellen raised her head and blew it away. "I'm not sure. The French are stubborn, almost like badly-behaved kids. Instead of enthusiastically helping us to get their country into shape, they put obstacles in our way. Out of spite they sabotage our work, blow up important infrastructure and even kill our men."

"But you have these deranged resisters in every country, even those who are on our side."

"It's different in France. While most of their people aren't brave enough to openly defy us, I know that secretly most every one of them cheers at the actions of the resistance. I really think we need to be tougher with them."

Ellen sighed, apparently done with talking, as she stubbed her cigarette into the ashtray, before leaning over and kissing him.

Much later, as she observed Wilhelm getting dressed, she asked, "When is the funeral?"

"Tomorrow. Would you like to come?"

"Actually, yes."

He looked at her, surprised. "Why?" Ellen was the most unsentimental person he knew and she'd always said the dead couldn't care less whether anyone attended their funeral or not, so her change of mind was surprising.

"New times, new rules." She left the bed stark naked and absolutely sure of herself as she crossed the room to where he was standing. "I, for my part, am welcoming our masters with open arms. If Reichsführer Himmler organizes a state funeral for your father, I'll be there to give my condolences and show how much I love our Führer and everything he stands for."

Wilhelm noticed the bitter tone in her voice. It was a topic they never talked about, not even in the privacy of her bed. Her preference for both sexes was considered abnormal and could easily land her in a concentration camp should the authorities ever find out about it.

"To use my brother's words: 'mingle and make valuable connections'. It can only help to know the right people." He placed a kiss on her cheek. "I'll see you tomorrow, then."

Out on the street, he wondered whether he should return to Reiner's place yet. As much as he feared running into his brother and being coaxed into another boring day with boring meetings, he decided that he needed a change of clothes. His friends wouldn't mind either way, but for his Christmas shopping he preferred not to be in uniform. Maybe he could even sneak into one of the shady bars off the Ku'damm first, and get so drunk that he wouldn't mind Reiner's condescending remarks or Erika's prim and proper disapproval of his loose morals.

Thanks to the spare key hidden under a stone, he managed to slip in and out of the house without anyone noticing. He spent the day with old comrades from the elite school known as Napola, or the National Political Institute of Education, drinking and talking about the war. In the evening he returned to Reiner's place, drunk enough not to fear the dinner conversation with the family.

"Oh, you decided to turn up at last," Erika said as she opened the door after he rang the bell. She was wearing a formless dark green dress that exposed her condition more than hiding it. Her chestnut hair was braided above her ears, pretzel style. Wilhelm thought that she would look so much more beautiful if she used some lipstick like the Frenchwomen did, but Hitler hated lipstick—and makeup in general—and had declared it un-German for a woman to artificially paint her pure Aryan face.

"Not too late, I hope?" He mustered a charming smile and stepped out of the darkness into the brightly lit corridor.

"You've been drinking." Erika squinted her eyes at him in disapproval. "Where were you last night?"

It had been many years since his mother had inquired about his whereabouts, and he certainly wasn't going to offer an account to his sister-in-law now. "About town."

"And you're out of uniform."

"I am on furlough." He felt the dread creeping up his spine. Had she always been like this? He couldn't really remember, since he'd never been at their place for longer than a family dinner before.

"Reiner takes great pride in appropriate wear at the dinner table."

"Really? And what exactly is inappropriate about my attire?"

"We have guests. I expect you at the table in your uniform, hair combed and with washed hands in five minutes."

He knew he shouldn't, but he couldn't help a rebuff at her patronizing ways and said, "Yes, ma'am."

She glared at him and her voice dripped with ice. "Be punctual."

Wilhelm rushed off to the guest room, where he changed into his uniform and combed back his hair with Brylcreem. He wished he'd stayed at the bar and drunk himself into oblivion. The more time he spent with Reiner and Erika, the more he understood Annegret choosing to run away. If he had to face the prospect of living permanently with his brother's family, he'd disappear without a trace as well.

Well, she should be happy without the oppressive embrace of her family. She had his blessing and he certainly wouldn't be bending over backwards to find her.

*

The next morning Wilhelm was sitting in the passenger seat of his brother's limousine, clad in his dress uniform, that had been impeccably ironed by Erika. She and Reiner were sitting on the backseat, having left their daughters at home under the care of a friend.

Wilhelm thought the children should have the opportunity to say goodbye to their grandparents, but Erika had insisted a funeral wasn't a place for small children and they would only disturb the other funeral guests.

They drove to the meeting point for the motorcade. The troop car with his father's direct subordinates went first, pulling an open trailer with the coffin draped in a huge swastika flag. Reiner's black staff Mercedes was directly behind, followed by a vehicle with friends from the SS. As they drove toward the cemetery, Wilhelm almost forgot about the sad occasion, such was the difference between Paris and Berlin, and in a good way. Every window in the city seemed to be flying the swastika, and passers-by stopped when they saw the motorcade, curiously looking and stretching their right hands proudly into the air, shouting a "Heil Hitler" whenever the official government cars came in sight.

Wilhelm rolled down his window to breathe in the admiration for the Führer and his SS. It would do the French good to adopt the admiring behavior of the German population and show the same unabated enthusiasm for their leaders.

After about half an hour they stopped near the chapel and eight SS men carried his father's coffin inside, where they put it beside the much simpler coffin of his wife.

Hitler himself had not been able to attend due to a conflict of schedule, but had sent a wreath. Reichsführer Himmler, a personal friend of Wilhelm's father, climbed the podium to deliver a lengthy eulogy about SS-Standartenführer Wolfgang Huber and his merits for the Third Reich. Wilhelm's mother was also commended for being a good wife and mother, raising three children for the Führer, the two sons having followed in their father's footsteps becoming highly valued members of the SS.

Involuntarily, Wilhelm held his breath, scanning the gathered crowd for Annegret, but to no avail. He was increasingly worried about her, since missing their parents' funeral was so out of character for her. Reiner might believe what he wanted, but Wilhelm was sure something was wrong with his sister, and it pained him to think she was somehow hurt.

After the moving speech, people got up to follow the coffin to the burial site and later to offer their condolences to the family. Nobody seemed to notice that Annegret was missing, or maybe they simply assumed she was too emotionally shaken to attend, although nobody publicly voiced this opinion, because it would be shameful for a good German woman to show this kind of weakness.

After most of the dignitaries had moved through the line, Ellen approached him, a Gestapo officer at least twice her age by her side. Wilhelm smiled on account of the clever move. Apparently, she'd put his advice to mingle into immediate action, and she'd chosen well. Having the Gestapo on one's side was always a good thing. He didn't bother with unnecessary jealousy, since he'd be off back to Paris in a week from now. "I'm so sorry for your loss."

"It's a great loss, not only for our family, but also for our country," he replied, shaking her hand and giving it a secret squeeze, meant to ask whether they were still on for the night.

"Of course," she said with a mischievous glimmer in her eyes.

"It was a shock when I heard about your father's passing," the man said by way of greeting. "You may not remember me, I'm Horst Richter."

"Of course, I remember your name, Herr Richter. Father always spoke most highly of you. Are you still at Prinz-Albrecht-Strasse?"

"No, about a year ago I was promoted to Reichskriminaldirektor and am now overseeing the education and library system. Unfortunately, that meant a relocation to Leipzig, which is nothing compared to Berlin."

Wilhelm's ears pricked up, since according to that young soldier's assurances, Anne had gone to Leipzig, but he decided not to make any reference to her. Having the Gestapo as friend was good, but there was no necessity to give them unasked for information.

"My father would be honored to know that you made it all the way over here to attend his funeral." His words felt so hollow and contrived, even to his own ears. Where he was now, his father probably didn't give a toss about who came to his funeral.

"Please forgive my asking, which of the two sons are you?"

"I'm Wilhelm. The younger one."

"Oh, the one in Paris, isn't that right?"

"You are well informed. And thank you again for coming."

"Wolfgang was a good friend and helped me out more than once. It was the least I could do. If you ever need my assistance, don't hesitate to ask."

"Thank you so much."

"Where's your sister, by the way? Annegret, isn't it?"

Wilhelm almost choked on his words, pondering what to tell the man in front of him. He couldn't well admit that Annegret had fled Berlin to an unknown destination, because that would only cast a shadow over the family's reputation. "She survived the bombing and is understandably very shaken. Currently she's recovering with a friend of the family in Leipzig." The moment the words left his mouth he realized his mistake. What if Richter took it upon himself to visit Anne to give her his condolences and found out something uncouth?

"What a coincidence. I'll pay her a visit," Herr Richter said, happy to help out an old friend. He pulled out a notebook and a pen, ready to take notes. "And her address?"

Wilhelm had difficulties keeping his breathing even. "I'm so sorry, I would have to ask Reiner."

"No need." Richter stuffed the notebook back into his breast pocket. "I'll find out myself."

"Please, there's no need…"

"That's an easy task for me. Comes with the territory." He guffawed about his own joke.

Wilhelm thought fast. Whatever Richter found out when visiting Anne, he had to keep the rest of the family out of any perceived affiliation. "I guess it does. Look, it's a bit embarrassing to say, but Annegret… She… She's… We don't exactly know where she is."

Richter looked surprised. "You don't?"

Wilhelm lowered his voice. "I believe she wanted to get away from Berlin. The death of our parents was too much of a shock for her. So if you could find her discreetly, we'd be incredibly grateful."

"Leave that to me. Discreet operations are my forte, after all."

Before Richter could elaborate, Wilhelm shot Ellen a glance and she immediately understood. "Horst, we should move on, there are more people wanting to give their condolences."

"Of course." Horst Richter bid his goodbyes and took Ellen's arm to lead her away.

After the last person had left, Reiner came to his side and asked, "What did Horst Richter want from you?"

"He was offering his sympathies." Wilhelm paused for a moment. "He's now in Leipzig and has offered to look for Annegret."

"Really? That's a stroke of luck. Let's hope he finds her and is discreet about it. We don't need any gossip about our sister, not now when I'm about to be promoted to Heydrich's department."

It was so much like his brother to reveal important news like this during his parents' funeral. But Wilhelm didn't rise to the bait. "Are congratulations in order?"

"Not yet, the official announcement will come after a suitable period of mourning."

CHAPTER 9

It had been snowing for days and the city of Leipzig lay under a thick white blanket. Margarete accompanied her aunt to the market for groceries. The next day was the first day of Hanukkah, but for obvious reasons they wouldn't celebrate.

"I thought we could buy a candle," Heidi suggested. "Everyone will think it's for Christmas."

Margarete was grateful for her aunt's attempts to keep the Jewish culture alive despite the difficulties. Heidi herself was Catholic, but had always celebrated the Jewish holidays as well with her husband, before the Nazis had taken him.

"I miss them so much," Margarete whispered, thinking of happier days with her family. As far as she knew, she was the only member of the Rosenbaum family still free—thanks to the despicable Huber family, who'd exploited her as a domestic slave. It had been a strange twist of fate that a gentile friend of her father's had mentioned Frau Huber's dire need for a maid. Margarete still remembered the glint in her eyes when the woman realized Margarete would work more hours than any other maid and didn't even have to be paid for her services.

Although, as badly as they'd treated her, she had to admit she'd only survived this long thanks to the protection of being in their house.

"I know, I miss Ernst, too. Every single day. Some days I think I can't breathe anymore, and the pain is so strong I want to ask them to put me on the next train just to be with him." They both knew it was a ridiculous wish, not just because Heidi had no idea even where they'd taken her husband or whether he was still alive.

The general public, and probably Heidi too, still believed in the myth of transit camps with subsequent relocation to the east—where exactly nobody dared question—but Margarete knew better. Back in October she'd overheard Herr Huber say the Führer wanted first Berlin and then Germany to be *judenrein*, clean of Jews, as if their mere existence somehow dirtied their surroundings.

Margarete reached for Heidi's hand and gave it a squeeze. "We may have to accept the fact that they are probably dead."

"Never."

"I know, it's so hard, but from everything I heard Herr Huber say, those who step onto one of the cattle trains are destined to never return."

Heidi turned to Margarete. "Whatever anyone else says, I will continue to believe my Ernst is alive until someone brings me his body."

"I will pray for him, like I do for the rest of our family," Margarete said and linked arms with her. At least this year she had someone to share the festive season with. For her it didn't matter whether they celebrated Hannukah or Christmas, as long as they sat together in loving spirit, praying for the return of their family members.

"Look over there." They had reached the market square and Heidi pointed at a stall selling nativity scenes, Christmas tree ornaments and candles.

Margarete followed her outstretched hand with her eyes, when the sound of harsh voices captured her attention and she stopped in her tracks.

Three Brownshirts were attacking two women who'd been walking down the street. Only when the women turned around, desperate to get away from them, did Margarete notice the yellow stars on their flimsy coats.

"Filthy vermin," one of the Brownshirts shouted, his baton hammering down on the back and head of the poor woman. "You'll get what you deserve. Soon all of Germany will be *judenrein!*"

Margarete paled at his vile words, indicating that not a single Jew would be left in Germany. Despite her new identity, she still was very much Jewish in her heart and soul, so the words hit her hard. She felt such sympathy deep inside for the two women being attacked in front of her eyes, because she knew it could have been her if it hadn't been for the lucky incident of that English bomb giving her an unexpected way out.

Every fiber in her body tensed and despite knowing better than to stare, she couldn't tear her eyes away from the scene. The three bulky men forced the women to kneel in the slush and emptied their bags onto the sidewalk.

"Where did you get this produce, you stealing lout?" a Brownshirt said, squishing a potato beneath his heel.

Margarete saw how the woman's shoulders shook with suppressed sobs. Since the Jews received such small rations, that one potato was probably a day's worth of food for her. When the baton crashed onto her head with a sickening crack, Margarete reacted automatically and jumped to help, but found her forward momentum stalled by a vice-like grip on her arm.

Almost unbelieving she glared at the hand gripping her and followed up the arm to the shoulder and the face of the person holding her so viciously. Aunt Heidi.

"Don't," her aunt cautioned her in a harsh whisper. "It will only risk blowing your cover."

Margarete puffed out a breath, feeling as if her entire self was being deflated into a sorry heap in the slush. Heidi, of course, was right, but that didn't make it any better. Even in her new identity as Annegret Huber, she was impotent to help another Jew and had to stand by watching how the two women were mistreated.

Heidi pulled her away from the ugly scene. "Don't look back."

Giving a last side-glance to the women being marched toward the main street, she reluctantly followed her aunt to the stall with the Christmas decorations. Still shaking with anger, she took a closer look at the things on display, hoping for some comfort. Instead she felt another wave of bile rising in her throat. Not that she particularly cared about the Christian holiday, but these abominations were simply too much.

A postcard adorned with a fir branch and the words "*Der Weihnachtsglöckchen traulich Läuten, möge uns allen Frieden bedeuten.*" May the cozy tolling of Christmas bells, mean peace for all of us. *Except for the Jews, of course,* she thought bitterly, tempted to take up a delicate red bauble with a painted black and white swastika and crush it in her hand.

"What about this one?" Heidi held up a simple, slender white candle. "Wouldn't that fit nicely with our decorations?"

Margarete didn't trust herself to keep her voice modulated and gave a weak nod. When Heidi handed the candle to the shopkeeper, the older woman said, "Wouldn't you want something more patriotic? These are my best sellers," pointing to an array of white and red candles with portraits of Hitler painted on them.

Even Heidi paled at this perversion of the Christmas spirit, but she had herself under much better control than Margarete. "Oh, they are beautiful, but I wouldn't dare to burn them, it would feel so wrong."

The shopkeeper nodded solemnly. "They are purely for decoration."

Margarete, though, almost wanted to buy one of the horrible candles with the sole reason to see Hitler's ugly head melting away. The idea gave her a surprising comfort. Meanwhile, Heidi had paid for the plain white candle and said, "Let's go. We still need to buy produce."

As they did their weekly shopping, Margarete couldn't get the scene of the two women being marched away out of her head and once they were on the way home, out of earshot of anyone, she asked, "Where do they take them?"

"Who?"

"The Jews. The two women they attacked earlier."

Heidi slowed down to look at her niece. Margarete had never seen her this tired and hopeless. It was as if her aunt had aged several dozen years in just one second. "The city council has placed the school building in the Yorkstraße at the disposal of the Gestapo, to be the collection and accommodation point. I was there right after they took my Ernst, but I wasn't allowed in. The school is surrounded by a fence and the SS patrol the perimeter day and night. There was no way to get inside, or outside, for that matter."

She gave a heavy sigh. "Only once I saw his dear face looking out of the window on the second floor. But as soon as I had blown him a kiss, the SS shooed me away and warned me never to return unless I wanted to get into trouble myself. A friend of a neighbor works in the city administration, and I heard from her that Ernst was on the first transport out of Leipzig. She didn't know where to, since she isn't privy to classified information, just that his name was amongst those to be relocated eastward."

They had reached their home, but Heidi's fingers were shaking so fiercely, she couldn't put the key into the keyhole. Margarete gently took them from her hand and unlocked the door to the apartment building. Once inside the confines of her apartment, Heidi flopped onto the sofa, caught in her grief.

"I'm sure he's fine." Margarete knelt beside her aunt, trying to soothe her. She knew the relocation to lands in the east was a ruse being told to Jews and Germans alike to lull them into a sense of security. Herr Huber had always impressed on Reiner that the truth must not be revealed, because most Germans would be too weak and kind-hearted to approve such measures and might even stage some kind of protest that might upset the well-oiled deportation machine. A nuisance nobody needed.

"You think so?" Heidi looked at her with the trusting eyes of a small child and Margarete simply couldn't destroy her hope.

"I do. He's married to an Aryan, so that would make him a privileged Jew. Nothing will happen to him."

"You have no idea. I thought the same, but when I went down to the city administration to ask for Ernst's return, they told me that since we don't have children and it's just the wife who's of German blood, he will be treated like any other Jew. What's more, they told me since I had the audacity to marry a Jew, I could be treated like one of them, especially if I didn't stop causing trouble. That despicable man already had a yellow star in his hand, mocking me to wear it if I loved my husband so much." Heidi's eyes shone with unshed tears and her voice sounded like it came directly from her grave. "I gave up on him. I failed him. I stopped fighting for him in an effort to save my own miserable skin. Dear God, what have I done?"

"You have done nothing." Margarete hugged her aunt, as if Heidi were the child. "It's all them. The horrible Nazis are doing this, not you. They are the bad ones. You are just trying to survive."

"But at the expense of my Ernst…"

"Nothing you could have done would have changed his fate. What would he have gained if you were deported, too?"

"We would be together."

"I don't think so." Years of eavesdropping at the Huber household had taught her that families were torn apart on arrival in the labor camps, where males and females were strictly separated, usually never to see each other again. But she couldn't tell Heidi any of this. "Ernst would have wanted you to be safe and living your life."

Sobs were the answer and Margarete decided it was best not to say anything else, except for non-committal murmurs of comfort. Much later, when she was lying on the sofa, her eyes remained wide open in the absolute darkness of the room behind heavy blackout curtains. The decision to impersonate the daughter of an SS officer had been done on impulse, but every day it weighed more heavily on her conscience. Being Annegret was so wrong.

Desperate for comfort, she reached deep into the upholstery for her amulet. Tracing her fingers across the levied branches of the Tree of Life, she felt her mother's presence. She was somewhere, on earth or in heaven, watching over her and guiding her through this difficult time.

"I don't know what I should do," Margarete whispered near to tears.

Of course her mother didn't answer, but her memory went back to the time when she had first sent her to work for the Hubers. "My darling, it may seem hard, even unfair, and it breaks my heart to send you away, but believe me, it is your best chance to get through this. We lost all income when the SS took our haberdashery, but with the Hubers you'll get at least board and food."

Margarete scrunched up her nose. On the few occasions she'd met her mother in the park while running errands for the Hubers, she'd never told her how little food she actually received and how bad her accommodation was, because she hadn't wanted to upset her. Mother had enough grief with the precarious situation of their family. God only knew how they had scraped by, and having Margarete fed and safe had taken a huge burden off her shoulders.

She furiously rubbed the backside of the pendant with the inscription "Mazel Tov," wishing good luck. Had she been the lucky one in the family? At first glance, yes. She was here with Aunt Heidi, currently safe from deportation, unlike her parents and her siblings and their families, who'd received the order to gather for relocation not long ago, in October. But was Margarete really lucky? She was in a precarious situation too, hiding under a frail disguise and pretending to be one of the people she hated most. How could that be considered lucky?

CHAPTER 10

After another day out with old comrades from Napola, Wilhelm arrived back at his brother's house just in time for dinner.

"You finally decided to deign us with your presence?" Reiner said in a derisive tone.

"I had important meetings to attend to." Wilhelm took a seat beside his niece Adolphine in her highchair, unwilling to rise to the bait. In reality, the meetings had consisted merely of eating, drinking and talking about women.

Reiner sniffed. "Are you drunk?"

"I'm certainly not, but even if I were, it would be none of your business." The rage was making Wilhelm's carotid artery pulsate furiously.

"That's where you are wrong, everything in my house is of my concern. And, if you haven't noticed, since our father is dead, I'm now the head of the family. Therefore *everything* that happens here is of my concern."

Wilhelm rolled his eyes, thankful for Erika who stepped to the table, a plate with steaming hot roast pork in her hands.

"Reiner, could you please cut the meat, while I bring the rest?" She put the plate down and rushed away, serving potatoes, sauerkraut and gravy.

Despite loving the French cuisine, Wilhelm salivated for a good old-fashioned German *Braten*. He inhaled the scent of pork mixed with tangy kraut and closed his eyes, memories of his childhood surfacing.

Before the war, when they had spent much time in their country house, the housekeeper Frau Mertens had always prepared the most delicious Sunday roast for the Huber family. It was such a shame they didn't have servants anymore, since most people had been re-allocated to jobs considered important for the war efforts. Nowadays nobody had housemaids, gardeners, cooks and nannies. Even some mothers had to go to work in the factories, when their rightful place in life was looking after the three Ks: *Kinder, Küche, Kirche*: children, kitchen, and church.

He couldn't fathom why their husbands would allow them to work outside the house. As much as he loathed Reiner for his condescending ways, at least that part he got right. As soon as they'd married, Erika had left her job in the accounting department of some insurance company. Apparently she'd made quite the career for herself, while waiting to find an appropriate husband. But now she was the perfect mother and wife, always eager to serve her husband.

Maybe getting married wouldn't be such a bad thing after all? While he couldn't fathom being with only one woman for the rest of his life, that might change with age. Or he might fall in love with someone and actually didn't need the variety he currently enjoyed.

The ringing of the telephone interrupted his musings. Everyone at the table looked at each other.

"Who could that be?" Reiner asked. Every decent person knew not to call during dinner time.

"Shall I get it?" Erika stood up to walk toward the hall, where the telephone stood.

"If it's important, get me, otherwise tell the caller to try again in an hour." Reiner picked up a forkful of sauerkraut, and stuffed it into his mouth. "Erika really is a great cook, don't you think so?"

"She definitely is." Wilhelm actually thought her food was average, but he would never dare to criticize his brother's wife.

Erika returned to the dining room and said, "It is Horst Richter, from the Gestapo in Leipzig, he said it was important."

Reiner sighed and walked the few steps into the hallway, leaving the door open. Wilhelm knew his brother hated to be interrupted during meals, but Reichskriminaldirektor Richter was not only an old friend of their father's, but also ranked much higher than Reiner, so it would be exceptionally impolite not to take the call. Not to mention the fact that Richter might have news about Annegret.

"Reiner Huber here, what a pleasure to hear from you… Are you sure…? Oh, that's wonderful news, then… Of course, let me check my schedule and get in touch with you in the morning… Good evening." When Reiner returned to the table his face was unreadable.

Wilhelm knew better than to ask what Richter had wanted, because that would only give his brother a reason to drag out a response. On the other hand, seeming disinterested might anger Reiner enough to keep the information to himself altogether. He had to tread carefully between showing too much interest and not enough.

"He sent a rather large wreath for the funeral, did you thank him?" Wilhelm tested the waters.

Reiner glared daggers. "We didn't talk about that. And weren't you supposed to send thank you cards to everyone important? I can't believe you could have forgotten the Reichskriminaldirektor."

It was so typical for Reiner to throw in Richter's rank in an attempt to make Wilhelm feel guilty. He put on a nonchalant façade. "Naturally, I have sent him a thank you card, but he might not have received it yet and it would have been a nice touch to thank him in person, too. After all, he went to the trouble of calling."

Reiner brusquely turned his head. "Erika, could you please serve me another piece of roast?"

Delaying tactics. It never got old with his brother. At least Wilhelm now knew Richter had given him some important information, or Reiner wouldn't be so flustered. Waiting until Erika had served, Wilhelm said, "So, what did he want?"

Too agitated to keep the news to himself, Reiner said, "He believes he has found our sister, which is a great relief."

"That's such great news," Erika interrupted, which earned her a scolding stare.

"Don't get your hopes up yet, because he's not a hundred percent sure. Annegret Huber is quite the common name, but there's a girl her age who arrived from Berlin not long ago and is living with someone named Heidi Berger."

"Heidi Berger? Never heard that name before. Is she a friend of Anne's?" Wilhelm asked.

"I honestly have no idea. Also apparently Anne now works in the university library."

"She's studying there?" Erika asked.

"Our sister? She was barely interested in anything enough to even read a book, let alone study. No, she's working there." Reiner furiously massacred the pork on his plate.

"Then it can't be her. For one, she's never worked a day in her life and secondly, she's more interested in music, nightlife and men than in books." Wilhelm couldn't really blame her, since his interests were the same. Except for the working, of course, because unlike the doted-on apple of his father's eye, he had to work for his living.

"Richter thinks differently and he wants me to travel to Leipzig to see for myself." Reiner put a piece of meat into his mouth. "Does he think I have free time to spare? My schedule is full for the next ten days and a trip to Leipzig would cost me an entire day. For heaven's sake, we have a war to win!"

"You work so hard." Erika patted Reiner's arm. "How could Annegret put us in this predicament? I am glad she is alive, of course. But how could she think taking a job was a smart idea? Someone in her position should be concentrating on charitable works and other things to support the war effort."

Looking at both of them, Wilhelm actually understood why his spoiled sister might have preferred to join the working population to living in their house, and since he didn't have to worry about her being dead or gravely injured anymore, he secretly congratulated her for her guts. But why Leipzig? He had a sudden idea. It would kill two birds with one stone. "I'll go."

"You?" Reiner's mouth was hanging agape.

"Yes. Since I'm on furlough I don't have meetings scheduled."

"But the reading of the will?" Erika interjected.

"Damn!" Wilhelm ignored Erika's glare at the swear word. He hadn't thought about that bit. "When is it?"

"The day after tomorrow in the morning."

"I'll be back by then."

"You'll never get the travel permits and train tickets in time. Not even with my help." Reiner paused a moment, frowning. "Although… I could… I won't be needing the car all day. Alright, I'll send it for you, and then you'll be in Leipzig in no time at all. If this woman is indeed our sister, the two of you can be back before the reading of the will."

"It's a plan, then," Wilhelm said, looking forward to having a day and night away from his brother. If he found Anne, they might even hit the streets together for a night out on the town and have the driver bring them back in the early morning. It wouldn't be his first night without sleep.

CHAPTER 11

Margarete was working her way through the cart of books students had returned to the library when Frau Merz came looking for her.

"There's someone here asking for you."

"Someone's looking for me?" Margarete didn't know anyone in Leipzig except for Aunt Heidi and her neighbor across the corridor, Olga. But neither one of them would disturb her at work.

"Yes. He said he was from the Gestapo."

Margarete almost fainted from the panic. Someone must have found out about her true identity and called the Gestapo on her. She scanned the library for a way to escape, but there really was none. The only exit door was behind the reception desk, where the Gestapo were presumably waiting to arrest her. Two emergency exits were in the back of the room and another one in the basement, but all of them were secured with loud sirens, and Frau Merz had impressed on her to never use them, save for a real emergency, because they would alert police and firefighters.

Plus, she probably couldn't run fast enough to reach the door, and the Gestapo might have men positioned outside, since they never came unprepared or with just one officer. No, she had to meet him and hope for the best. Maybe she could lie her way out of the situation?

"Come along, don't keep him waiting," Frau Merz said rather impatiently and stepped aside to let Margarete precede.

She nodded, swallowing painfully, while trying to put on a brave face. "Maybe it's that charming young man I met the other day? He wanted to go out with me." She looked at Frau Merz for confirmation, but immediately had her hopes crushed.

"No. No, this is an older man. Reichskriminaldirektor Richter. You did deliver the list on time, didn't you? I really hope he's not here because the list was somehow faulty. You did write down anyone requesting a restricted book, didn't you?"

"Of course," Margarete managed to say in a neutral tone, despite the fear creeping up on her. On two instances she'd *forgotten* to write down the name and address of a person when it was clear that they didn't need certain books for academic reasons. Did Frau Merz suspect something? If she survived the encounter with the Gestapo officer, Margarete promised herself she would be much more careful from now on.

"Here she is," Frau Merz announced with a chipper, yet anxious, voice.

He said, "It won't take long. Is there a place where we can talk without being disturbed?"

Margarete was too frightened to answer, but Frau Merz hurried to say, "Certainly, Herr Reichskriminaldirektor, you can use one of the study rooms over there." Those rooms were usually reserved for professors studying restricted books, but the irony was lost on Margarete, since she had difficulties keeping her legs from giving out from under her.

Once inside the small room, he closed the door behind them and gave her a long, probing look before he asked, "You don't remember me?"

"I'm afraid not." She had no idea what he was talking about or what he even wanted from her. Or maybe this was simply a scare tactic the Gestapo used to get a quicker confession. And it worked, since she was about to spill all her secrets, if only he stopped giving her that scrutinizing stare.

"But you do know who I am, right?"

No, no, no. She had no idea, who he was, but suddenly she remembered Frau Merz's remark and made up the rest. "You are Reichskriminaldirektor Richter, head of the Gestapo in Leipzig and, among other tasks, responsible for the office overseeing the usage of restricted books."

He smiled and his gaze warmed up to her. "I see your father taught you well."

My father? Good heavens, what does he have to do with this? She opted for a nod and a smile, waiting for Herr Richter to bring some light into this strange visit.

"I'm so sorry for your loss and I want to let you know, that I'm always willing to help, should you ever be in need."

Margarete had to put a hand against the wall, to steady herself. He wasn't here to arrest her. On the contrary, he believed she was Annegret and wanted to help. Her mind raced, trying to be just like Annegret and act like she would in such a circumstance. Despite living in the same household for two years, she'd always been too occupied working for and hating the family to closely study their behavior. But one thing she knew, Annegret wouldn't be afraid of a Gestapo officer, no matter how high up, and especially not if he was a friend of her father's.

"Thank you. It was a shock." She added the appropriate amount of distress into her voice, before looking up again. It was harder than she'd expected, and the moment she met Richter's eyes, she recoiled in fear.

"Is that why you ran away to Leipzig?"

His words, said in a caring tone, sent new chills down her spine. All her life she'd lived in fear of the authorities, and she was helpless to stem the anxiety rising inside her chest. But she didn't have the luxury of being scared, she had to snap out of it and begin acting the way Annegret would. Sad over the loss of her parents, but still haughty and entitled.

"There was nothing left of my parents' place."

"You could have stayed with Reiner."

"Oh… I didn't want to impose. His wife is heavily pregnant and…" Margarete thought quickly. "She doesn't particularly like me."

"Why didn't you come to me first thing when you got here?"

For heaven's sake, why would anyone seek out the Gestapo voluntarily? "I don't know."

"You should have told the registration office that your father was SS-Standartenführer Wolfgang Huber. I'm sure they would have been able to accommodate you, so you didn't have to work, either."

Margarete was getting desperate; this conversation might be benevolent on his part, but it was leading into dangerous territory. Somehow she needed to make it clear that she couldn't ever go back to her family. She sighed, and cast him an apologetic gaze. "You're probably right, but I was so shocked after the bombing, and seeing my parents lying dead amongst the rubble, my only thought was to get away."

"Well, that is understandable, Annegret, but…" he put a hand on her shoulder and it cost her all her willpower not to flinch away "… you really should have told me. Your father and I were good friends and even though I haven't seen you or your brothers in almost a decade, you must have known I would help."

"I guess… I was just too shaken by the events… I'm only just getting my bearings."

He shook his head. "It didn't leave a good impression that you weren't at the funeral. People have been asking questions."

The funeral! Margarete hadn't thought about that. Annegret was the apple of her father's eye, she certainly wouldn't have missed paying her last respects to him. "Nobody told me."

He gave her a skeptical look and said, "Maybe because your family doesn't know where you are?"

The blood vanished from her head as she realized the implications of his words. That darn man was onto something, and being the Gestapo officer he was, he wouldn't stop until he got to the bottom of things. Forcing tears to her eyes was an easy task, given the horrible fear that was holding her in its grip. "Please, Herr Richter… My brothers can't know where I am."

"You must know that they are very worried about you?"

"But… You have no idea… They will surely kill me." Her voice was shrill and her anguish was real.

"Annegret, please calm down. Whatever has happened, I can help you. Please, tell me what you're afraid of. I'm sure I can take care of it."

She swallowed hard. What could she actually say to get him off track, since he seemed determined to help her? "That's so kind of you, and my father would certainly appreciate it. But if you'll just leave me be and don't tell my brothers, I'll be fine."

Once again, he gave her that scrutinizing gaze that seemed to disrobe her right in front of him, exposing every little secret she owned. Just when she thought she couldn't stand it anymore, he cleared his throat and asked, "Are you with child? Is that why you ran away?"

Margarete reddened with indignation. How could this man even suggest such a thing? Did she look like a tart who offered herself to the first man who came along? Shame spread through her veins, since she knew that a woman fell pregnant after sharing the bed with a man—who should be her husband—for some time. "I'm not… What do you think I am?" she said outraged, ready to give him a piece of her mind, when a frightening thought occurred to her. Could she be carrying Reiner's offspring? Nobody had ever explained to her how exactly these things worked, and her mother had always warned her to keep her legs crossed at all cost and never let a man give her as much as a kiss, because this was the beginning of more sinister things. How sinister, she hadn't been able to imagine back then.

"I... I..." she stuttered. "I..."

Richter took her hand with surprising kindness and said, "Did someone take advantage of you?"

She nodded, unsure, what to say. The fear, the tension and the horrible prospect worked together to make more tears spill down her cheeks.

"Now, now. This is not the end of the world. We'll arrange for a quick wedding, and nobody will be the wiser."

A wedding? Another wave of panic made her gag. Whom was she supposed to marry? And... Annegret's brothers would surely attend the ceremony and recognize her... No, she had to avoid a wedding at all costs. "I can't."

"But whyever not? This kind of thing happens all the time. If it's done before you show, there will be no uncouth gossip either."

For a fleeting moment she wished he'd be the ruthless Gestapo officer people were afraid of, and not the kind and caring man trying to help a friend's daughter out of trouble. Then she had an idea.

She kept her eyes downcast as she whispered, "He said he loved me, but when I told him, I found out he's already married with two children and a third one on the way." She looked up to Richter and pleaded. "I swear it, I didn't know. It was never my intention to break up a family. I know how much the Führer values the German wife."

"It's not your fault. He was the one to deceive you. Who is it?"

Fear filled her once more. She couldn't tell the truth, because the man who'd taken from her what wasn't his to have was the brother of her new self. "I... He... He's very high up in the SS. I don't want to get him into trouble."

Richter's lip twitched. "That's noble of you, although this man should have known better than to seduce the daughter of a fellow officer. Aren't there enough easy women populating the cabarets and bars of Berlin?"

Margarete forced herself to nod and wiped her cheeks dry with her fingers. "If my brothers ever find out, they'll kill me, they might even go after him. No, I can't possibly tell them."

"And you can't marry the father." Richter rubbed his forehead in deep thought. "That complicates things. But... at least he's a certified Aryan. What does he look like?"

Whatever did he want to know this for? She shrugged and described Reiner. "He's six feet three, blond hair, green-brown eyes, broad shoulders... A model of a good Aryan man." She forced a dreamy expression onto her face. "And so handsome. Strong, but kind. Determined. Always willing to sacrifice himself for his Fatherland." She felt like she was being sucked down into quicksand. With each lie, she was digging herself deeper and deeper into a pit that would eventually swallow her up.

Richter gave her a stern look. "What you did was stupid and reckless. It's not a behavior any well-raised German woman should ever engage in."

Shame sent a heated blush from head to toe. It wasn't a behavior she had ever willingly engaged in.

"Nevertheless..." his voice became kind again, "I'm going to help you. Your father was a good friend and I owe him. That the father is SS, will make things easier."

Margarete nodded, although she had no idea why that would be the case.

"How far are you along?"

She didn't have the slightest idea and took a wild guess. "A month or two?"

"Good. Here's my plan. You'll keep working as usual, while I start making arrangements for you. As soon as you show, you'll move into a Lebensborn Institution. They will take care of you, and once the baby is born, it'll be given to a good German family, after which you can return to Berlin and make amends with your brothers."

Margarete had never heard about Lebensborn, but nonetheless nodded to his suggestion. As long as he wouldn't tell Annegret's brothers, she was safe, at least for the time being. "So you won't tell my brothers?"

"No, I won't. Your secret is in safe hands with me. And now, get back to work, or Frau Merz will become suspicious."

"Oh my God, yes. What should I tell her?"

"Nothing. Let me take care of it. You simply keep pretending everything is alright."

"Thank you." Margarete couldn't believe she was thanking a Gestapo officer, who was helping her to hide from Annegret's brothers.

She spent the rest of the afternoon on tenterhooks. Horst Richter had given her both a ray of hope to get out of this and the awful worry that she might be carrying Reiner's child under her heart. A child from one of the SS men she loathed more than anything in the world.

A wave of nausea rolled over her, as if to prove the horrible suspicion. Weren't most women sick in the early stages of pregnancy? If only her mother had been more specific in these things, instead of leaving her ignorant about what really happened between a man and a woman after marriage and how exactly children came about.

She couldn't wait to finish her work and, after a hurried goodbye to Frau Merz, she raced home to have a very awkward but necessary talk with her aunt.

"Aunt Heidi?" she called as soon as she opened the apartment door.

"In the kitchen."

Margarete took off her gloves, scarf, hat and coat and hung them on the rack beside the door. Then she unlaced her shoes and put them in an orderly fashion beside Heidi's. This was rather embarrassing, and while she needed clarity, she feared the way this conversation might go. What if Heidi was repulsed by the things she had done and threw her out? Things like that happened. A neighbor girl had found herself in the family way and her parents had sent her away. Nobody ever mentioned her name again, just like nobody ever talked about the Jews that vanished overnight.

"What do you know about the Lebensborn?" Margarete asked, jumping a bit when her aunt turned around with wide open eyes, swinging the cooking spoon in her right hand.

"The Lebensborn? Are you in trouble?" Heidi asked aghast.

Margarete's shoulders slumped and heated shame ran through her body from head to toe. She'd thought she would never again have to be reminded of the things Reiner had done...

"Dear God, help us! When did that happen?"

"I don't know. Not really." Margarete fell on the kitchen chair and buried her head in her arms while telling her aunt the entire sordid story, interrupted by sobs. She began with Reiner's attacks, and ended with recounting her conversation with Richter earlier that day.

"Are you sure?"

"No. How does a woman know before she shows?"

Heidi sighed, pushed the pot from the stove and moved the second chair next to Margarete, before she sat down. "What exactly did your mother tell you?"

"Not much. That I should never show myself naked to a man until after marriage. Then, my husband would tell me what I had to do."

"Nothing else?"

"No."

"Did she explain to you about your monthlies?"

If that was at all possible, Margarete blushed some more and buried her head deeper into her arms on the table. How could she even talk about such things? "That it's a monthly curse all women have," she whispered barely audible.

"When was the last time?"

"Right before I came here."

"Thank God!" Heidi said with such fervor, Margarete raised her head. "You can't be pregnant then."

"But why?"

What followed was a lengthy explanation about things that happened in a woman's body and how the clearest sign of being in the family way was being late on the bleeding.

But the relief was soon mixed with a new fear. "But if Herr Richter finds out, he'll tell Annegret's brothers where I am."

Heidi covered her mouth with her hand. "Then we're both as good as dead."

Desperation took hold of her and suddenly the idea of having to bear Reiner's child didn't seem so awful anymore. "He must not find out."

Heidi stared at her with unbelieving eyes.

"Richter offered to find me a place to stay when I begin to show and once the baby is born, give it up for adoption. Then, I could return to Berlin to make amends with my brothers."

"But you're not with child. He will discover the truth soon enough and then God help us all."

Since Margarete was not well versed in these things, even with her new knowledge, she asked, "How long until I'm supposed to show?"

"It's different with every woman. Some don't show until very late. Four months at the most, I would guess."

"That's plenty of time. He might get transferred to some other place, or maybe now that the Americans have declared war, it will all be over by then?" Margarete knew she was clutching at straws.

"We can't rely on this. You have to leave. Go someplace where nobody knows Annegret and her family won't find her."

"And where could that be? Half of Europe is under German rule. The Gestapo have their spies everywhere, and surely an SS man's daughter can't simply vanish?" Desperation was taking hold of her. Perhaps going along with Richter's outrageous suggestion hadn't been such a great idea, after all. But on the other hand, what else had she been able to say to keep him from telling Annegret's brothers her whereabouts?

Both women were quiet with their thoughts. Finally, Heidi spoke again. "We won't solve this tonight. You are safe for at least the next two months, which gives us time to come up with a plan. For now, go to work and play along. We'll talk about this more and come up with a solution before it's too late."

Margarete nodded and then hugged her aunt. "Thank you."

CHAPTER 12

Wilhelm went downstairs for breakfast, where the rest of the family was already waiting for him.

"Did you have a good sleep?" asked Reiner.

He ignored the underlying insult. "I slept very well, thank you. It was a late night."

"Where have you been?" Erika asked.

"Out and about." He had no intentions of filling her in about his escapades of the night before.

"When will you find yourself a good wife and settle down?" Erika asked insistently.

Wilhelm gave a pointed glance at Reiner and said, "Not every man settles down after marriage."

Erika paled. "What are you suggesting?"

"Nothing." Reiner glared at him. "My brother is just being his usual annoying self, because he's jealous of my success."

Erika seemed mollified and beamed again. "Has Reiner told you about his latest coup?"

"And what would that be?" Wilhelm wasn't really interested in whatever great thing his brother had achieved. Why couldn't his family understand that he'd be happiest if everyone left him alone?

Reiner ruffled his feathers like a peacock doing a mating dance. "I've been invited to present at the Wannsee Conference."

"Isn't my Reiner wonderful?" Erika said as if it were somehow her doing that Reiner was rubbing shoulders with Reinhard Heydrich himself, and would no doubt present some boring concept for whatever boring thing the top brass were talking about at this conference.

"Your Reiner certainly is beyond wonderful. When is the conference?"

Erika took the praise without acknowledging the irony in his voice and poured coffee into his cup.

"In January. We're going to put a final solution to the Jewish question. I'm sure you'll be informed about the results once we have reached a conclusion," Reiner said.

Wilhelm ignored the intended insult. "The headquarters in Paris will be so pleased to get rid of these vermin. Any ideas yet?"

Reiner smirked. "Top secret, little brother. But I promise you'll be the first one to hear, once I'm cleared to talk about it."

"That is so exceedingly generous of you." In reality Wilhelm couldn't care less which way the Jewish problem was solved, as long as he never had to set eyes on one of those horrible creatures again. The world would be a much better place without them.

"I could get you into a more important position, if you only had an ounce of ambition. Father was so disappointed by you." Reiner glanced at his wristwatch. "Sorry, but I have to get going. I'll send you my car after I arrive at the office."

Wilhelm sighed to himself. All he really wanted was an easy office job that didn't involve any hands-on activity beating up or killing people, and enough money to lavish it on the good things in life.

"Thanks. And see you tomorrow at the reading of the will." Wilhelm smiled. After tomorrow he would never have money problems again.

Several hours later, he was sitting in the back of Reiner's staff car, reading the newspaper, when the driver addressed him, "Herr Oberscharführer, your brother just sent a message over the radio that you should please give him a call immediately."

What could Reiner want? "Well, then leave the Autobahn and find me a telephone booth in the next village."

"Certainly."

Ten minutes later, the driver stopped in front of a yellow phone booth and Wilhelm got out to dial Reiner's office number. The secretary put him right through.

"You can come back," Reiner said.

"What happened?"

"Horst Richter called. That woman he mentioned is not our sister."

"Did he meet her in person?"

"What do I know?"

"So how does he know it's not her?"

"He's Gestapo, and while they aren't the brightest heads, they do know how to fish out suspects."

"Anne is not a suspect."

"Stop arguing with me and come home. Richter insists we don't go looking for her."

"But why?"

"Maybe because he knows that SS officers generally have more important things to do than gallivant?"

"Look, I'm already halfway there and I have arranged to meet a few important people." Wilhelm had already made plans to meet a few former comrades from the Napola. "Aren't you the one who always tells me to mingle more? How would it look to backpedal now?"

Reiner sighed. "Well then, by all means. Go to Leipzig, but please just don't offend Richter by going on a wild goose chase after a woman who's not our sister."

"You think I'm stupid enough to do such a thing?" Wilhelm pretended to be indignant, but in reality he would do just that. Have a look at the young woman himself, and find out whether she was Anne or not. Some gut feeling told him she was hiding from the family, and, who knows, she might have duped Richter into believing whatever reason she'd offered him for her need to get away from Berlin.

"Don't be late for the reading of the will," Reiner warned him, before he hung up.

Wilhelm returned to the car and told the driver. "We can continue our way to Leipzig." He relaxed into the backseat and continued to leaf through the newspaper, while listening to the radio. It was full of glorious victories for the Wehrmacht.

"Rommel is cunning as a fox," the driver said with admiration.

"The Desert Fox. Such a shame he couldn't attend my father's funeral. The two of them always held each other in high esteem."

"Yes, Herr Oberscharführer, I'm sure he would have wished to pay his respects."

Wilhelm chuckled. "But he's better placed in Africa, lambasting the British cowards with lightning speed."

"Such a shame we only have one of him, or we would have won the war already."

They were reaching the outskirts of Leipzig and he turned his attention to the surroundings. It was a sight of pure beauty, since the obnoxious Englishmen hadn't dropped their bombs over the city and, in contrast to Berlin or Paris, there were no ruins to be seen. Even the few people they met seemed to be more upbeat, waving at the dark limousine flying swastika flags on both sides of the front spoiler.

Wilhelm leaned back in his seat, tempted to roll down the window to graciously wave at the spectators the way he'd seen Hitler doing. But since he wasn't here on official business, he decided to keep the window up. He didn't want the driver to go running to Reiner, telling tales.

His brother might have graciously loaned him the automobile for the journey, but Wilhelm didn't have any illusions about where the driver's loyalty lay and that he would report every single detail not only to Reiner, but probably to the entire chain of command.

As they arrived in front of the hotel, he gave the driver time off until the evening, before he waved at one of the bellboys to carry his overnight bag to his room and walked into the hotel bar, ordering a drink. Usually he didn't drink this early in the day, but he felt strangely anxious about the confrontation with the girl who might be his sister. If it was Annegret, she would most certainly refuse to return to Berlin with him and make a scene, a behavior he blamed entirely on his father doting on her his entire life, instead of teaching her the way a good woman was supposed to behave.

He changed into civvies, and carefully checked for the driver before heading out of the hotel and down the street to the university library with a sense of anticipation in his chest. Nothing might come out of it, but the whole thing stank. Someone like Richter didn't make mistakes and it was more than strange that he'd called again to prevent them from going to Leipzig to see for themselves.

At the Bibliotheca Albertina, he didn't take time to appreciate the amazing architecture, but walked straight into the office to the right and spoke to the librarian sitting behind the reception desk with one swollen foot propped up on a stool. "Good afternoon. I am looking for Annegret Huber."

The woman gave him a suspicious glance. "We don't allow personal visits during work hours."

Wilhelm cursed himself for not wearing uniform. That brazen woman wouldn't have dared contradict him. "I'm her brother,

Wilhelm Huber, and I came all the way from Berlin to alert Annegret about our father's reading of the will."

"Oh! She never told me that her father had died."

"She is probably still too shocked. It was such a tragedy, for all of us," Wilhelm hurried to say, inwardly groaning. "May I talk to her for just a minute, please?"

"I'm afraid she left on her lunch break."

"When will she return?"

"She should be back in," the woman glanced at the clock on the wall, "in exactly thirty-five minutes."

"Great. You won't mind me waiting in here, will you?"

She gave him a scathing look. "This is a university library. We don't encourage loitering."

What was wrong with this woman? In Paris no civilian would have dared to speak to him out of tone. But here? Did this librarian really think she had anything to say? He swore never to take off his uniform again. For a split second he entertained the idea of showing her his ID card, but then thought better of it, since he'd come to Leipzig to have fun. Not dignifying her with an answer, he clicked his heels and saluted, "Heil Hitler!" Then he suppressed a chuckle, when the woman hobbled to her feet, returning the salute before sitting down again with a pained grimace.

That'll teach her to talk back to a member of the SS.

He walked a few hundred yards to a small park, where he spied a young woman who looked awfully familiar. But that couldn't be his parents' maid. His mind must be playing tricks on him. She was walking straight toward him, her eyes cast to the ground in a pensive way. The woman wore a beautiful dress—ruling out the idea it could be her, because Jews only ever wore old and drab things. No, it couldn't be Margarete, because this pretty girl, while she looked similar, had a completely different presence than the dull and stupid Jews who always lived in fear.

He was about to walk in another direction when she looked up and their eyes locked. He knew the exact moment when she recognized him, because her striking hazel eyes filled with sheer panic. Something was wrong with her. It didn't take long for him to notice what it was: she wasn't wearing the yellow star. It was a crime and he should report her for it.

And he would, but first he'd interrogate her. Maybe she knew about his sister? It seemed improbable, but if Annegret was in some kind of trouble, she might have confided in their former maid and perhaps even taken her with her? It wouldn't hurt to ask a few questions. Wilhelm frowned as he tried to put the puzzle together, but sprang into action as she made to run away and grabbed her arm.

"You can't get away, Margarete. It would be better to tell me the truth," he said with rightful anger.

"I… I'm visiting a friend."

"Jews don't have friends. And why aren't you wearing your yellow star?"

She looked down at her jacket with growing panic, and he increased the pressure on her arm to make sure she knew who was in charge. "Please, it must have dropped off. I'll go and get another one."

"I'm wondering…" he licked his lips, "if you aren't maybe hiding your real identity, pretending not to be a Jew?"

"No… no… I would never."

He saw sweat break out on her forehead and was now certain she was hiding something. "I was told you died in the bombing." His voice was cold as ice, imitating the way he'd watched some of the Gestapo agents talk when interrogating suspects of the French Résistance. While he usually avoided being present during the gorier parts, he was now happy for the experience, since it would come in handy getting the truth from this cunning Jewess.

"I… didn't… die, as you can see. The authorities must have made a mistake."

He let it go for a moment, since lecturing her on how German authorities never made a mistake wouldn't help getting information out of her. Instead, he smiled, hoping to lull her into a false sense of security and said with his kindest voice, "I'm not after you. I'm not even on duty. I came here to look for my sister. Have you by any chance seen her?"

She winced as if he'd physically hit her. "No."

She was lying. That much he knew. But why? "Are you sure?"

Margarete shook her head, swallowing heavily. "I have no idea where Fräulein Annegret is. I haven't seen her since the bombing. Please, Herr Huber, you must believe me. She's not here."

"Well, then it looks like I made the trip in vain," Wilhelm said and released her, not missing the relief that came over her.

Recovering her composure, she said in a much more confident voice, "I'm sorry I can't help you, but I really do need to get back to work."

He decided to let her go, partly because his definition of fun didn't include rounding up cute young women and handing them over to the police, but mostly because he was sure something was fishy here and he fully intended to follow her and find out more. When she walked straight into the Bibliotheca Albertina, his suspicions were confirmed. How could she not know about Annegret when they both worked at the same place? Maybe she and Richter were involved in some kind of sinister plot, highly unlikely as it was. In any case he was determined to find out.

CHAPTER 13

Trembling with fear, Margarete walked toward the library. Wilhelm Huber was here, looking for Annegret. She debated whether to run away or pretend nothing had happened and take up her work again.

Since she had nowhere to run or hide, she opted for the latter, hoping to come up with a plan. Wilhelm was no fool, it wouldn't take him long to put the pieces together. Her breathing was labored, because she fully expected him to come rushing into the library with an armed contingent of Gestapo officers.

"Fräulein Huber, what is wrong? You are so pale?" Frau Merz appeared in front of her.

It took all of Margarete's strength not to dissolve into a bawling puddle. "I'm sorry, I must have stood up too fast. I became dizzy, but it seems to be passing." She reached for the rolling cart full of books needing to be filed. "These need to be taken downstairs."

"Are you sure you're feeling well?" Frau Merz asked with a gaze that seemed to go through her.

"I am. Thank you. It was nothing, really." She clasped her hands around the handle of the cart and pushed it to the back of the reading room, intending to escape into the basement, where she could take refuge amongst the tall bookcases, protected from prying eyes. But even downstairs in the basement amidst the usually soothing presence of thousands of books, she couldn't calm her racing mind.

She dawdled as long as she possibly could, but had to return to the reading room to collect more returned books and sort them into the proper shelves. Trudging up the stairs with a racing heart, she reached the landing just when the door opened from outside and Frau Merz stood there. "Oh good. You have a visitor."

Margarete's heart sank to her boots, but she somehow managed to ask, "Who is it?"

"Your brother."

She felt the color drain from her face and her eyes frantically darted around the room, searching for an escape. But she already knew there was none. Without any better idea, she pasted a delighted smile upon her face and followed Frau Merz to the office, like a lamb to the slaughter.

"Herr Huber, here's your sister."

The moment Wilhelm recognized her, his eyes flashed with rage and Margarete involuntarily ducked her head. Desperate not to blow her cover she said in her most chipper tone, "Dearest brother. It's so good to see you."

The expression in his eyes turned from furious to dumb-founded, to unbelieving, but at least he didn't shout her betrayal to the winds. It was a thin thread to hang on to, but deep in her heart she hoped he would find it in himself not to expose her. He'd always been the nicest family member, never explicitly hurtful toward her, although she hadn't missed his appreciative glances upon her body either. But in contrast to his brother, he'd never acted upon those urges. If only she could talk to him alone, he might let her escape.

She turned to Frau Merz and asked, "Would you mind if I talked to my brother for a few minutes in private? It won't take long, I promise."

Frau Merz nodded. "Five minutes, not a single second longer. You can use the room for the stationery, you'll not be disturbed there."

"Thank you." Margarete turned toward Wilhelm and motioned for him to follow her. The moment she closed the door of the small windowless supplies room behind them, he grabbed her arm violently and hissed, "What kind of sick game are you playing?"

"Please, listen to me."

She could see the rage in his face and knew he'd rather strangle her, but he nodded. "If you don't tell me the truth, I swear, you'll wish you'd never been born."

She shuddered. "Please, Herr Huber, you must believe me. This is a big misunderstanding."

"Where's my sister?"

"Annegret is dead."

He seemed to deflate in front of her eyes and she was almost compelled to feel sympathy for him. The poor man had just lost his parents, and now his sister. But then she steeled her heart and remembered how much pain his kind had brought over her people, and herself. His own father had been about to deport her to one of the camps, for God's sake. This family didn't deserve her sympathy. They all deserved to burn in hell for eternity.

"No, she isn't," he whispered.

"She died in the bombing, along with your parents."

"That's not true! They never found her body. She went to Leipzig, she's here, working at the library." He was talking himself into a rage and she saw a mad flicker appear in his eyes.

"I'm the one they believe to be Annegret Huber." It might not be the wisest choice to tell him about her deceit, but he'd figure it out anyway. With her admission she might appeal to his humanity and plead for her life. "It was my chance to survive."

The mad flicker in his eyes intensified. Usually they were greenish-brown like those of his father and his brother, but now they turned into a sparkling emerald green. She looked right into them and saw a hidden kindness deep in his soul. For the shortest moment she felt a deep attraction to him, a connection of two lost souls. But she pushed the thought away. Wilhelm might not be sadistic and cruel, but he was still a Nazi—and her very life lay in his hands at this moment.

Before she could say another word, he attacked her, pushed her against the wall, holding his arm across her shoulders so she couldn't move. "You killed my sister! Admit it! You killed her! Why?"

Behind his fury was so much pain that she stopped being afraid of him. He wouldn't kill her, at least not right now. "Please, Herr Huber. Hear me out. I didn't kill her. She died in the bombing. I was caught beneath a staircase, which saved my life. When I crawled out of the rubble, I saw her and… I just wanted to live."

"What did you do?" He released his grip, sagging into a picture of misery in front of her eyes.

He probably already knew, but she would explain it to him, praying he'd not turn her in. If only she told him her situation, he might find a shred of humanity in his heart and let her go. It was her only chance.

"Your father had disclosed that he'd have me deported by the end of the week. Please, I beg you, you must know what really happens in these camps. How people are starved, mistreated and worked to death. I know you have kindness in you and you never really agreed with the cruelties committed against civilians… please…"

But it didn't work the way she'd hoped for, because with every word she said, he looked at her with more hatred in his eyes. "You're a Jew. You're debasing the memory of my sister by posing as her. I won't stand for it." He turned around and left the small room, while Margarete grappled to come to terms with the death sentence he'd just issued her.

CHAPTER 14

Wilhelm rushed from the small room, shaken to his core. He would have never believed that their former maid, a Jew no less, could be brazen enough to impersonate his sister—and beg for his understanding. Who did she think she was? Nothing but a piece of trash that Hitler rightly wanted to rid Germany from.

If he ever needed any proof that the Jews were evil, now he'd found it. An obscure urchin pretending to be the respectable daughter of a high-ranking SS officer. He seethed at the very thought.

In his hurry to call the police, he bumped into an older man walking into the huge entrance hall.

"Excuse me," he said, not looking up.

"Wilhelm Huber, is that you?" a familiar voice said.

He raised his head and recognized Horst Richter. "Herr Richter, what a coincidence, I was just about to call the police."

Out of the corner of his eye, Wilhelm noticed how Margarete was trying to slink away, but Richter had already seen her. "Annegret, come here."

The woman had an expression of raw horror on her face, but obeyed and carefully inched closer.

"I told Reiner that neither of you needed to bother coming here," Richter said, while ushering the three of them into the reception office. He turned to Frau Merz, and said, "Would you please leave us alone for a moment and make sure nobody disturbs us?"

The poor woman paled when she recognized the head of the Gestapo and quickly said, "Of course Herr Reichskriminal-direktor."

"I'm glad I came, because otherwise I would never have found out about this heinous deed. This woman is bringing shame over our family." Wilhelm wasn't furious anymore, instead he gloated over the fact that Richter would soon have to give him credit for figuring out a horrible deceit that Richter himself had been taken in by. No doubt the older man had been seduced by Margarete's big hazel eyes into believing she was simply a random woman sharing the name with his sister.

But now, he, Wilhelm, the underestimated second son, would prove to the world that he was cleverer than the rest of them.

Richter nodded. "Please, don't be so harsh in your judgement. Your sister—"

Wilhelm interrupted him, "This woman is not my sister. She never was."

"Don't say such awful things that you might later regret." Richter looked at a very pale Margarete and then back to Wilhelm. "Family bonds can never be untied, no matter what."

"This woman is not my sister. My father housed her and was kind to her and see how she paid him back! By debasing the reputation of our entire family."

"Enough of this," Richter said. "I understand your outrage, but everything will turn out just fine. You return to Berlin, tell your family you didn't find Annegret and let me handle the rest."

Wilhelm stared at Richter, not quite understanding what was going on. Seemingly he knew about Margarete's deceit, but why was he protecting her?

"This is not the first time something like this has happened and, I assure you, the matter is best left in my hands. Your sister is doing a great service for the Reich, something no one will ever know about."

"A service for the Reich?" Wilhelm got his wires crossed, not understanding a single word Richter was saying. All he noticed was the relieved expression on Margarete's face. If she was in cahoots with Richter, it wouldn't serve him well to stir up a hornet's nest.

"Yes. See it as a sacrifice for Führer and Fatherland. And let me take care of the rest. I've already started to turn the wheels."

"Well, if you think so, I'm most certainly not arguing. We all need to make sacrifices for Führer and Fatherland." Wilhelm's mind raced as he tried to find some reason why Richter would be coming to the aid of a destitute Jewish girl. Even in his high-up position it was a crime that could well end his career, or worse. The only explanation he could come up with was that the old man was bewitched by the young, beautiful woman.

On second thoughts, an illicit affair between the two of them made a lot of sense and he decided to make discreet investigations into the matter and use the knowledge when the time was right. Nothing could be better than a few dirty secrets that one could then use to blackmail another man if necessary.

While his money problems would be solved tomorrow after his father's will was read, he might still one day need a little push in his career. Maybe a promotion, or at least the guarantee of a safe position far away from the front if things became worse. The more he thought about it, the more tempting he found the idea. An entire universe of possibilities if he played his cards well.

Wilhelm smiled and deliberately used Richter's first name, which would normally be disrespectful, because the older man had to offer it to the younger one. "I'm sorry, Horst. I should have heeded your advice and not come here. Please, take my apologies and rest assured that I won't interfere with whatever you have in mind." He turned to look at Margarete, observing her closely. Without the drab clothing and the yellow star, she was a striking beauty and he could well understand why Richter had been seduced by her. What puzzled him was whether the Gestapo officer knew she was a Jew, or if he believed her to be the daughter of his late friend. For his purposes, Wilhelm realized, it didn't make a difference either way.

"Take care… Annegret. I'll be in touch," he said with a brooding look at her. He could tell by the way Margarete's eyes filled with panic that she had heard his unspoken warning and left the library with a spring in his step.

CHAPTER 15

After the roller coaster of emotions she'd gone through during the past hour Margarete was more exhausted than if she'd run ten miles. She still couldn't quite fathom what exactly had transpired, except that somehow Herr Richter hadn't believed Wilhelm when he'd claimed she wasn't his sister.

Unable to keep herself together one more second, she decided to leave it to him to deal with Frau Merz, and come up with a believable explanation. "Excuse me, Herr Richter, but I should get back to my work."

He gave her a wink. "We do need valiant women like yourself. Please don't hesitate to contact me whenever you feel the need."

Frau Merz gave a surprised look and even as Margarete fled from the room, she overheard Richter saying something about a siblings' quarrel, but everything had been sorted out.

She managed to stay clear of the head librarian most of the day, and after her workday ended, she rushed home and collapsed in tears upon seeing her aunt.

"Dear Margarete, whatever happened to you?"

"I must pack."

Before she could gather her things, Heidi took her arm and led her over to the couch, where she pulled her down to sit. "This Gestapo officer again?"

"No… worse…" She sobbed.

"Tell me. Maybe we can find a solution together."

"We can't. My cover got busted. Wilhelm Huber was here."

"Annegret's brother?" Heidi asked in shocked horror.

Margarete nodded. "Yes. He knows. He recognized me. He even accused me of murdering his sister and then he said he'd report me."

"Good heavens! You should have run away immediately, you still can—"

"Auntie, I… I really don't know what happened, but just as he walked off, Herr Richter came along and…" Heidi's gasp echoed from the walls of her tiny apartment "… he didn't believe Wilhelm when he said I wasn't his sister. On the contrary, he scolded him for being so cold-hearted and told him that he would take care of everything and I was doing a great service to the Reich."

Heidi shook her head, her face filled with fear.

Margarete hugged her and whispered, "I don't understand why he didn't insist. I mean, he tried to tell Herr Richter that I wasn't his sister. But I guess Richter misunderstood and thought Wilhelm was just trying to disown me because of the supposed pregnancy." She was quiet for a moment and then, almost to herself, asked, "But why didn't he press the issue and insist upon an investigation? He just let it go and agreed to go along with Richter's plan. I don't understand it."

"This is very strange, indeed. What do you think could be the reason?"

"I'm not sure what or whom to believe anymore."

"Well, regardless, it's no longer safe for you here. You need to get away and the sooner the better."

"But where will I go?"

Heidi thought for a long minute before she spoke again. "I have a friend who lives in Toulouse, in the free zone of France. She's German but married a Frenchman shortly after the Great

War. I will send her a letter tomorrow, but you cannot wait for an answer. You must leave in the morning. By the time you get there, my letter will have arrived explaining everything."

"I can't just show up on a stranger's doorstep," Margarete argued.

"You don't have a choice. Besides, I know my friend and she will surely help you once you appear on her front porch. You don't have any time to waste."

Margarete wasn't convinced that crazy idea would work out, but she didn't have any other options at the moment. "My French isn't good." In truth, her French was probably good enough for her to get along, but traveling all the way to Toulouse on her own? While pretending to be Annegret? And without valid travel papers? This was completely nuts, and not even the papers of a Nazi brat would protect her if she came to a control stop, which was bound to happen. "It'll never work."

"It's the only way. Wilhelm Huber could return anytime, and he might bring his brother or other relatives to prove you're an impostor. Richter will not help you then. You really need to leave Germany, and as fast as possible."

Margarete thought about that while she helped prepare a simple supper for them both. Much later, lying on the sofa and not finding sleep, she reached for the amulet between the upholstery and held it in her hand. The silver quickly warmed to her touch as she traced the branches of the Tree of Life with her thumb. She would have to file off the inscription, because it was too conspicuous. It broke her heart, but it had to be done.

Since she couldn't sleep anyway, she tiptoed into the bathroom and took out a metal nail file. It was hard work and seemed impossible at first, but after half an hour of arduous work, she'd removed the inscription "Mazel Tov" and turned the back of the pendant into a rough surface without any trace of the incriminating Hebrew words. Looking at it, she felt as if all good luck had truly deserted her along with the inscription, but then she smiled.

Because she'd come up with a fantastic idea. She wouldn't just run away, no. She would go in style and with all the required paperwork needed for a trip to France.

CHAPTER 16

The next morning Wilhelm returned to Berlin. Sitting on the backseat with a newspaper in his hands, he appreciated how much more comfortable traveling by private car was than having to use the train. Though he didn't actually read the newspaper, because he was busy mulling over the unanswered questions he'd been left with, and whether to tell Reiner and Erika anything about the strange events of the day before. Before he even realized it, they'd reached Berlin and the driver stopped in front of Reiner's detached house.

"Oh good, you're just in time to go to the lawyer," Reiner said instead of a greeting.

"That was the plan." His brother's words had confirmed Wilhelm's decision to keep his mouth shut. What Reiner didn't know; he couldn't use for his own benefit. "Let me quickly refresh myself and change into a new shirt. I'll be back in five minutes."

"I pressed your shirts and your dress uniform," Erika called after him as he rushed up the stairs, taking two steps at once.

While he changed into the freshly washed and immaculately ironed dress shirt and slipped on his uniform trousers with a sharp crease, he had to give Erika credit. Nobody put a sharper crease in a pair of trousers than she.

"Are you done? We don't have all day," Reiner called from downstairs.

"Ready." Wilhelm walked downstairs much slower than was necessary, just to anger his brother. "Thank you so much, Erika, for taking care of my clothing. You did great work."

Erika looked embarrassed at the compliment and cast her eyes downward. "I'm just doing my duty."

Once again, Wilhelm settled into the backseat, musing whether he might be able to arrange for an automobile and a driver to take him back to Paris, after the reading of the will. His father had amassed fortunes in his position as SS-Standartenführer and in less than an hour a huge chunk of it would be his.

They stopped in front of a representative building on the prestigious boulevard Unter den Linden. Naturally, the family lawyer, Dr. Hansen, was one of the most esteemed in the capital who catered to many high-ranking Nazis.

The young secretary ushered them into the meeting room and Wilhelm noticed Reiner's hand lingering on her backside for a few seconds. Just moments later, Dr. Hansen, a man in his fifties appeared.

"Gentlemen, before I begin, let me convey my condolences for the loss of your parents. Your father was a true hero, a man who dedicated his life to our country and our Führer. His sacrifice will not be forgotten."

"Thank you, Dr. Hansen, we are disconsolate. But rest assured, we are determined to work even harder for Germany's victory. His death will not remain unpunished. Heil Hitler!" Reiner saluted and everyone, including the cute little secretary followed suit.

Then Dr. Hansen took a seat at the immense oak table that took up at least half of the space in the office. Reiner and Wilhelm settled to either side and the secretary at the foot end, a shorthand notebook and a pencil in front of her.

"Where is your sister?" Dr. Hansen asked.

On the way here, Wilhelm had filled in Reiner on the official version of events, including that he'd met Horst Richter, who'd repeatedly assured him the woman in Leipzig wasn't their sister.

Reiner answered. "Annegret is staying with a friend of the family. She's still in shock and unable to leave the house."

Apparently the idea of Annegret disconsolately crying and being unable to leave the house didn't make much sense, because the lawyer gave both of them a scrutinizing stare, before he said, "I thought her to be made of sterner stuff."

Wilhelm hurried to add, "She was in the bombing herself and was severely injured. She's still not out of the woods."

Reiner cast him an angry glare, but Wilhelm didn't care. It was the perfect setup for Annegret's demise, should the need arise.

"Well then… I will read the will in her absence."

As was to be expected, Reiner inherited most of their father's fortune, including the country house with the valuable art collection, vast lands in Prussia, a small cottage in the Black Forest and another one near the Führer's Berghof in Obersalzberg.

Dr. Hansen pushed his glasses up on his nose and continued to read, "My second son Wilhelm and my daughter Annegret both receive a trust fund."

"How much is it?" Wilhelm asked impatiently. That was a lot better than he'd hoped for. Should Reiner keep all the real estate, and even the requisitioned paintings and tapestries. He would gladly take the cold, hard cash. And lots of it. He already fantasized about all the things he could afford starting the moment he walked out of this office. First thing, he'd buy himself a huge signet ring to show his new wealth to anyone he met, and maybe an incredibly expensive fountain pen layered in gold. Just two of the accessories of a wealthy man.

But the lawyer put a damper on his dreams. "Not so fast. I'm sorry to say, your father included several conditions for both you and Annegret to access your trust funds."

Wilhelm rolled his eyes. That was so much like his father to torment him even from his grave.

"The inherited funds of a quarter million Reichsmark each will remain under the custody of my trusted lawyer Dr. Hansen until the following stipulations are met: Wilhelm will gain access to his trust fund upon getting married and producing a male heir."

Wilhelm jumped up, sending deadly glares into Reiner's triumphantly gleaming face.

"Please sit until I'm done," Dr. Hansen said with a placating gesture. "Annegret will gain access to her funds upon the day she turns twenty-five, or on the day of her wedding, whichever occurs earlier. In case of getting married, her brother Wilhelm will oversee the usage of the funds in her name and gain access to one fourth of his own trust fund."

He was seething with fury, but remembered the lawyer's warning and didn't dare to interrupt him again.

"In the event either one of them dies prior to obtaining access to their trust fund, it will be given to the charity for SS widows to be distributed for the good of the country. In case my first son Reiner dies without a male heir, a trust fund of one hundred thousand Reichsmark will be set up for his wife and children, while the rest of the estate reverts to Wilhelm, and in case of his demise, to Annegret. If neither of my children survive, the estate will go to the charity for SS widows." The lawyer put the will down and glanced at both men. "That is all of it."

Wilhelm couldn't hold back any longer and surged to his feet. "He can't do that!"

"I'm so very sorry. I tried to convince your father that this wasn't the best implementation of his will, but he was adamant it was for the best. He was convinced you weren't responsible enough to handle such a large amount of money just yet and would only squander it. In fact, he told me that he hoped a wife and offspring would help you to become a better man, which is why he stipulated the conditions."

"And what if my future wife only produces girls?"

"Then I'm afraid you'll never get your hands on the money."

"How can this even be legal?"

Dr. Hansen sighed. "I advised your father against writing this will, because it does indeed have some points that could be critiqued. Believe me, I would have liked him to have a straightforward will including two trust funds for you and your sister without any stipulations."

"I'm going to sue." Wilhelm was completely outraged.

Reiner tried to placate him. "Wilhelm, please. Think about all the negative publicity."

"You would say that! You've got it made."

"I swear, I had no idea."

"Please, gentlemen, calm down." Dr. Hansen raised his voice above theirs. "I agree with Wilhelm that the will is unfortunate, but at the same time I have to warn you that Reiner is right about the negative publicity, and," he paused, pointedly looking from one to the other, while that stupid secretary shorthanded every word spoken in this room, "no court in its right mind would take on this case. Your father was a highly respected official and no judge would want to besmirch his memory."

"Damn bastards all of them," Wilhelm mumbled quiet enough that the secretary couldn't hear it. He'd understood the lawyer's backhanded threat very well and bowed his head. "Please excuse my outburst. Nothing would be further from my mind than negating my father's last wishes." He smirked. "It will spur me on to find a willing woman to impregnate. In fact, I may start right away."

The young secretary gasped in shock, giving him slight satisfaction, before he slammed out of the lawyer's office and stomped down the street without waiting for Reiner. As far as he was concerned, he had nothing to talk about with his brother. At least he hadn't told anyone that Annegret was dead, because then her share would have gone straight to the charity for SS widows. They didn't deserve the money: it should be his.

CHAPTER 17

Margarete got up early, braided her hair into two plaits that she slung around her head like a crown. She used Heidi's lipstick, smudging it on her cheeks, well aware that Hitler disliked painted lips, but every good German maid had to show off rosy cheeks for the healthy and strong look disseminated by the propaganda.

"Aunt Heidi, can I borrow your red scarf?" Margarete asked, since she was out to impress.

"Sure," Heidi answered absentmindedly, but tore her eyes wide open when her niece stepped out of the bedroom to present the results of her efforts. "Whom exactly are you trying to impress?"

"Horst Richter."

"What? I thought we agreed that you're leaving the city today."

"I will, but first I'll go and get travel permits."

Heidi shook her head. "Do you really think that's a good idea?"

"It's much better than running away without valid papers. I wouldn't make it past the first checkpoint."

"Not if you are careful and avoid them."

Margarete looked at her aunt. "You and I both know this escape to Toulouse is a suicide mission without proper protection. And Richter will give it to me. It is the only way."

"It's too dangerous. What if Wilhelm Huber has told him the truth after all?"

"Then Richter's men will show up here or at the library any time. But before this happens I need to take my chances and convince him to expedite a travel permit for me."

"Godspeed, my girl. Tell Simone to write to me with the words 'The winter is such a beautiful season in southern France'. Then I will know you arrived safely at her house." Heidi kissed her forehead as she prepared to leave.

"Thank you, Aunt Heidi. I promise, I'll be careful. And we'll see each other again when all of this is over. It won't be long anymore, now that the Americans have declared war."

"From your lips to God's ears. I will miss your company." Heidi hugged her and pressed some Reichsmark into her hand. "Take this, you'll need it."

"I can't possibly…"

"Yes, you can. Promise you'll be careful."

"Promise." Margarete left the apartment and headed for the Gestapo headquarters in the Karl-Heine-Straße, holding her head high even as her blood felt like it was freezing in her veins. Walking into the lion's den wasn't something that came easy to her, a girl who'd been raised to fear all officials and especially the Gestapo who harassed the Jews at every opportunity.

She took a deep breath and channeled Annegret's character. For the next half an hour she needed to be bold, self-confident and courageous if she wanted her plan to work. Entering the large building, she felt the panic rising in her and swallowed hard to force the forming lump in her throat down.

"Good morning," she said to the uniformed man behind the reception desk.

"Good morning, what can I help you with?"

"I need to speak with Reichskriminaldirektor Richter," she said with as much confidence as she could muster.

"Do you have an appointment?"

"No, I don't. I'm the daughter of his late friend and I'm afraid it's a matter of urgency."

"I'm afraid he doesn't usually see personal contacts during office hours."

"Please tell him Annegret Huber is here."

"Very well." The young man picked up the phone.

"Please excuse the disturbance, Herr Reichskriminaldirektor, but there is a young lady here to see you. She says her name is Annegret Huber and it's a matter of urgency." The young man listened and then nodded sharply. "Right away, Herr Reichskriminaldirektor." He hung up the phone and stood up. "Follow me." Moments later she was ushered into a large office where Horst Richter stood by the window behind his desk.

He greeted her warmly, dismissing the young man with a wave of his hand. "Annegret. Come and sit down. What brings you here this early?"

She had carefully rehearsed her words, but now that she was actually here, his presence intimidated her and she felt goosebumps appear on her arms. "Herr Richter, I've been up all night worrying… Now that Wilhelm knows I'm here, he's sure to tell Reiner, who is well known to be tenacious. He might come here and…" A few pressed-out sobs would help make her case. "I'm afraid of what he might do."

Richter came around his desk and stood beside her. "Reiner can be stubborn, which is normally a good trait, but in this instance, I can see how it would be concerning."

Margarete nodded. "I spent all night thinking about what I should do and whether maybe I should leave Leipzig for someplace small and quiet. And I think that would be the best option."

"I already inquired with the Lebensborn, but institutions like them don't work that fast. They need to do medical exams, and you'll have to divulge the name of the father." He must have seen her flinch, because he added, "Amidst the greatest secrecy, of course. Nobody will ever find out, it's just to make sure he is in fact an Aryan and hereditarily healthy."

Margarete's eyes became wide.

"In case he's not, which I don't believe, because as you said he already fathered two healthy children, the Lebensborn doctors will help you to take care of your problem."

Even though she wasn't actually with child, Margarete paled some more at the thought of it. Abortion was strictly forbidden, except for Jewish and other undesirable women, of course, who were often forced to have the procedure against their will. Many women did not survive the ordeal that usually was given without much consideration for the mother.

"Don't you worry, Annegret. I regret even telling you this, because as I said, the father of your child has already proven his value to the German nation." He patted her arm. "It's just a precaution to make sure no undesirable objects are accidentally born and given to deserving Aryan citizens."

"I… I appreciate the thoroughness, but I'd rather leave Leipzig today. I don't feel safe here anymore. Reiner… he is capable of anything, especially now when he's deeply in grief over the death of our parents."

"Hmm." Richter was quiet for a long time and then nodded. "You might have a point. Even if Reiner won't do you any harm, we certainly don't want any negative publicity. Both he and I have powerful adversaries who are only waiting for the slightest perceived flaw. And his sister bringing shame on the family could stall his career. It might even cast a shadow on his children's origin, because some people might argue if he can't keep his sister in line, his own wife might stray outside her conjugal bed as well."

"Do you really think?" Margarete hissed, shocked by his words.

"No. I suspect that Reiner is capable of showing his wife her place. But bad tongues blabber." He stepped behind his desk again. "Going someplace small and quiet is probably the wisest option at this point."

Why are you helping me? The question was on the tip of her tongue, but she swallowed it down. He'd already told her that he wanted to help his late friend's daughter. Although she couldn't reconcile his friendly manner toward her with the image of the ruthless Gestapo man without the slightest trace of compassion and even less patience he had in the general public. She cleared her throat and instead suggested, "I was thinking maybe I could go to Toulouse."

"Toulouse? Isn't that in the free zone in France?" Richter asked her, a puzzled look on his face.

"Yes, but Marechal Petain is on our side, isn't he?"

"He certainly has proven his willingness to work with us. But why would you want to travel that far away?"

"My mother, may she rest in peace, had an old friend who lives there. I know without a doubt that she would be willing to help me."

"Going to stay with someone you know would probably be more convenient. What is this woman's name?"

Margarete felt frozen with fear. She couldn't very well give him the true name of Heidi's friend. Racking her brain, she suddenly remembered Frau Huber talking about a woman she'd known as a girl, before the last war. They had met during a skiing vacation in Switzerland and Frau Huber had stayed in touch with her until recently.

"Caroline Dubois," Margarete offered the name.

Richter tipped his chin and shook his head. "I thought Caroline Dubois was dead?"

"Oh, no. My mother received a letter from her only a week before the bombing. I'm sure she would be willing to help me."

"Very well. Do you have her phone number? I'm happy to call and verify that she still lives there and make arrangements…"

"I'm sorry." Margarete shook her head. "I'm very bad at numbers and Mother always kept it written down… but I know where the house is." She allowed a sad expression to cover her face, thinking that would be how Annegret might have reacted.

Richter gave her a stern, almost fatherly look. "I will agree to help you do this, but if you arrive in Toulouse and find that Mrs. Dubois is no longer living there, you must immediately place a phone call to my office and I will reach out to the local authorities to facilitate your return."

"Thank you. I can't tell you how much I appreciate your help. I was very foolish to get myself into this situation, but I promise to make amends and be the most useful German woman our Führer could wish for." She all but vomited, saying these words.

"I will see that you have the proper travel papers to take with you, including a personal recommendation from me."

"Again, I owe you my thanks. My father would appreciate everything you have done for me," Margarete said.

"Wait here." He stepped from his office and was only gone a few minutes before he returned with several documents in his hand. "These are your travel papers to the free zone in France, as well as an endorsement letter from me. And here are my phone numbers both in the office and at my home. If you run into any problems, I expect you to let me know. I will also expect you to let me know when you have safely arrived. Until then, I will worry about you."

Margarete took the documents and promised to keep in touch. As she left the Gestapo headquarters, she felt the sweat running down her back and soaking her chemise. She'd confronted the devil and lived to tell the tale. Now, if her luck would just hold out until she arrived in Toulouse. Only then would she relax enough to take a deep breath and let down her guard.

The travel papers tucked into her pocket along with a generous amount of Reichsmarks that Richter had given her, she returned to Aunt Heidi's apartment to grab the few things she owned. She'd leave the only relative behind who was still free, and would from now on have to depend on the help of strangers.

Heidi's apartment was empty, with only a note from her aunt lying on the kitchen table. She took the piece of paper and felt the soft texture, before reading it:

> *Sorry, but I had to go to work. I'll keep you in my thoughts and prayers. Godspeed.*

Margarete sighed and took the small suitcase Heidi had given her last night, packed all her belongings, mostly clothes from Heidi, because Margarete herself had lost everything in the bombing. She tucked the note into her purse along with the money and then took out her amulet from between the upholstery.

She turned it back and forth, scrutinizing her work. She fought with herself, but couldn't leave it, since without her amulet to draw strength from she'd be lost away from home. The backside felt rough to the touch, but there was no evidence of a previous inscription. And the Tree of Life itself was innocent enough; anyone could have such an adornment.

Having packed her belongings, she walked to the train station, eager to get away from Leipzig. Herr Richter had warned her that all trains would be full due to the upcoming Christmas holidays and Wehrmacht soldiers on leave crisscrossing the Reich, but she'd insisted that she would somehow find her way.

As she thought about him, she couldn't help but be puzzled. Horst Richter was the epitome of a Nazi. A Gestapo officer whose reputation of cruelty and ruthlessness preceded him. A man who was feared by enemies and friends alike, but mostly by anyone Jewish, communist, or critical of the regime. But to her, he'd been nothing but kind, warm and caring.

How could a man have two faces so different to each other? It shook her perception of the world to the core. Until a few days ago she'd considered all Nazis vile monsters, and now all of a sudden, they were nice to her. How could that be? And why could they value one human life and not another one? How could they be friendly to one stranger, but spit on another one, when the only difference between the two people was a yellow star sewn onto their clothing?

Her head was hurting and she pushed the confusing thoughts aside. Nazis were inherently bad, if they showed random kindness occasionally, that didn't change a thing. A good person had to be kind to everyone.

CHAPTER 18

The last three days had passed in a blur. From the moment he'd walked out of the lawyer's office without a single penny to his name, Wilhelm had been drinking, partying and losing himself in the arms of any woman who would have him.

He didn't even bother to hide his drunken ways from Erika who gave him the evil eye, every time he came through her door and walked to the guest room without a greeting, to fall on the bed face down and sleep off his inebriation.

Two days from now his leave would come to an end, and he would have to return to Paris, poor as a church mouse. He got up from his bed—still fully clothed—and staggered into the bathroom. The reflection in the mirror caught him unprepared and he all but hit the vagrant staring at him. He hadn't shaved in three days, his blond hair was tousled and the brooding green-brown eyes women loved so much were bloodshot. Even the birthmark under his left eye seemed to add to his dirty and unkempt look. What a disgusting sight! If it weren't for his uniform, any police officer would certainly pick him up and send him to a concentration camp for being a work-shy, loitering asocial.

That thought sobered him. The uniform would only protect him for so long, and SS men who dishonored it weren't above being sent the same way the vagrants went. Then, not even his father's good name would help him.

He put his head under the tap and turned on the faucet. Cold water gushed down, slowly clearing his clouded mind. He'd have to pull himself together. This was not the end of the world. He still had his salary to live on, although without the additional allowance coming from his father whenever sorely needed, he'd have to tighten his belt.

It was a shameful thing he was forced to do. A man raised with all the money in the world suddenly thrust into the poorhouse. His comrades would laugh their asses off. He shook his head, turned off the water and began to shave. Once he looked presentable again, he returned to the guest room to change into civvies, leaving his uniform scattered on the floor. Erika would take care of everything and when he returned, he'd find it hanging behind the door, cleaned and ironed. At least some things still functioned properly in his life.

Erika appeared in the hallway like a ghost the moment he walked down the stairs. "Good afternoon, Wilhelm."

"Good afternoon." He took his greatcoat and hat.

"You're going out?"

"Yes."

"Where are you going?"

He didn't like her accusatory tone. "You're not my wife, I don't owe you an explanation."

She looked rightfully contrite. "You haven't even eaten yet."

"I'll grab a bite somewhere. Don't wait for me with dinner." He put on his hat and left her standing in the hallway. He knew he was being unfair, but he resented her for Reiner's fortune. If his brother were an honest person, he'd have given him an allowance, but no. Of course Reiner thought his brother could survive well enough on a meager salary, while he himself lived in the lap of luxury with his family.

He walked aimlessly through the streets of Berlin until he stood in front of Ellen's building. She'd commiserate with him.

"Oh, Wilhelm, what a surprise, come in. I thought you might have left for Paris already."

"Not until the day after tomorrow."

She took his hat and coat and hung it on the rack. "Coffee?"

"Yes, please."

Several minutes later she returned with two steaming cups and placed them on the coffee table in front of him. Not one to beat around the bush, she asked, "How was the reading of the will?"

"Catastrophic."

"Are you going to tell me or do I have to worm it out of you?"

He chuckled. It was so refreshing to be with Ellen, because she never held back. Their mothers had been friends and they'd even entertained the idea of a wedding between Ellen and Wilhelm, until the day Ellen had started an explosive affair with another woman. While Wilhelm couldn't care less who else she slept with, the fine Berlin society had been outraged and Ellen had become persona non grata. Thanks to her good looks and influential lovers, though, she'd never been punished for her crimes.

"Well, as was to be expected, Reiner got most everything, while Annegret and I are stuck with a measly trust fund of a quarter million Reichsmark."

Ellen whistled through her teeth. "That's an amount not to be frowned at. I'd better get us some champagne."

"That'll have to wait." He put a hand on her arm to keep her from rushing into the kitchen.

"And that is… why?"

"My rotten Father has put in stipulations."

She broke out into laughter. "Don't tell me he's going to force you into marriage with some old Prussian nobility to get your hands on the money? That kind of stuff only happens in cheesy romance novels."

"It's worse than that. I have to marry and produce a male heir if I want to get access to the money."

She slumped back in her plush wing chair. "How heinous! I would have offered my hand in marriage, you know that, but having a child and raising it? That would completely ruin my career."

"I'd never ask that from you. It's a shitty bargain, either way. If my future wife only ever produces girls, I won't get a single penny."

"Poor Wilm." She moved over and sat on his lap, moving her hands over just the right places for him to forget his sorrows.

Much later they were lying in her bed, smoking, when he said, "There's one more thing."

"Good or bad?" She stretched out one of her long legs and wiggled her toes that were painted in a dark cherry red.

"I don't know." He rolled her on top of him, and locked eyes with her before he said, "Promise you'll never tell anyone."

"You know I won't. Not even if the Gestapo come to pull out my fingernails."

"Good God, woman, don't even joke about that."

"So, what's the big secret?"

"Annegret. She got a trust fund too, and the only stipulation for her is to get married and then… I'll be the custodian over her money until she turns twenty-five."

Ellen clicked her tongue. "How convenient. Although, how you're planning to force your spoilt sister to marry someone is beyond me."

"You're terrific!" He kissed her on the lips. He hadn't actually thought of forcing Annegret to get married, but now that Ellen mentioned it, it seemed like a great idea. And he already knew how. A Jew on the run would do anything to save her life. He'd just have to return to Leipzig and offer her this way out. He'd even go to the trouble of finding a nice and respectable husband for her and offer them a small monthly allowance to buy their silence. The more he thought about it, the more excited he got about implementing his plan.

"Now you just have to find her."

He paused for a moment and decided not to tell Ellen the entire truth, just in case the Gestapo did come to pull her fingernails at some point in the future. "I already did. She's hiding out in Leipzig."

Ellen raised an eyebrow. "Why didn't you tell anyone?"

"Because she's under the protection of Reichskriminaldirektor Richter."

"Do you think he's her lover?"

"He's at least double her age," Wilhelm said scandalized, even though he'd suspected the same. But for some strange reason he hated the thought of Margarete being with another man.

"Oh, come on. Older men are often much better lovers."

He sighed. He couldn't tell Ellen that an impostor had taken his sister's place. "She's my sister, for God's sake. But even if he's her lover, why would he want me to pretend she isn't in Leipzig until he's taken care of everything."

"Wilm, are you really that naïve?" Ellen giggled, wiggling on top of him. "Don't tell me it has never occurred to you that your precious little sister might be pregnant?"

He stared at her in disbelief as the realization trickled into his brain. Then he rolled her off of him and stood up to walk to the window. After looking out into the darkness for several minutes, he turned to look at Ellen. "And you think Richter is the father?"

"It's obvious, isn't it?"

Wilhelm replayed all of his interactions with Horst Richter, before he said, "It does make a lot of sense. That's why she disappeared. She's Richter's mistress and that's why he's willing to go to such lengths to protect her. And their illegitimate child."

"See? It all makes sense now."

The one thing that didn't make sense, was why Richter was having an affair with a Jewess. Or had Margarete somehow lured him into believing she was Annegret months ago? But how?

"But how does that help me?" he said, returning to the bed.

"Maybe you could offer Richter a better solution. Find a husband for his mistress and the baby will be born to a legitimate father. I could help you find a gay man in need of protection if Richter is worried about her being unfaithful to him. You earn Richter's gratitude. He's rich and powerful enough and will be happy to give you some compensation in exchange for you taking care of all his problems. Everyone is happy. The End."

"You act in too many love stories," Wilhelm said and smiled as he stroked her soft skin. "But you're brilliant. It's the perfect plan. Can I make a phone call?"

"Be my guest."

He got up again and walked into the sitting room, where the telephone stood on a small table next to the wall.

CHAPTER 19

Horst Richter had been right. Due to the overcrowded trains and priority given to Wehrmacht soldiers, it had taken Margarete an entire week to arrive in Paris with more stops, deviations and changes of trains than she cared to remember.

Completely exhausted from queuing up for tickets, standing for hours on slow regional trains, sleeping on benches in waiting areas, she wished for nothing more than to freshen up, sleep and feel like a human again. But she hesitated to spend her precious money on a hotel and decided to continue her journey to Toulouse. Once there she could relax all she wanted.

Stepping off the train, she felt completely and utterly lost. Gare de l'Est had to be the biggest train station she'd seen, since in Germany it was forbidden for Jews to use public transport and this journey had been her first one on a train, except for the journey to Leipzig as Annegret.

Thankfully the German administration had put up signs in German everywhere, so she didn't have to fall back on her rusty French. Still, the sheer amount of people going to and fro left her completely disoriented. Like on all the train stations she had passed through, plenty of men in different German uniforms were standing around, some obviously passengers waiting for their respective trains while smoking and chatting, whereas others occupied an official function, checking papers and tickets of the travelers. Between them she spotted the odd French policeman in dark blue uniform and that peculiar hard-brimmed hat.

She pondered asking one of them for the way to an affordable, yet safe, hotel for young women. But just as she set out toward him, she stopped again. Annegret would never ask a Frenchman for anything. Why should she?

Margarete took a deep breath, steeled her spine and adopted an air of confidence as she walked up to the pair of SS men checking papers. "Excuse me, *meine Herren*," she said with her most convincing smile. "I'm headed for Toulouse, could you tell me where to find the train?"

They stared at her as if they'd seen an apparition. After an endless time during which she fought the urge to take to her heels, the younger one finally said, "Your papers, please."

She handed him Annegret's identification, her nerves tingling as he took his sweet time to scrutinize it. "Annegret Huber. A comrade of mine has a sister called Annegret, and his name is Wilhelm Huber. You aren't his sister, by any chance?"

The blood in her veins froze and her heart missed a beat as she answered in the most nonchalant way she could. "I'm afraid not. Huber is quite a common name."

"You're right," he said, giving her a friendly smile. "Tough travels?"

Despite having used the train toilet to make herself halfway presentable, she still must have looked exhausted. "Yes. Due to the holidays I've been on the road for a week."

"Poor girl." He cast her a flirtatious smile. "Your travel permit, please?"

A heavy burden fell from her shoulders as he returned Annegret's identification and she gave him the travel permit and personal recommendation signed by Horst Richter.

He gave a low whistle. "Yours must be quite the important trip. Why are you going to Toulouse?"

Richter had impressed on her not to divulge any personal information about her condition or otherwise.

"I'm sorry, I'm not allowed to say. If you need further information, please contact the Gestapo headquarters in Leipzig and they will tell you what you need to know."

He swallowed and said, "No worries. Your papers are perfectly fine, I was just trying to help."

No, you were trying to pry. "I do understand. Now, could you please indicate the platform where the next train to Toulouse departs?"

The older officer joined the conversation. "I'm very sorry, Fräulein, but this is Gare de l'Est and trains to Toulouse leave from Gare Montparnasse."

She wanted to scream with frustration as exhaustion overwhelmed her and she could barely stand upright. "How far is that?"

"It's really not that far, about three and a half miles. But we've had to close down the entire area due to resistance activity and there's no way of getting there except on foot."

"On foot?" Margarete shrieked. She couldn't contemplate crossing a foreign city on foot, without a map, and with roadblocks everywhere. "Isn't there another way?"

"I'm afraid not. Since most trains out of Paris will be delayed with searches anyway, I'd suggest maybe you spend the night here and travel in the morning."

She sighed. A bath and a bed seemed like paradise right now. Maybe she had to bite the bullet and spend some of her money on a hotel. "Would you be able to direct me to an affordable, yet clean and safe, hotel for tonight?"

"Sure. See that exit over there?" Margarete nodded. "Just across the street is a nice hotel called Pension Kaiser that only caters to Germans. You should be fine there."

"Thank you." Margarete hurried to get away from the SS men. Despite having nothing to fear from them with her identity as Annegret, she still had damp hands and goosebumps all over.

She found the hotel without any problems and walked inside. Much to her surprise, the young woman at the reception desk spoke almost perfect German and it took only two minutes to register her and show her to her room. The receptionist also gave her instructions how to get to Gare Montparnasse and informed her that trains to Toulouse only went in the morning.

Margarete fell on her bed and slept for sixteen hours straight. When she was woken up by the grumbling in her stomach she noticed with horror that it was already too late to go to the Gare Montparnasse and she would have to stay another night in Paris.

Making the best of the situation, she ran herself a bath and scrubbed off the dirt from her week of traveling from her skin and hair. Then she relaxed in the tub, until the water cooled down and she had to emerge. At least here she was safe from the Huber family and had little to fear, since the chance of anyone recognizing her was slim.

The grumbling in her stomach became more forceful and she decided to venture out into the city to grab a bite to eat and do a bit of sightseeing. Apparently she wouldn't even need to practice her French, because most signs were in German and many Parisians spoke her language.

"*Guten Tag, Fräulein Huber*," the receptionist greeted her and then asked, "Will you be having dinner in the restaurant tonight?"

Still shy about dining out all on her own, she said, "Yes, please."

"It will be served between seven and nine p.m."

"Thank you."

Margarete set out into the cold sunshine to spend a carefree December afternoon in the splendid city of Paris. Just the knowledge that nobody here knew her made her feel lighter than she could remember.

Paris was everything she had heard it would be, and so much more. It was truly the city of love, light and *savoir vivre* and she found herself wishing she could stay and explore more.

CHAPTER 20

Wilhelm sat in his apartment in Paris, moping about his bad luck and how all his spectacular plans had evaporated into thin air. On his train journey back he'd taken a detour via Leipzig to find Margarete and make her an offer she couldn't refuse.

But she had disappeared and neither Horst Richter nor Frau Merz from the library would admit to knowing where she was. Richter had said something about her visiting a sick friend in the country, and Frau Merz only knew that the *Reichsarbeitsamt*, the national work office, had requested Annegret for an assignment of utmost importance for the Fatherland. Obviously Richter was behind all of this and had whisked Margarete away before anyone became suspicious—or before Wilhelm had the opportunity to return and expose her. Although he still wasn't sure whether Richter knew of Margarete's true identity or not.

Tonight was Christmas Eve and for lack of families, he and his comrades had decided to throw a spectacular party at the restaurant in the Pension Kaiser. The fancier places were all booked by higher-ranking officers and it irked him no end that he hadn't been invited to any of those.

The tinkle of the delicate antique mantel clock tore him from his thoughts. It was his newest acquisition, an exceptionally beautiful piece in bronze gilt. The Rococo style clock showed the most graceful adornments with foliate designs, and a vase of flowers on top of the beautiful white enamel dial.

It had been outrageously expensive, even after reminding the previous owner how much he depended on Wilhelm's goodwill to keep his position as kitchen staff for the SS headquarters. Not that Wilhelm actually had any say in hiring decisions, but the woman didn't have to know that.

He smiled and traced the beautiful mantel clock with his fingers. Paris truly was the center of good food, precious antiques and fashionable women. He could consider himself lucky to be part of its administration, and he'd be a happy man if it weren't for the lack of money to enjoy the city's delights to the fullest.

When it was finally time to get ready for dinner, he combed his hair back with Brylcreem, put on his dress uniform, greatcoat and gloves and walked the ten minutes through the mostly empty streets in Paris.

He'd never before seen the city so empty and assumed the French people were all at home celebrating Christmas. For just one night and one day, everyone would forget about the war going on and be happy with friends or family. Although, the French really didn't have reason to complain. Despite their stubborn behavior they were treated royally by the new administration, and should rather be thankful for all the advances in efficiency and punctuality they were being taught. In time, this nation would become a jewel in the Great German Reich that would ultimately stretch from the Atlantic Ocean in the west to the Pacific in the east.

His comrades were already waiting and soon enough all his worries were washed away by plenty of wine and food. The mood in the restaurant was glorious. He raised his glass to make a toast, when the words caught in his throat.

A young woman stepped into the restaurant and all heads turned to size her up. She definitely wasn't Parisian, since a Frenchwoman would never have been caught dead in such drab clothes, but she was... Margarete.

What on earth is she doing here?

For a moment, he panicked, afraid she'd been sent here to expose him. It took him but an instant to realize how dangerous it had been to go along with her deceit. If someone found her out, he'd dangle from a streetlamp alongside her. But the next second his eyes locked with hers and he recognized nothing but deathly fear.

Without even realizing what he did, he got up, walked toward her and said for everyone to hear, "Annegret, you could make it after all."

He made a show of greeting her with a hug and kisses on both cheeks the French way, before he turned around to announce to his comrades, "Everyone, I'd like you to meet my sister, Annegret. She just arrived in Paris to celebrate Christmas with me." As he led her to an empty seat at the table, he whispered in her ear, "Just play along and nothing will happen to you."

He felt the goosebumps forming on her arm beneath his hand and knew that she would do nothing to expose him, because whatever his punishment might be, hers would be a hundred times worse.

At the beginning the conversation was stilted, and he was over-conscious that the imposter by his side was not his sister, but as more wine flowed and more food was served, he all but forgot about that little detail and treated her much as he would have treated Annegret if she were still alive.

His mind though, relentlessly tried to work out why she was here and what was the best way forward. Ever since learning that Margarete had escaped to some unknown location, he'd cursed his bad luck, because without her, he'd never get his hands on his sister's money. As the shock and fear wore off, he began to see the opportunity.

What better way to hide her than in plain sight, while secretly looking for a suitable husband for her? The only problem in the equation was Reiner, who would be able to call the bluff, but he was busy in Berlin with his career and had hinted that he'd soon be off to someplace in Eastern Europe as Heydrich's sidekick.

"So, how long are you staying in Paris? I should hope at least until the New Year," one of his comrades asked Margarete.

"In fact, I had planned—"

Wilhelm quickly interrupted her. "Annegret is going to move in with me. The poor thing has been devastated by the death of our beloved parents and since their house was bombed to shreds, I suggested she join me here."

"Well, who wouldn't want to move to Paris?" one man asked cheerfully, completely oblivious to Margarete's glares in Wilhelm's direction.

"I couldn't possibly accept such a generous offer," she said slowly.

"And yet you did. What kind of man would I be if I didn't offer my own sister a home in a time of need?" He gave her a warning glance and just in case she shouldn't understand, he issued an unveiled threat not to keep contradicting him, "I have friends working at the registration office, so I can report your arrival anytime, dearest sister."

The expression on her face, a mixture of rage, fear and capitulation was worth gold and he relished the power he had over her. This woman would be putty in his hands, completely at his beck and call, because she was intelligent enough to know that he could end her life with a click of his fingers. Adrenaline rushed through his veins and he had a glimpse of understanding why Reiner worked so hard for his career. Having power was as intoxicating as drinking wine, and equally enjoyable.

"Welcome to Paris," Rudolf, a quiet, withdrawn man said, looking at her completely smitten.

"Paris is a lot more fun than Berlin. You'll like it here, even if you have to put up with Wilhelm," Karsten offered, and added with a wink, "I'd be most willing to be your tourist guide and show you all the best places." Karsten was known to flirt with any and all women, despite having a wife back in Germany. He certainly wasn't going to become Annegret's husband.

"My sister is not an easy woman, and anyone who dares to behave even the slightest bit inappropriately toward her will have to contend with me first," Wilhelm said, smiling to make it sound like a joke, but he knew his comrades understood the warning. Annegret Huber was off limits for anyone except her future husband, who would be carefully chosen by him.

For several seconds nobody said a word, until someone made a joke and everyone returned to the frothy conversation. Wilhelm participated only half-heartedly, because he was attacked by doubts about his brilliant idea to have Margarete move in with him. The advantages were that he could keep tabs on her, watching her every move while finding the best way to convince her into a fake marriage. On the other hand, every passing minute he didn't report her to the authorities would drag him deeper into a web of lies and would make his punishment harsher should she be found out.

He sighed, looking at the beautiful woman sitting beside him and trying to figure out what he should do. She looked and behaved so differently from the time she'd been his parents' maid. She'd been dressed in the drabbest threadbare clothes with the yellow star sewn onto them, her shoulders always hunched forward and her voice barely audible when she said, "Yes, Herr

Huber. Of course, Frau Huber. Can I serve you some more food, Herr Huber? Yes, I ironed your favorite dress, Fräulein Annegret."

He smiled suddenly, realizing something. Because, actually, Margarete was the solution to all of his problems. Since she had learned the housekeeping tasks under the merciless tutelage of his finicky mother, she would be far more accommodating than his rather stubborn French housekeeper—and cheaper, since he wouldn't have to pay her a salary. Even if he couldn't marry her off, he would still end up saving money.

This was his lucky break and he intended to grab it with both hands.

Reaching for the bottle of wine, he refilled both their glasses, then he stood to give a toast. "Merry Christmas to everyone. I'm so happy to be here with my friends and my beloved sister. We will win this war in no time at all, and then I hope we can all meet again and remember the wonderful time we had together in Paris."

"Sieg Heil!"

"Merry Christmas!"

"To our friendship!"

Wilhelm sat down again, satisfied at the turn his fate had just taken. Wine continued to flow and the atmosphere grew more raucous. Most of his comrades readied themselves for the after-party in the arms of their French mistresses, but he had different plans.

Tonight he'd show Margarete who held her strings in his hands and what was expected of her if she wanted to survive.

CHAPTER 21

Margarete couldn't quite figure out what kind of game Wilhelm was playing. He'd not exposed her and for that she was thankful, but she couldn't keep pretending one minute longer. When he got up and left the restaurant for the restroom, she saw her chance to escape.

If she had to, she'd walk all the way to the Gare Montparnasse and sleep there until morning when she hoped to board the first train leaving Paris southward. She put her napkin on the plate and pushed back her chair, giving a sweet smile to Wilhelm's comrades. "Thank you so much for letting me join you. But the journey was very exhausting and I should retire now."

"Don't go yet, the night is young," the young man opposite her said. Many of Wilhelm's comrades had given her appreciative glances, and some had even tried to flirt with her, before he'd put a stop to it.

The entire evening had been so confusing. Mere weeks ago, when she was still Margarete, no man had ever tried to flirt with her; on the contrary, they usually hurled insults at her or spat at her for being a Jew. Except for those who didn't care as much about *Rassenschande*, racial defilement, who openly leered at her, expecting to take what they wanted without her consent, because she wasn't even a real human being to them. She shuddered.

"I'm sorry. It was a pleasure meeting all of you. Merry Christmas." She walked as gracefully as she could manage from the restaurant while inwardly quivering with fear Wilhelm might return in time to thwart her escape. Once she arrived at the reception, she gave a furtive glance toward the exit onto the street. Five steps and she'd be out of here. She felt for Annegret's papers in her skirt pocket, fully determined to leave the suitcase with her belongings behind. But the blood froze in her veins, when she remembered that she'd left the money and travel permits in her coat that hung in her room, an unforgivable stupidity as she now acknowledged.

As much as she hated it, she had to return to her room on the second floor to grab her things, since she couldn't afford to leave without proper travel documents. When she raised the key to unlock her room, the door swung open and Wilhelm stepped out, holding her suitcase in his hands, a timid chambermaid two steps behind him.

"What are you doing with my suitcase?" Margarete asked.

A sly grin turned his lips up. "I took the liberty of asking the hotel manager to have someone pack up your belongings, since you're going to live with me… Annegret."

She felt herself sway, but the next moment, Wilhelm jumped to her side to steady her and said apologetically to the maid, "I'm afraid my sister has had a little too much wine. I'll get her home immediately." He pushed a banknote into her hand. "Thank you for packing up her things."

The young girl made a curtsy and quickly vanished.

Meanwhile Margarete had regained her poise and said, "I'm not going anywhere with you."

"It's your choice. Either you come with me, or I'll happily call the police."

She swallowed hard. "But… they will hold you accountable for being my accomplice."

For the tiniest fraction of a second she believed she saw fear in his eyes, but that passed and he was his usual cocky self again. "They may or they may not. In either case, this will be the end of you. And then… well, I'm told they have special treatments at the Avenue Foch for traitors like you."

Violent shivers ran down her spine, but she forced her voice to sound steady and calm as she asked, "What do you want from me?"

"I'll tell you when we're home. Now let's go."

Margarete's hatred of the hold he had over her intensified, but when he took her elbow and turned her around to head back down the stairs, she couldn't do anything but go with him. He was in control as he held her very life in his hands. One word from him about her subterfuge and she'd be meeting her death.

He led her out of the hotel and turned to the right, walking past the Gare de l'Est and then into a quiet side street. Whatever his motives were, she would have to go along with it and wait for an opportunity to get away. He might have saved her life, but he was still a Nazi and that deeply concerned her. It also confused her. He risked punishment if the deception was discovered because he was now actively engaging in the charade of pretending that she was his sister.

As they turned another corner, Margarete's fear about his intentions overtook her common sense and at the first occasion, she yanked her hand away and took off in the opposite direction. She darted around the corner and screamed in desperate fury when she realized the alleyway was a dead end.

With her shoulders slumped, she turned around, fully expecting Wilhelm to beat her, but he only laughed.

"The sooner you realize that I'm the one calling the shots, the better for you." He closed the distance between them, and took her chin into his free hand, forcing her to look at him. His voice was calm, but hard from the underlying steel as he said, "Don't you ever attempt such a stupid thing again. If I wanted to, I could break your neck here and now and leave your corpse lying in this filthy gutter and no one would know or care. Whoever found you would assume you were just another lousy whore trying to cheat a German soldier."

Margarete struggled to draw enough breath, because the fear was making her choke. "Please... Why are you doing this?"

"That's for me to know and you to find out when the time is right. For now the only thing you need to know is that you're going to live with me as my sister, keep house for me and do everything I tell you to." He smirked. "Just like you did at my parents' house, but without wearing a yellow star."

Another wave of terror crushed her soul and she briefly wondered if he intended to follow Reiner's example and force her to satisfy his other needs, too.

"Do you understand?" His breath brushed her cheek and she needed all her strength to nod. "Say it. Say that you'll always do as I say and not try to run away again."

"I... will do as you say. I... won't run away," Margarete whispered.

"Good. Now, I think it's better if I store your papers, since we don't want them to get lost." When she didn't react, he added, "Give them to me, now."

With trembling fingers, she reached into her coat pocket and retrieved the identification card that kept her alive and handed it over to him. Now she was truly and completely at his mercy. Her life belonged to him.

"Good girl. I'm sure we'll get along well, as long as you know your place."

Several minutes later, they reached one of the fancier five-story buildings and the moment he opened the front door, an elderly woman shot from her office. "Monsieur Huber, here is a letter for you."

"Thank you Madame Badeaux." He pushed Margarete forward and said, "This is my sister, Annegret, she will be living with me for a while."

The concierge seemed to be displeased, but couldn't well contradict her German tenant, so she smiled at Margarete and said, "Welcome, Mademoiselle Annegret."

"Thank you very much. I won't be a burden."

They took the elevator and minutes later Wilhelm unlocked the door to his third floor apartment. His parents' house had been plain and functional with mostly monochromatic furniture, with just a few personal touches in the living room, a stern, uninviting, even threatening feeling in the office that belonged to Herr Huber, and a complete disarray of stuff in Annegret's room. Somehow she'd expected his place to look similar and was therefore taken aback when she stepped into the living room that looked like one of the fancy chambers in royal castles she'd seen in Frau Huber's women's magazines.

"How beautiful," she said with genuine admiration. From the giltwood mirror hanging on the wall, to the delicate oak escritoire with the spectacular bronze gilt mantel clock to the royal blue chaise longue with a floral pattern, the room was spectacular in its tasteful elegance.

"You like it?" A proud smile broke out on his face, making him look that much more handsome. "I've hand-collected these pieces, visiting countless antique shops, flea markets and pawnshops. You have no idea how much rubbish you have to sort through to find a truly unique piece."

She didn't like the way she warmed to him and reminded herself that Wilhelm Huber was the bad guy. His good taste didn't make him a good man. "Very nice, Herr Huber."

"You must call me Wilhelm."

"Certainly, Herr Wilhelm." She slightly bowed her head to express her agreement.

"Not Herr Wilhelm. Wilhelm. Don't forget I'm your brother and I want you to address me like that at any time, even when the two of us are alone."

"Yes… Wilhelm." It was utterly disrespectful to call him, an SS officer and Aryan, by his first name and she involuntarily flinched, waiting for the inevitable dressing down, but instead he gave her a pleased smile.

"You're a fast learner. Now give me your coat."

She obeyed and slipped out of the coat, watching how he hung it on the rack next to the door, where he'd put her suitcase as well. Just when she was about to relax, he slipped off his own coat, and shoes, before he locked the door and pocketed the keys. "This is just a precaution, until I know that I can trust you."

"As you wish." She shrugged, hoping to convey the message that she didn't care either way, although she cared a lot. Simply knowing that she was locked in here with him, with no way to even jump out of the window, had her toes curled with fright.

Wilhelm though seemed to have forgotten about her, because he walked straight into the adjacent room, his bedroom, and took off his tunic. When he began unbuttoning his shirt, Margarete quickly turned around, intently studying her fingernails, while she stood in the middle of the room unsure of what to do.

A deep chuckle drew her from her frozen state. "Aren't you going to change?"

Her cheeks flushed with horrible shame. He did not expect her to, or did he? Her voice was but a croaking whistle when she finally turned around and asked, "Where am I supposed to sleep?"

"Well, I would invite you to my bed, but since you don't seem to be open to that suggestion, you can have the chaise longue."

Despite his condescending tone, she breathed out in relief—for less than two seconds, because then he removed his dress shirt and unbuckled his belt. Apparently he had no intention of closing the door to his room, so she took a tentative step toward the chaise longue, but he stopped her with a wave of his hand. "The bathroom is through the bedroom."

More blood rushed to her head, as she tried to keep her poise. "Thank you." As quickly as she could, she raced to her suitcase and carried it through his room, then locked herself inside the bathroom to change into her night dress, hoping he would have fallen asleep by the time she came out again.

But when she finally tiptoed into his bedroom, he was sitting at a small desk, waiting for her and pointed at his bed. "Sit."

She sat down on the edge, barely touching the bed, her small suitcase like a protective wall on her lap. "What do you want?"

"Don't be afraid, I'm not going to hurt you. For the time being, you are going to stay with me. I'll register you with the authorities and keep your paperwork, just in case. You will keep my household and do everything you did at my parents' house, except that you won't be allowed to go outside until I know that I can trust you not to do anything stupid."

Margarete nodded, forcing herself to breathe.

"From now on I will call you Anne and treat you as my sister, at all times. You have to actually become her, or this will never work. Do you understand?"

"Yes," she whispered, still unsure why he was even helping her.

"Deep down in your heart you must forget that Margarete Rosenbaum ever existed and you must become Annegret Huber. You must embrace her. Her personality. Her good traits, and her bad ones, too. You are her now. One mistake and you will die." He must have noticed her growing anxiety, because he gave her a reassuring smile. "Nobody in Paris except me knew her, but we can never be sure that someone from our past won't show up. Therefore, it's absolutely crucial that you never slip from your role for even one second. Do you understand?"

"I do." She swallowed hard, as the truth of Wilhelm's words sunk in. She'd had some practice living under Annegret's name, but if she was truthful, she'd never tried to become the spoiled Nazi girl for longer than a few minutes. And now that girl would be her. Always. "I will try my best."

"Trying is not enough." He stood up, walked the few steps over to her, took the suitcase from her clasped hands and set it aside, before he got on his haunches, and fixed his greenish-brown eyes on her. "You *are* Annegret Huber. Every second of every day. Inside this apartment or out. With officials or friends. With Germans or French. Every time. All the time."

Again, she nodded, grateful for his advice. Looking back now at her performance over the past weeks she understood how lucky she'd been not to get caught, because her behavior had been so different from how the real Annegret would act. "Please, tell me why you're helping me?"

He stood up, looking down at her. "I'm not doing this for you, but because of your little secret with Horst Richter."

"You know…?"

"I'm not dumb. Anyone can see that you are in the family way. Richter is the father, isn't he? That's why he helped you get away from Reiner and me."

Margarete stared at him in disbelief, as she unraveled the web of lies. Horst Richter believed she was pregnant by a married SS officer and helped her out of respect for an old friend. Wilhelm, though, believed she was pregnant with Richter's child. And he must hope to gain some kind of favor from helping the high-ranking Gestapo officer to get rid of the evidence of his little indiscretion, willing to sacrifice the honor of his supposed sister for his own benefit.

She sighed, hating to be a pawn in the game of powerful men. Although, technically, Annegret was the pawn and she was… nonexistent. At some point she would have to tell him the truth, that there was no baby, but until then she would play her role better than any of the actresses on Goebbels' *Gottbegnadetenliste*, the list of God-gifted artists. And she would start this very moment.

"I never believed anyone would find out."

"Never underestimate me," Wilhelm said with a proud expression on his face, which gave her an insight in how to treat him in the future. "Now, I suggest you go to sleep and we'll talk some more in the morning."

CHAPTER 22

Wilhelm was woken up by an unusual noise in his apartment. He glanced at the alarm clock on his nightstand and momentarily feared he'd overslept. But today was Christmas Day and for two days all public offices were closed.

Then he saw her. Margarete—*Annegret*, he corrected himself— had gotten up early and was busy preparing breakfast in the tiny kitchen. He got up and went to the bathroom, where his robe was hanging. Living with a girl who was pretending to be his sister meant he couldn't walk around his own place half-naked anymore.

When he stepped into the living room, he noticed that she'd already set the table for two, which was a good sign. Apparently his speech yesterday had had the intended effect and she would be taking this charade seriously. He'd made it sound as if he was telling this only for her benefit, but in reality, he was scared, too. If she was found out, he would hang as well. Throughout the night he'd barely slept, wondering whether passing the Jewess off as his sister had been such a great idea.

Not insisting when Richter had brushed his accusations away was one thing, but actively hiding a Jew… The Gestapo would have a field day with him. And he had witnessed how much some of those sadistic brutes enjoyed their work.

He truly had no idea what had possessed him last night when he'd seen her at the Pension Kaiser and introduced her to everyone as his sister. But whatever his motives, there was no way back now. She held his life in her hands, as much as he held hers. He just hoped she would never realize it.

"That smells delicious, Anne. What did you cook for breakfast?"

Margarete blushed slightly and answered. "Pancakes with apple compote." She busied herself, serving him and he relaxed a bit. "Would you like coffee, or tea? I found both in your kitchen."

"Coffee." He'd not even finished speaking, when she raced back into the kitchen to fulfill his order. His mother had truly trained her well and he leaned back in his chair, content about the advantages of this arrangement, since he surely could get used to having a live-in maid who catered to all his needs and wishes.

"Your coffee. Would you like anything else? Otherwise I'll make your bed now, Herr Huber." Her voice was clipped and he could see the anxiety on her face. This would never work. He jumped to his feet, knocking over his chair. She raced to pick it up, tripped over her feet and spilled the coffee all over the expensive white linen tablecloth adorned with delicate golden Christmas embroidery.

She stood there, trembling and her eyes downcast, like a misbehaving child might when awaiting punishment.

"You useless klutz! Look what you have done! Do you have any idea how much this tablecloth cost? No, you don't because you're nothing but a Jew, not worthy to walk on this earth!" The moment the words left his mouth, his shoulders sagged and he picked up his chair from the floor before sinking onto it. "I'm sorry. Sit."

Margarete cast him a stubborn gaze, but didn't move.

"I said sit!" He raised his voice just enough to make her follow his orders. When she took her seat at the table across from him, he exhaled deeply. "I'm truly sorry. We both need to play our role to perfection, not only you. I want to help you and your baby, but I won't risk my own career to do so." He already was in knee-deep, but she didn't have to know that. "You'll stay in the safety of this apartment until slips like the one that just occurred don't happen anymore. You must behave like Annegret. You must become her. You can never for one second forget that you are her."

"I'm sorry, Herr—" She caught herself, and said, "I mean, Wilhelm?"

"On second thought, you better call me Wilm. That's what Anne always said." He didn't tell her the other, less flattering sobriquets his sister had invented during their childhood.

"Wilm." She said it hesitantly, as if finding out whether she actually was allowed to speak in such a disrespectful manner with him. She would have to learn a lot. He almost pitied her, but then decided she should be grateful for the chance he was giving her. What Jewish girl wouldn't dream of being the daughter of a rich and influential SS-Standartenführer?

He smiled encouragingly at her. "It's not so hard, is it?"

"No, Wilm. What else do you expect me to do or not do? Yesterday you said you wanted me to keep your household, but Annegret never did a stroke of work in her life."

Did he only imagine this, or was she smirking?

"That might be true, but what you may not know is that since the death of our parents she's destitute and depends on the charity of her brothers. The way I see it, she could either put up with Reiner, who inherited the entire family fortune, or she could choose to live with her favorite brother Wilm in Paris. But since I have to subsist on my salary, she would have to adapt and learn how to keep a household." He smiled. "We all need to do our bit for the war effort."

"We certainly do."

*

In the afternoon, the telephone rang and he answered it. "Wilhelm Huber."

"It's Erika. Merry Christmas to you."

"Merry Christmas to you, too. Did the children like their presents?" He chatted a few minutes with Erika, aware that Margarete was cleaning the kitchen and could hear every word. Therefore he took the telephone, unraveled the cord and walked into the bedroom, shutting the door behind him.

The two people who must never know that Annegret was living with him in Paris were Erika and Reiner.

Thankfully, Erika kept it short, because long distance calls were incredibly expensive and said, "I'll pass you on to Reiner. He wants to talk to you."

"Merry Christmas, little brother. Such a shame you couldn't stay with us. There are important things happening in Berlin right now," Reiner said in his usual patronizing way.

"Wishing you the same. But duty calls and I have to do my bit for the Fatherland here in Paris."

"Have you received any news about Annegret?"

"I'm sorry no. I had hoped she would show up at your place."

"No. Who knows what that girl is up to? I can tell you one thing for sure, my daughters will be raised with better discipline."

"I'm sure they will." Wilhelm had no intention of getting into a fight with his brother, even though he didn't wholly approve of his education principles.

"You don't seem concerned about Anne's disappearance."

"Neither do you."

"If I were you, I'd be starting a search party this very minute. If she doesn't get married before her twenty-fifth birthday, you'll not see a dime of Father's money, since you'll never be able to produce a legitimate male heir." Reiner laughed as if he'd made a funny joke.

"You should know that feeling. Though at least you can still hope that, after two girls, you might finally be man enough to produce a son."

"You filthy little rat."

"You are welcome." Wilhelm hung up, hoping Reiner was mad enough not to bother him in a long, long time. At least, until Annegret was safely married and he'd gained access to her money.

Suddenly a frightening thought occurred to him. How would he prevent Reiner from meeting Annegret, possibly for years? He groaned and decided that was a problem he would solve when it arose.

CHAPTER 23

She'd spent five days locked inside the small apartment. After the Christmas holidays Wilhelm had been in his office most of the day and wherever else he went in the evenings, leaving her alone.

He'd impressed on her to never answer the phone, for fear it might be Reiner calling and she'd cleaned the small place from top to bottom twice already. She'd laundered and ironed his clothes, dusted every little knick-knack in the apartment, scrubbed the bathroom until it shone, and now she was bored.

Wilhelm loved hunting for antiques, but he didn't have a single book in his apartment that she might read to pass her time. The one exception was Hitler's *Mein Kampf*, and she wasn't valiant enough to even take that thing into her hands, since it was a symbol of the oppression of her people.

So, she sat at the window, staring down onto the street, where people milled about. Jealousy at every single one of them her foremost feeling, since they had an actual life, outside the confinement of four walls.

When she heard the key turn in the lock she jumped up in fear. It wasn't dark yet and Wilhelm never came home before five p.m. What if someone had found them out?

The next moment, the door opened and she could barely restrain herself from throwing herself into Wilhelm's arms, so relieved was she to see him instead of a bunch of Gestapo officers coming for her.

"What happened?"

He grinned from ear to ear. "Get your coat. We're going shopping."

"Shopping?" So far he'd always bought groceries on his way home from the office.

"Yes. You need proper clothes, and new shoes. A hat and—"

"I don't need any of those things."

"A new haircut wouldn't go amiss either. You can't go outside in that peasant garb."

"But that's all I own, and I never go outside, because you keep me locked up in here."

He cast her a stare that was hard to make out. "Do you even listen to me? I said we're going shopping."

"But I have no money…" She shook her head.

"Consider it a loan on the trust fund you'll receive once you turn twenty-five."

Her eyes widened in shock, since she'd had no idea. He didn't actually expect her to live as his sister, keeping his house for the next five years?

"Forget what I said, it was a joke," he said hurriedly, but his demeanor gave the impression he'd accidentally told her the truth. Perhaps that was his real motive in helping her out? To get his hands on Annegret's money? In any case, it didn't matter.

"This is Paris, and my sister has to look the part if anyone is to believe our story."

"Well then, let's go shopping." In reality, she itched to leave this place that had become her cage. Eagerly, she slipped into her coat, which earned her a shake of his head.

"That thing is atrocious. Anne wouldn't wear such a sad piece of clothing for her own funeral. Whom did it belong to? Your great-grandmother?"

"My aunt. With the rationing…"

"Well, here there are ways to get fashionable clothes you can't get in Germany. Sometimes it does pay to be with the SS," he said cheerily, making her shudder.

They took the elevator downstairs, where Wilhelm cut the concierge short, who was about to launch into a lengthy interrogation about why Annegret hadn't left the apartment all these days.

The moment they stepped onto the street, Margarete inhaled deeply. The air smelt foul with coal smoke from heating, but to her it was a breath of freedom. Her eyes darted around, taking in her surroundings with a hint of awe and wonder.

"Paris is so beautiful," she said as they walked beside each other.

"It is. I fell in love with it the day I arrived. And despite the war and the stubborn French resistance, there's so much beauty here."

She decided not to contradict him, although she could certainly understand why the French weren't elated to be occupied.

He took her to all the places where German officers could buy beautiful things for their wives or mistresses—and she never saw a single French customer frequenting these stores. Her heart filled with sympathy for the people who were marginalized in their own country, almost like she had been in Germany when she was still Margarete.

Her feet were hurting and her head whirling from all the new things Wilhelm bought for her. He had a surprisingly fine eye for elegance and soon enough she left the choices to him and the sales lady, since he paid for the purchases anyway.

She didn't even want to think about the huge amounts of money that changed hands, but as she left the umpteenth store, decked out in a new royal blue woolen dress, stockings, ankle boots, a soft and cuddly coat with fur collar, a matching bonnet, and gloves, she couldn't help but be amazed at her reflection in the mirror.

"You look amazing," Wilhelm said, warmth lingering in his gaze and his voice.

"Thank you. I already feel different, wearing the new things. It may sound strange, but the moment I slipped into this beautiful dress, I felt more confident."

"It's not strange at all, because clothes do change a person, and the way one is perceived. Why do you think every man and his dog wears a uniform?"

She cocked her head, looking at Wilhelm. "Because it makes them look better?"

He chuckled and she felt a wave of warmth rushing through her. He'd been so kind to her, she often forgot to consider him the enemy. "That's only part of the reason. It makes you feel more confident and authoritative, just like this absolutely gorgeous dress does with you, but more importantly, a uniform makes everyone else see you differently. Passers-by don't see the insecure boy, but the assertive man."

She wondered, whether he was talking about himself, but despite her growing confidence, she didn't dare to ask him. Instead she opted to return the conversation to neutral ground again. "Paris truly is the city of fashion, not even the high society ladies in Berlin can measure up to the average Frenchwoman. I don't know how they do it."

"Well, you can compete with any Frenchwoman now, Anne." He hugged her warmly, the way a big brother would do, and Margarete relaxed against his chest, barely noticing how the insecure, persecuted, and anxious girl she had been slipped from her existence and she truly became Annegret. A young, beautiful woman who had all the opportunities in the world, because she belonged to the so-called Aryan master race.

"Should we eat a brioche somewhere? You look tired." Wilhelm was in an exceptionally good mood today, and since it was her first day out, she would certainly not deny herself an opportunity to taste one of the famous French pastries.

"I'd love to. Thank you again, for everything."

His eyes lingered on her body much too long. "Your transformation is remarkable. With your new hairdo and makeup nobody would ever guess…" Since they were in public, he didn't vocalise what they both knew he was thinking. *That a month ago you were my parents' maid and a Jew.*

"We need to get one more thing for you," he said, sipping his coffee.

What else could there possibly be? Careful not to annoy him, she imitated the way he sipped his coffee and said in Anne's high, clear voice she'd practiced for days, "What else do you have in mind, Wilm?"

He abruptly set down his cup on the saucer and stared at her. "Say that again!"

"What else do you have in mind, Wilm?"

"That was fantastic! How did you do that? I mean, I really thought… you know who… was talking."

She beamed with pride. "I practiced for hours and hours when you were gone, to get it just right."

"It does sound perfect." He smiled. "You're ready to be introduced to society, Annegret Huber. We just need the perfect dress for you."

"More perfect than the one I'm wearing?"

"That one's nothing compared to the one I have in mind. We're invited to a New Year's party by the military governor of Paris and you'll be the star of the evening."

She paled at the prospect of being on show with the high brass scrutinizing her every move. "Do you think that is a good idea? There might be someone who knows me from Berlin."

"I doubt it. Anne never mingled with military people. She was more interested in actors, directors and other artists. She had this misguided idea she could be an actress, as if our father would ever allow her to take up such an indecent profession. Kissing a man for everyone to watch on the silver screen. Scandalous!"

"I still think you'd better go alone," she said, a tight knot forming in her stomach even entertaining the idea of having to rub shoulders with dozens of upper crust Nazis.

"Don't worry, I have great plans for you."

That answer made the anxiety in her stomach explode.

CHAPTER 24

"The cab will be here any moment now," Wilhelm said.

"Are you sure I should be going to this with you?" Margarete's stomach was tied into one huge knot, despite the gorgeous, figure-hugging, confidence-boosting gown worthy of a princess that she was wearing. The bright red dress made her stand out, when all she wanted was to cover up and go unnoticed.

"Yes. People have asked me why I'm hiding you. They might get suspicious that something is wrong with you."

"You could tell them I'm not feeling well."

"And raise more suspicions?"

She cast her eyes downward, since he still believed she was in trouble. "Or you could say I already have another invitation."

"And offend the military governor? No one, and especially not Annegret Huber, turns down an invitation to his party." He patted her arm and said in a much more conciliatory tone, "You'll be fine. You have mastered to perfection looking, speaking and acting like Anne. By the way, we need to present you before you start to show, or people will notice right away."

"How do you know this?"

He gave her a sly grin. "I've made discreet inquiries and people experienced with delicate situations have said so."

"You have done what?" It took her all her strength to keep her voice even.

"Did you think I would leave this to chance? If my other plan doesn't manifest in time, it's most important to keep up appearances. I won't let you bring shame on the Huber family."

Once again she was confused as to why he'd been hiding her, since he was so preoccupied by his family's honor and hated the Jews so much. What exactly could be a motive strong enough for him to risk his own life by hiding her?

"Care to let me know what your other plan is?" She kept her voice nonchalant, almost disinterested, in an effort not to let him see her inner turmoil.

"Getting you married."

His words took a while to trickle into her brain, but once they had, she burst out, "I'm most certainly not!"

"Do you love Horst Richter?"

"Of course not." The words left her mouth before she could think them through, and he looked puzzled at her reaction.

"So, why don't you want to marry then?"

"Because…" Did she really have to explain her reasons? Why would she want to marry a man she'd never met, while she wasn't even her true self?

"See? There's no good reason to refuse. It will solve all our problems; it just has to happen quick enough to pass Richter's child off as his."

"This is so sick." Her legs became wobbly and she had to grab onto the bureau standing behind her.

"You'll still do it. And tonight, you'll have the opportunity to charm your future husband." He looked out the window and added, "Our cab has arrived."

Margarete was burning with fury, when he took her arm and his warm breath brushed her cheek as he whispered into her ear, "Never forget that your life depends on your compliance."

"I don't," she sighed. "But will I have to be Annegret for all eternity?"

Seemingly surprised, he led her into the elevator waited until the door closed before he answered. "Honestly I never thought about that."

It was so much like him, not to consider this small detail, since it wasn't his identity that was at stake. "Maybe we could tell him who I really am?" she suggested.

"Most certainly not. It's way too dangerous. The less people know about you, the better for everyone." He gazed at her and she suddenly had the impression that he actually cared for her, because his features became soft and his voice warm when he continued. "I'll make sure your husband is a good man who treats you well."

She opened her mouth for an answer, but in that moment the elevator door opened and Madame Badeaux launched at them like a torpedo. Margarete could swear that woman had a little alarm going off whenever one of the tenants used the elevator.

"Good evening, Herr Huber, Fräulein Huber. You're going out?"

Wilhelm indulged her. "Yes, Madame Badeaux, my sister and I have been invited by the military governor to a New Year's reception. Our cab is already waiting."

And before the concierge could reply, he opened the door for Margarete to step outside. They spent the journey in silence and soon arrived in front of the Hotel Meurice that was decked out in the most wonderful and elegant Christmas decorations, albeit with the ubiquitous swastika flags hanging prominently in every room.

They checked their coats and weaved their way through the guests, and Wilhelm made a point of introducing her as his younger sister to everyone they met. When it was time to sit for the first course, they were placed next to an SS officer with a very elegant, dark-haired woman on his arm.

"Gerald, this is my sister, Annegret, Anne this is my comrade, SS-Oberscharführer Gerald Nadler."

"It's my pleasure, Fräulein Huber. Please call me Gerald, since your brother and I have become good friends here in Paris." He bent down to kiss her hand.

Margarete had practiced her reaction countless times in front of the mirror and fell right into her role play. "Thank you so much, Gerald. Please call me Anne. Everyone has been so welcoming, I feel completely at home in Paris already." Did she imagine this or had the beautiful woman on his arm just given her a vile glare?

The next moment, Gerald said, "This is Paulette."

"A pleasure to meet you," Margarete said and offered her hand for the other woman, who looked absolutely stunning in a shimmering white dress that contrasted wonderfully with her tanned Mediterranean complexion. Her black hair was done in a fancy updo, with single curls hanging down from her temples. The dark brown eyes and the full, red lips completed the picture of elegance, and once more Margarete was impressed by the Frenchwomen.

And there was no doubt she was French, even before she uttered her first word; whilst the way she looked at Gerald with enthralled admiration made it clear they were in a romantic relationship.

"Welcome to Paris, Fräulein Huber," Paulette said in a delightful accent that made the German phrase sound like a melody.

"Please call me Anne. Everyone does." Out of the corner of her eyes, Margarete noticed that Wilhelm shot her a surprised, but entirely approving glance.

*

The evening wore on and, as Wilhelm had predicted, Annegret was the star of the evening. It wasn't often that a well-bred German Fräulein came to live in Paris, and naturally all the eligible bachelors outdid one another to charm her. French girls were well enough for diversion, but a man who wanted to marry and start a family had to look among his own kind. One man in particular, Ludwig Greiner, seemed especially smitten with her and flirted outrageously.

Even the married men wanted to make Anne's acquaintance, and thus she was asked to dance more than a dozen times. Wilhelm observed how she gracefully waltzed across the floor in the hands of his boss, Obersturmführer Bicke.

Dancing was another thing he'd insisted she practice and the two of them had spent countless, albeit rather pleasurable, hours with dancing lessons in his apartment. It was amazing what a little bit of time and attention had done to change the cute, but drab and clumsy maid into a beautiful and confident woman in her own right. Maybe Hitler was wrong and under the right tutelage the Jews could be converted into valuable citizens—at least some of them.

"Your sister is so very delightful! Where have you been hiding her all this time?" Bicke said.

"She only arrived recently to live with me after the tragic death of our parents."

"Again, my sincerest condolences." Bicke took Margarete's hand and pressed a kiss on the back of it. A kiss that lasted much too long to be polite. "We must meet more often, Anne."

Margarete cast him a bright smile. "I'm sure my brother wouldn't object."

A sharp pang of jealousy hit him. Bicke of all men! He couldn't let her fall for his boss, since he needed to marry her off to some stupid and desperate bloke who was broke enough to accept another man's child in exchange for a considerable amount of her inheritance. Ideally a common soldier whom he could threaten with a transfer to the Afrika Korps should he cause problems for Wilhelm.

"Anne is still grieving the loss of our parents and it was hard enough to drag her to this party tonight. But I'll see what I can do."

At least she had the decency to look contrite at his rebuff. But Bicke didn't seem to understand that his flattery wasn't welcome, because he said, "It would be my honor to show you the beauty of Paris and take your mind off those horrible events. We're all grieving for your father, he was such a wonderful man."

You didn't even know him!

Thankfully it was announced that dessert was now ready and everyone should return to their seats. They arrived first and while they were alone, he hissed at her, "What were you thinking of, flirting with Bicke? You're not some tart. You're my sister."

She gazed at him with a measured expression, as if sizing him up. "Didn't you want to marry me off in a hurry? He's quite handsome and seems very gentle."

Anger exploded inside his chest and he wanted to slap her for even entertaining the idea of being with another man, when it was him who… He was surprised at his own thoughts, since he most certainly wasn't the least bit interested in her. While pretending to be his own sister, she still was a Jew. Two very good reasons not to have romantic feelings toward her. He took a deep breath and murmured, "He's not suitable. Whom you're going to marry will be my decision, and mine alone."

"Certainly, my dearest brother," she said in the soft, submissive voice she used to placate him, but he'd seen the flicker of rebellion in her eyes and didn't like it one bit.

"We'll talk about your behavior at home," he said and put on a pleasant expression to greet Paulette. At least that woman knew how to be obedient, since Gerald blabbed nonstop about her extraordinary compliance in catering for his every wish.

The table filled and when everyone was seated, the waiters served the most delicious crème brulée Wilhelm had ever eaten. Wine and liqueurs flowed abundantly and soon enough it was midnight.

The military governor had arranged for fireworks and everyone walked outside to celebrate the beginning of another successful year. Hopefully it would bring the same number of fantastic victories for the Wehrmacht, and by the end of 1942, Europe would be one peaceful country united under German rule.

Just before dawn they arrived at his apartment and he fell on his bed exhausted, his head whirling with thoughts and worries. None of the men in attendance had been suitable to marry Margarete. Some might not care about raising a bastard, but he knew for sure that every single officer at the party wouldn't hesitate to hang both of them should he find out her real identity.

Once again, he wondered what on earth had possessed him to help her out, because not even the considerable inheritance was worth dangling from a rope. His heart squeezed at the thought of anything happening to her, and although he didn't understand why he'd suddenly developed a soft spot for a Jew, he found himself wanting to do everything in his power to protect her. Even if that meant marrying her off to another man… She'd made a stellar appearance during tonight's event in looking like a veritable fairy-tale princess in her red gown, the shimmering white skin, the brown hair combed in the latest Parisian fashion and her vivid, intelligent, lovely hazel eyes.

Going in circles, his thoughts arrived back where they'd started: finding a suitable husband. Ellen was right. The groom had to be as desperate for protection as Margarete was. Someone who'd be shipped off to a concentration camp if his secret was found out. Just how should he go about finding such a man?

He couldn't well telephone Ellen and ask for her help, since one could never be too sure the line wasn't tapped. Much later, when he fell asleep, he still had no idea.

CHAPTER 25

A few days later Wilhelm returned in the evening with a bag full of groceries.

"Look what I got!"

She smiled, because she actually liked it when he came home to spend time with her, and not only because she was incredibly bored in the small apartment on her own. "Let me see."

He removed a huge piece of meat from the bag and held it up. "I specifically asked the butcher for beef, since…" He didn't have to finish his sentence for her to understand that he'd done it out of respect for her, because Jews weren't supposed to eat pork.

"We weren't very religious at home, so I wouldn't have minded, but thank you so much for your consideration." She took the bag from him and walked into the kitchen.

He followed her and lingered in the doorway. That wasn't unusual per se, because he sometimes liked to watch her cook or chat with her. Today, though, it felt different. His gaze bore deep into her back and she felt goosebumps breaking out all over her skin.

After a while, he cleared his throat and said, "Can I trust you?"

"What?" She turned around, her hands bloody from the beef she'd been seasoning.

"Can I trust you not to run away?"

She sighed. How often had she contemplated the idea of escaping her captivity in his apartment? Just two days ago, he'd forgotten to lock the door when leaving for his office. But as much as she yearned for freedom, she also knew she wouldn't be safe anywhere in Paris, or possibly in France. "Much as I hate to admit it, I have realized that the safest place for me to be is here with you."

A genuine smile crossed his face. "I… you… I mean… what I wanted…" He broke off, took a deep breath and tried again. "What I meant to say is I want you to feel at ease and do things you enjoy. Therefore, if I don't have to worry about you doing something foolish…"

"I promise, I won't," she quickly said.

"… then I'd maybe ask Gerald's friend Paulette to take you out and teach you the ropes? Show you around, help you go shopping for groceries, teach you some French?"

Margarete was touched. "That would be nice."

"Good." He seemed relieved and turned around.

"Wait!" Since he'd been so kind, she suddenly felt the urge to tell him the truth. But the moment his eyes locked with hers, she chickened out. "You must be eager to change out of your uniform."

"That can wait. You wanted to tell me something."

"It really wasn't that important."

"It sounded very important to me." He closed the distance between them and put a hand on her shoulder, which pierced her marrow and bone, since he normally meticulously avoided touching her. "Don't be shy and tell me what troubles you."

"There never was a child." There, she'd said it. With bated breath she waited for his reaction, but nothing happened apart from a confused frown.

"What child?"

"Mine. I wasn't ever pregnant."

Finally he seemed to understand. His brows knitted together. "That can't be. Horst Richter said you were."

"It's a long story."

"We better sit down, then."

She turned around to wash and dry her hands, before she followed him into the living room where she settled on the chaise longue while he poured two glasses of cognac for them.

"Does Richter know?"

She shook her head. "He believes that I, or rather Anne, got taken advantage of by a married man. Then he felt compelled to help me—her—due to his friendship with your father."

"So, he wasn't your lover?"

"Hell, no!" The mere thought of the Gestapo officer, who was at least twice her age, made her shudder.

He cocked his head and looked at her intently, seemingly pleased that she wasn't with child. After taking a sip from his cognac, he slowly said, "That will make it so much easier to find a husband for you."

"Why do you still insist on marrying me off, now that I won't damage the reputation of your family?"

"Well, I guess since we're laying our cards on the table, I should probably tell you. It's all about money."

Margarete hissed in a breath. "This is a joke, right? Who would pay you for protecting me? I don't have any influential friends."

He chuckled. "You're right, nobody would pay a single *Pfennig* to protect you. Annegret though… she has inherited a considerable trust fund and will gain access to it when she turns twenty-five or the day she marries."

"That's why you've been trying to match me up with all those sleazy men!" The warm feelings she'd had for him mere seconds ago instantly dissolved and left nothing but stale disappointment.

"I'm sorry. No decent man would marry one of your kind, so I needed to find someone who'd be willing to keep his mouth shut even after he possibly found out…"

Her shoulders trembled with shock and she had the hardest time not to cry at the realization of the disgusting game he'd been scheming, with her as the pawn.

"So, did you find anyone willing to agree to your conditions? And after the wedding, I suppose you'd pay him off and keep the rest? Were you ever going to tell me?"

"I'm telling you now." He scratched his chin.

"I see." For the first time she looked at the precious antiques in his apartment with a collector's eye. They must have cost a fortune—undoubtedly more than a soldier, even an SS-Oberscharführer—could afford. Deprived of the extra money his father had regularly sent him, he'd grabbed the opportunity with both hands. While she despised his ulterior motives for helping her, she could actually understand his reasons.

"It would be beneficial for both of us."

"What would keep me from finding a husband myself, getting married and keeping my money once I pay him off?"

"The fact that you're just a woman."

"What exactly is that supposed to mean?" She was seething with fury. She couldn't even believe that she'd thought Wilhelm might be a nice person just minutes earlier.

"It means that my father thought a woman's place was in the kitchen and therefore I will become the custodian for Anne's, or better, *your* money once you get married, until you turn twenty-five."

"I'd rather rot in hell than do your bidding!" She knew it wasn't true, but her anger was too strong to see reason at this moment.

"Be my guest. Shall I call the Gestapo?"

"You wouldn't dare!" she screeched.

"You're right, I wouldn't, because I care too much about you," Wilhelm murmured the last words and Margarete felt as if someone was sucking the oxygen from the room. His confession was both heartwarming and frightening at the same time. This wasn't supposed to happen. There could never be anything between an SS officer and a Jew. Not in Germany, not in France, and not in any other place on this earth.

"I can't do this," she said and escaped back into the kitchen.

He followed her and she could feel his eyes boring into her back while he lingered in the doorway. It was quite unnerving and she wished he'd just leave. When she finally put the meat into a pan, she turned around, ready to take him on, but he looked at her with such an amount of pain in his eyes that she wanted to wrap her arms around him and console him. For obvious reasons she did nothing of the sort.

"My father made sure in his will that I wouldn't get a single penny until I had a family of my own and was therefore, in his eyes, mature enough to use the money wisely. Getting my hands on Anne's trust fund was my financial salvation… but… I never actually thought this through. I intended to get you married, take possession of Anne's money and never think about you again. But during the past weeks, I've come to see that you're an actual human being—and a nice one at that." He gave her a sheepish look. "And I started contemplating what would happen to you after the wedding. You know, that this is forever, right? There will be no way out, not ever."

"Not even after the war?"

He gave her a confused glance. "Hitler isn't going to change his opinion about the Jews, just because the war is over. So, yes, you'll have to be Annegret for the rest of your life."

Her shoulders sagged in defeat. She'd been riddled with remorse about denying her culture, her upbringing, her very identity, but had always consoled herself that it was only for a short period of time, until the war was over. She'd never once contemplated the outcome Wilhelm apparently took for granted: that Germany would win this war and the Jews would be persecuted until the end of time.

"I can't do that." Her voice was little more than a whisper.

"Of course you can. And I will help you, since I have a new plan."

Despite herself she gazed up at him, putting all her hopes into whatever he had cooked up.

"Anne's money will save both of us, because after the war we'll use it to escape to some place where nobody knows us. Maybe South America? How does that sound?"

"You want me to escape with you and live in a faraway continent forever?" Margarete was already feeling homesick.

"Would that be such a bad thing?" His breath brushed her face and made her skin tingle.

"I... I don't know."

"You could even be Margarete again, because nobody will know that you are a Jew."

It was too much to take in and her head felt dizzy with all the revelations of the past fifteen minutes. In an urge to get away from him and his suggestions, she said, "I'd better make dinner or we'll go hungry tonight."

CHAPTER 26

Wilhelm kept his word and gave her Annegret's papers. "Now you can come and go as you wish."

She was truly grateful to him for giving her the freedom to go out in Paris and live like any normal young woman her age. Once in a while she pondered running away, but always tabled the idea because without help, and a new identity, there was no way she'd go undiscovered for more than a few days. And, if she was honest with herself, she was afraid of the unknown and would rather stay in relative safety with Wilhelm.

Sometimes they went out together to the theater or a concert and one day he invited her to accompany him to the flea market where she saw him show an enthusiasm and joie de vivre she hadn't seen in him before.

He stopped in front of a stall with small statues and Margarete couldn't help but admire the white marble sculpture of a woman about twenty inches high.

"You like it?" he asked, beaming.

"It's so beautiful." She traced her finger across the sculpture's dress that was carved with such delicate care it seemed to be of transparent silk instead of stone. On her head and in the pleats of her skirt the woman carried roses and next to her, on a small pedestal, sat a basket full of roses. Despite the fact the roses were made of white marble, Margarete could almost smell their alluring scent and see the luscious red color.

"Yes, a fine piece." He turned around to the saleswoman and bargained the price with her in surprisingly good French. Once he'd paid for it he pressed it into Margarete's hand. "It's yours."

"No, I can't possibly accept this."

"But I want you to have it."

She knew she should not accept such an expensive gift from him, but she'd fallen in love with the sculpture the moment she'd seen it and now that her fingers touched the cold, yet soft marble that warmed beneath her touch, she couldn't resist. "Thank you, Wilm."

When they left the market, she said, "You should have become an art dealer."

He turned around and gazed at her with the saddest expression she'd ever seen on him. "That's what I wanted to be, but my father thought it more appropriate for me to have a career in the military."

"I'm sorry." She meant it. Under different circumstances, in a different country, it felt like perhaps he and she might have been friends.

The weeks passed and life in Paris became routine. Every day, she became more like Annegret, to the point that she sometimes forgot who she really was. It was comforting and frightening at the same time and she wished so much for a person she could confide in.

Just once, she wanted to talk about her inner turmoil and the sense of betrayal she often felt when realizing how she was shedding her whole identity, perhaps forever. But she had nobody whom she could trust.

Certainly not Wilhelm, despite the fact that she had to admit she enjoyed spending time with him, and actually looked forward to talking every night when he came home after work. But he wouldn't understand what she was going through. While he never said anything unpleasant about Jews in her presence, she knew he considered them lowlife criminals and a threat to the Reich.

Her only other friend was Paulette, who'd turned out to be quite pleasant company. In the beginning it had been Wilhelm's proposal to go out with Gerald and Paulette, but it hadn't taken long for Paulette to invite her to spend some girls-only time together, which Wilhelm had actually encouraged. But not even with her could Margarete be honest. Too much was at stake.

She was dusting the living room with all the exquisite artwork on display when someone knocked on the door and she glanced at the clock with surprise. It wasn't even noon yet and she wasn't expecting visitors. Wiping her hands on her apron she went to open the door, amazed at herself for not feeling the slightest trace of fear.

"Paulette? What are you doing here?"

"Can I come in, please?" The usually chic woman stood in front of the door, heaving like a locomotive, her hair in disarray and her makeup smeared.

"Of course," Margarete said, stepping aside and locking the door behind her. She liked the Frenchwoman, even though she'd been a little skeptical when they had first been introduced. Margarete couldn't understand why a beautiful woman like Paulette would willingly choose to sleep with a Nazi. But then, she considered her own circumstances, and while she wasn't sleeping with Wilhelm, she was still with him because he protected her.

"Do you want to freshen up?" she asked with a gaze at Paulette's untypically disheveled state.

"Yes."

"I'll make coffee for us, and I might still have some bread from breakfast." All Parisians were hungry during these difficult times and even though, thanks to Gerald, Paulette probably didn't have to endure hunger, Margarete suspected that she was giving most of her rations to friends and family.

When Paulette returned from the bathroom looking immaculate again, she also seemed to have recovered her self-confidence. "I'm so sorry to unexpectedly drop in on you, I shouldn't have."

Despite her efforts to sound detached, Margarete sensed her underlying panic and looked at the woman she considered a friend. "Has something happened?"

"No." Paulette shook her head violently, her black curls bouncing.

"I won't tell anyone. Maybe I can help you. Has Gerald done something…?"

"No, no. Gerald and I are fine." Paulette was fighting with herself, and Margarete could follow her inner turmoil by the expressions on her face.

"Please. I want to help. You've been so kind to me, especially teaching me French. You've shown me around, explained to me how life in Paris works." *And I still don't know why you've been doing it, because normally French people aren't welcoming toward Germans.* "If there's anything I can do, please tell me."

Paulette took a moment, until she finally said, "There's one thing. If someone ever asks, could you say you and I spent the morning together?"

"Of course." The words left her mouth, before she could even consider the consequences, and when she observed the silent wave of relief washing over Paulette's body, she couldn't take it back, although she was now one hundred percent sure something was amiss.

Paulette also grasped the momentousness of Margarete's decision, because she added, "Probably nothing will come of it, but if you think Wilhelm would object…"

"No, no. He won't. He's quite protective of me, but he likes you and thinks spending time with you is good for me."

"Can I... ask you something?" Paulette's voice had a very disquieting tone to it, but Margarete decided not to dwell on it.

"Go ahead."

"Is... I'm sorry, but is... oh God, this is more difficult than I thought. Is he somehow...? I mean... has he ever hurt you?"

"What? No? We don't agree on everything, but I'm very thankful that he's letting me live with him." Margarete wanted to jump up and run away, because this conversation was heading into dangerous territory. Usually she evaded all inquiries into Annegret's family, because Wilhelm had instructed her that the fewer details people knew, the better. It wouldn't do any good if someone remembered a certain event from Anne's childhood in a different way than she'd told it.

"It's just... Please don't be angry with me... I really like you. It's just I've noticed him looking at you in a way that... let's say... feels a bit unbrotherly."

Margarete somehow managed to laugh lightly. "Oh no, you're imagining things. He's my brother and we've always been very close, but I can assure you there's nothing, absolutely nothing other than sibling love between us."

"It is just that he seems almost jealous when he sees you with another man, but at the same time he seems to be hell-bent on matching you up with someone—yet not the most eligible kind of man, if I may say so?"

This was definitely getting dangerous. "I appreciate your concern, but there really is nothing. Wilhelm has always been a stern protector of my honor and hates it when any man has designs on me. In this way he's exactly like my father who believed no man was good enough for me." Paulette seemed assured, but Margarete had to get this idea out of her mind once and for all.

If anyone as much suspected Wilhelm and she weren't siblings, she'd be dead in a blink of an eye. "You must never repeat these atrocious accusations. Are we clear?"

"Forget I said anything," Paulette said, but just before she left the apartment, she whispered into Margarete's ear. "If you ever need to get away from him, I know people who can help."

Margarete decided to be more careful and steer clear of Paulette for a few days. It wouldn't do for the Frenchwoman to dig into her complicated relationship with Wilhelm, or worse, find out her true secret. A woman who collaborated with the Nazis would surely be appalled and report her to the authorities.

A few days later she went grocery shopping and since the sun was shining she decided to take the afternoon off from her housekeeping duties and simply enjoy herself. Walking idly along the Seine, she realized that this was the first time since Hitler's *Machtergreifung* in 1933 that she had spent an entire day without a single care in the world. Taking on Anne's identity and living in Paris had been nothing but a revelation of how life could be without harassment, oppression and ostracization.

It was almost too wonderful to be true. As Annegret Huber, she was protected in many ways from the horrific reality all around her. It could have been the perfect life, if it weren't for the nagging doubt of being someone she despised, always fearing she'd actually become as heartless, selfish and cruel as Annegret had been.

That evening she returned to the apartment, to find Wilhelm already waiting for her.

"Where have you been? I was worried about you," he said instead of a greeting.

"I was walking along the Seine. I started near the Louvre and walked all the way to the Bois de Boulogne. Paris is so beautiful and I had the most marvelous day," she said, brimming with the need to share her happiness with someone.

"You should have been back before dark."

"I'm sorry. I completely forgot the time and when the sun went down, I raced back home as fast as I could. Can't you be happy for me?"

"Happy?" He gave her the once-over before he asked, "Did you meet a man?"

"What?" she asked, appalled that he would think such a thing. In fact, nothing had been further from her mind. She'd simply enjoyed the wonderful sunshine grazing her skin and the harbingers of spring in the huge park.

"Did you sneak away for a secret tryst?" The vein in his temple was pulsating furiously.

"No! I would never." Margarete was both hurt and angry that Wilhelm would think so little of her. She watched him as he paced back and forth several times and suddenly realized that he seemed jealous. Had Paulette been right? Was he secretly in love with her?

Wilhelm stood opposite her, a grimace on his face as if she'd just punched his guts. But the expression disappeared as he schooled his features and said, "I don't believe you."

"Then don't. I was out walking along the Seine, all on my own." She looked at his face that she knew was handsome, although now she could only see cold rage. "I'd never give myself to a Nazi. They're nothing but lowlife criminals, the worst of the worst, heartless monsters who think they're above anyone else," she screamed at him, not caring that his face turned into a deeper crimson red with every insult she flung at him.

"Stop. Now," he said with a voice harder than steel, and cold enough to send shivers of fear through her.

Wilhelm was not a violent man, but now she feared what he might do to her. "I'm sorry, I shouldn't have insulted you."

"No, you shouldn't have. And you will never do so again, or I will denounce you and cheer while they drag you away in chains."

She stamped her foot before challenging him. "Don't use empty threats on me, because if you report me, you're in as much trouble as I am." The Nazis didn't treat anyone kindly who was suspected of helping Jews.

"If I were you, I wouldn't want to test that theory." Wilhelm snagged his coat off of the hook by the door. "Don't you ever defy me again. You'll do what I tell you to do; when I tell you to do it." Then he slammed out of the apartment, leaving Margarete in a state of open-mouthed disbelief.

For the past weeks she and Wilhelm had formed a friendship, even an attraction to each other, and in just a few moments, he'd torn the fragile trust to pieces and shown his true colors. He was not the slightest bit better than the rest of them.

Maybe she should be happy that it had come to this showdown, because now at least she knew she could never be truly safe with him. Despite her comparably convenient position as his sister, in his apartment, the constant hide-and-seek was beginning to take a toll not only on her, but apparently also on him, since she'd noticed his mood was getting ever more volatile.

As dangerous as it was, she had to leave Paris and hide someplace far away in the country, where nobody knew who Annegret Huber was. Or better yet, she needed to shed her identity once again and become someone entirely else. An inconspicuous young woman, maybe from the region of Alsace, where people spoke a mixture between French and German that would explain her accent. But for that plan, she needed new papers. Just whom to ask for help?

Wilhelm didn't return and it was way past midnight, when she settled onto the chaise longue to retire. In the early hours of the morning, she woke feeling a rough tug on her arm.

"What's wrong?" she asked sleepily into the darkness.

"You can't stay here."

CHAPTER 27

Earlier that day

Wilhelm answered the ringing phone in his office.

"Surprise, it's your brother," came Reiner's voice through the line. Instantly Wilhelm was a bundle of nerves, expecting him to ask about Anne. He'd still not decided how to tell him, but one thing was sure: he couldn't hide her presence indefinitely and one day Reiner was bound to hear about her staying with him through the grapevine.

"What a pleasant surprise."

"Stop pretending to be charming, you're talking to me."

"Well then, bugger off, if you prefer that."

Reiner chuckled into the phone. "Actually, the opposite is going to happen. I'm coming to Paris next month."

"You what?" Wilhelm shrunk in his chair as if someone had squeezed all air from an inflated tire.

"Isn't that great? I'll stay for three or four days and who would be better suited to introduce me to everyone, especially some young ladies after work?"

Wilhelm groaned. "Sure, I can do that. If you give me exact dates I can even get us tickets for the Moulin Rouge."

"Now, that sounds good, doesn't it? I'll stay in the Hotel Meurice, but I'm hoping to—"

Wilhelm quickly interrupted him. "What's the reason for your visit?"

"Way above your pay grade. I can only tell you this much: the wind for the Jews in France is going to change. Heydrich has had enough from locals dragging their feet. I'll be presenting the results of the Wannsee Conference regarding the 'Final Solution of the Jewish Question' and will oversee immediate implementation."

"That sounds promising."

"It is. I shouldn't be telling you, but since you'll be invited to my presentation anyway… We found a final solution for the Jewish question. The idea is to put them to use first. The able-bodied objects will be led eastward on road construction projects. Undoubtedly a vast majority will drop out through natural selection. Thus we only have to eliminate the remaining rest."

"You're killing them all off?" Wilhelm couldn't hide the shock in his voice. Never had he believed it would come to that. Emigration—definitely. Deportation to hostile regions in the east—fine. Putting up with high death rates in the work camps—acceptable. But actively killing those who survived the ordeal?

"What did you think? Those objects will be the most resilient ones and if we let them go free, they will become the nucleus of a new, and more virulent strain of the Jewish race. It's necessary to destroy that seed."

"I see…" Wilhelm was fighting against the bile rising in his throat. Although there wasn't any lost love between him and the Jews he abhorred the idea of murdering them in cold blood.

"The implementation will start immediately, combing Europe from west to east, starting with France."

"You're starting in France? Why?" Wilhelm felt a heavy weight squeezing the breath from his lungs, thinking of Margarete, and the concentration camps being built in the east where people were being worked to death.

"It's obvious, isn't it? We start where the more valuable people live. Scandinavia, Benelux and obviously France. Once we've rid them of the nefarious Jewish influence, these nations will be so much better equipped to accept the German superiority and work with us for a peaceful Europe."

"The French are putting up much more resistance than expected."

"Of course they are, because the World Jewry is kindling hatred with their conspiracy against our country. But once all the Jews are eradicated, this problem will go away and the French will be soft as lambs, you just wait and see."

"That will be refreshing." Wilhelm was tired of the attacks and assassination attempts all over France.

"Anyhow, I'm giving you this advice to advance your career: volunteer for a raid on the Jews ahead of the announcement, deliver it quickly and when the next opening comes up, I'll put in a good word for your promotion. How does that sound?"

"Perfect." Wilhelm was glad Reiner couldn't see him grimacing, since he had no desire at all to get his hands dirty and round up Jews. Brutality was something he'd rather leave to someone else, like the Gestapo brutes who seemed to enjoy it so much.

"Oh, and haven't you forgotten to tell me some important news?"

"Me... there's really nothing to speak of..."

"I'd say the fact that Anne finally showed up and is living with you is quite something to speak of, don't you think?"

Wilhelm all but fell from his chair. He somehow had to limit the damage and thought quickly. "I told you! Don't you remember? You must have forgotten about it, because... it was on the same day your new baby was born." He knew that Reiner was more than a little bit peeved that the newborn was just another girl, and hoped to distract him by rubbing that fact under his nose. "You were so excited with the birth of your third daughter and all that."

Reiner snorted into the phone. "I most certainly would remember if you'd told me anything about our sister. But now I'm wondering what reason you had to keep this little detail from me. What kind of mischief are the two of you cooking up?"

"Reiner. Don't be ridiculous, why would I keep Anne's visit to Paris from you?"

"It's more than a visit, though, isn't it? I have it on good authority that she's been with you since New Year."

"Anne has been with me, but she is insisting on looking for another place, since she hates it in Paris. She's been telling me for quite a while now that she rather wants to return to Berlin."

"It will be quite difficult for her without money. Or has she found a wealthy suitor yet?"

"Look, Reiner, your accusations are beyond ridiculous. I told you, but since you never really listen to what I say, this is entirely on you." Wilhelm was desperately fighting to keep some credibility. His brother was suspicious enough as it was.

"It doesn't matter anyway. Next month during my visit to Paris I'll be checking up on both of you. And then I'm taking her home with me, I think. It can't be doing her any good gallivanting around France. And what kind of light does that throw on me?"

"A caring family father devoted to his wife and three infant daughters?" Wilhelm suggested with the tiniest trace of glee in his voice.

"Don't talk nonsense. Make sure Anne doesn't get into trouble and tell her I'm giving her the choice to either live in my house or in a *Faith and Beauty* boarding school."

"Anne would hate the discipline in a boarding school."

"One more reason to live in my house. Erika can teach her all the skills needed to be a good wife and mother."

"I'll tell her and I'm sure she'll be delighted to meet with you. Don't forget to advise me on the exact dates of your visit so I can make arrangements."

Wilhelm wiped the sweat from his forehead as soon as he hung up the phone. Under no circumstances could Reiner meet Margarete, or the deceit would be discovered immediately. And he wouldn't put it past his brother to turn them both in.

His mind was running in wild circles, but for the life of him, he couldn't think of a way to keep them both safe. Too many people knew about Anne and would surely ask questions if she simply disappeared. Except… maybe if there was a valid reason. One month gave them just enough time for a whirlwind romance, a wedding and a honeymoon far away. More urgently than ever, he needed to find an appropriate husband for her, and with the funds from her inheritance he'd ensure she was safe.

Options were limited, but a honeymoon in neutral Spain might do. There she could wait it out, until he had access to her funds. Switzerland, for one, would welcome her with open arms if she carried a coffer full of money with her. Or if they denied her entry for some reason, he could arrange for a boat ticket to South America, nobody would ever go looking for her down there. He didn't even flinch at the considerable cost involved, because right now he cared more about her safety than about the money he would get from this.

Still pondering the details of his plan to get Margarete into safe territory, he was disturbed by a knock on his office door.

"Come in."

His boss, Obersturmführer Bicke entered, wearing his hat and coat. "Will you have lunch with me?"

Nothing was further from his mind, but he still nodded. "Of course, Herr Obersturmführer. Would you kindly give me five minutes to lock up all documents?"

"I love your attention to detail," Bicke said, taking a seat and watching Wilhelm's every move.

"Thank you." Wilhelm finished locking the filing cabinets and took the key with him to hang it in the key safe in the secretary's office, wondering what Bicke could want from him. The two had never been on friendly terms and it was unusual for Bicke to ask him out to lunch.

Once they'd settled in La Tour d'Argent, one of the fine Parisian restaurants catering exclusively to German officers, Bicke said, "You might be wondering what this is about."

"Indeed I do, Herr Obersturmführer."

"We've been working long enough together, I think it's time to do away with formalities. Please call me Karsten."

Wilhelm was surprised, since Bicke was one of the old school who insisted on the usage of the polite *Sie.* "I would be more than pleased, Karsten. And please call me Wilhelm." Just in time wine arrived, and they drank to their new friendship.

As the first course arrived, Karsten said, "I've heard your brother is coming to Paris."

"Yes, he called me this morning to announce his visit."

Karsten looked contrite. *Aha, hence the new friendliness.* Wilhelm was now sure his boss had listened in on the phone call and made a mental note to be even more careful what he said, never once uttering a critical word about the regime.

"We've been advised about his visit for a while now, but nevertheless I wanted to use the opportunity and put you in charge of the operation at Drancy. It'll be of value to have someone we can trust to be the liaison to Heydrich's department. The Gestapo of course have claimed authority, but we insisted on an SS officer with equal rights."

Wilhelm had difficulty swallowing down his food and took a moment to answer. Drancy was the internment camp where several thousand Jews were being held before deportation. He did not wish to dirty his hands with the conduct of a camp, much less in collaboration with one of the Gestapo brutes, but he also knew that he didn't have a choice.

"I'm very honored you should think of me for this important position, and I'm all too willing to be the liaison to Heydrich via my brother. But I'm afraid I'm not the ideal person for this position."

"Whyever not?" Karsten raised an eyebrow.

"For one, I'll be hopelessly outranked by the Gestapo and you know how they like to steamroll over our organization. The leader of Drancy should at least be a commissioned officer, to be able to keep them at bay."

Karsten laughed. "We think alike. When my boss told me about this idea, I told him exactly the same." Wilhelm didn't dare to breathe. Did this mean, he was off the hook? But Karsten's next words shattered his hopes. "As of now, you're promoted to SS-Untersturmführer. Present yourself at the old man's office in the afternoon and you'll receive the formal paperwork."

Margarete will never forgive me for this. His thought surprised him. Since when did he care for the approval of a Jew? He forced a pleased expression on his face and said, "I can't tell you how very honored I am. And I'll most certainly do everything to make you proud of my work."

"Good. Perhaps we should have a small celebration on the weekend? You could bring your sister as well."

"I'm certain she would love to come." Except, Wilhelm knew, she'd hate nothing more than to find out about Wilhelm's new job and for some reason he wanted to see her happy. He spent the rest of his afternoon in a foul mood, worried sick about Margarete, about Reiner's forthcoming visit, and also his new responsibilities at Drancy.

He finished work early and raced home to tell Margarete about Reiner's upcoming visit, but she wasn't home.

CHAPTER 28

Margarete was asleep on the chaise longue when she was woken by a rough tug on her arm. It took only a few seconds for the memories to return. She'd been out and Wilhelm had been waiting for her in a foul mood when she'd returned home. After an awful row, he had rushed out and she'd finally fallen asleep alone in the apartment. Now he had returned.

"Do you know what time it is?" she asked, trying to make sense of his behavior from the evening before and now.

"Three in the morning."

She sat up, pulling the blanket around her to shield her bare arms from his view, although it was almost completely dark, with only the tiniest sliver of moonlight coming inside through a gap in the blackout curtains. "And could you please stop pacing like a caged lion, because you're making me feel dizzy just hearing you stomping in circles."

"Sorry." He stopped for all of three seconds and then started again. "Reiner is visiting."

"What?"

"He called my office yesterday to announce his visit." He finally stopped pacing and flopped beside her on the chaise longue, his breath unmistakable evidence that he'd spent the night in a bar drinking.

"When?"

"Sometime next month."

"If he sees me it's all over." She shivered and neither of them said another word, trying to figure out their next steps.

"You must disappear for a while."

"But how and where?" Truth be told, the thought of being all on her own in a foreign country frightened her. While staying with Wilhelm hadn't been her first choice, she'd grown used to the comfort and protection he offered her. It was a most troubling thought, but she actually *liked* living with him and secretly considered him a friend, despite the fact that he was a Nazi.

"I don't know yet, but we'll find a way." In the darkness she could only see his contours, but his voice was surprisingly warm beneath the obvious worry. It encouraged her enough to ask the question she'd been wanting answered for such a long time.

"Why are you doing this for me? Again? You don't even like me."

He was quiet for a long time, before he spoke. "I do like you. A lot more than I probably should. You're so… different. I never thought… I mean… you're supposed to be a bad person."

"Me?" She was dumbfounded, but only for a moment. The two of them never mentioned her race, and quickly changed the topic whenever Jews came up in the news. She knew he still believed the Nazi propaganda: about how her people were the source of all problems in Germany, the conspiracy of the World Jewry that was to blame for the Great Depression a decade earlier, not to mention them being responsible for the hyperinflation of the Weimar Republic, unemployment, and even the loss of the last war. Hitler conveniently blamed the Jews for every problem under the sun and claimed without them, Germany, and the world, would finally be whole again.

"I must admit, I never really considered you to be… an individual. At my parents' place you were the maid, someone who took care of their needs, without actually being someone yourself. But now… since you've been living here… I've realized just how great a person you are. You're kind, funny, intelligent, pretty, agile. You're not only a good housewife, but also an interesting companion. You can sing and dance, cook, entertain my comrades, have an eye for antiques, speak French… You can do everything as well or better than any German girl."

"That's because I am a German girl," she couldn't resist saying.

"And that's exactly what baffles me. You're not supposed to be. Hitler says—"

"We both know what that idiot says!" She jumped up, the blanket falling from her shoulders as she paced the room, oblivious that she wore nothing but a semi-transparent white cotton nightie. When she passed the mirror, she caught a glimpse of her silhouette, gleaming in the darkness. But she was too angry to care, two steps on and she bumped her bare foot against something hard. "Ouch!"

"Now you had better be the one to stop pacing. Sit with me." His voice had an amused tone to it and enraged her further.

"No. I'd rather stand."

"Do as you wish, although I should tell you that your gown is a little see-through in the moonlight."

Blood rushed to her cheeks and left a hot trail in its wake. Although he couldn't see it, she energetically shook her head. "Why do you still believe what this man says?"

A sigh was his only answer.

They both kept silent for the longest time, and she started to shiver from the cold air in the apartment, but she didn't dare to move, or talk, or even let her teeth chatter.

"You still need to disappear for a while," he finally said.

"I was actually on my way to Toulouse to a friend of my aunt when you spotted me in the Pension Kaiser." She tentatively stepped from one foot to the other.

"You must be cold, come here."

But wild horses couldn't drag her next to him, since she didn't trust herself after his unexpected confession. "I can't. We can't. Ever."

He got up and moved toward the kitchen. "Get back under the blanket, or do you really want me to explain to Reiner that his beloved sister froze to death because she was too stubborn to stay warm?"

She was thankful for his attempt to lighten the mood and slipped under her covers, giving him a wide berth. As soon as she had settled, he spoke again.

"You can't go to Toulouse, because now that Reiner knows you're here it would be too dangerous for that friend of yours. For any trip to the free zone you'd need proper papers, which we can't get overnight."

"I have a travel permit, signed by Horst Richter," she said meekly.

"But that is dated months ago. Most probably it wouldn't work. The least the control posts would do is to ask the authorities here if they're still valid. And then Reiner would find out… no… you need to stay within the occupied zone, where I can issue the proper travel permits myself."

Margarete suddenly remembered Paulette's offer to help if she ever needed to get away from Wilhelm. She fought with herself whether to tell him or not, since he was still a Nazi. But after a while, she decided it was her only chance.

"How about Paulette? She has family in the countryside."

"I didn't know that… It is a good idea…" Wilhelm was talking more to himself than to her, until he raised his voice again and asked, "Are you sure she'd be willing to take you, though? I mean, there's no love lost between French and Germans. Even though she's Gerald's amour, I'm quite certain her family doesn't know about that."

"I could pretend to be in some kind of serious trouble."

"Yeah, maybe you could pretend to be a persecuted Jew?" He chuckled, indicating he was not seriously considering such a bold move. Still, it gave Margarete pause for thought.

"I'm not sure she'd help me if she knew. But she might help me because we've become good friends and she likes you. We just need a good reason to tell her."

"I'm not keen on getting her involved, but let's talk about this idea in the morning. Good night."

"Good night, Wilm."

CHAPTER 29

Wilhelm was pacing the room, waiting impatiently for Margarete to return. She'd insisted on talking to Paulette alone, "woman to woman" she'd called it. For the umpteenth time he checked his wristwatch, struggling to believe that not even one minute had passed since his last check.

To make sure it wasn't broken, he compared it to the mantel clock in the sitting room and then walked into his bedroom to pick up the alarm clock. Nothing. All three of them seemed to have banded together against him and simply refused to move their hands.

With a deep sigh he walked to the Louis XIII cabinet and poured himself a brandy. And another one. Finally he heard steps and then the key turn in the door.

"What did she say?" he asked Margarete even before she'd closed the door behind herself.

"Good afternoon to you, too." She smiled, seemingly enjoying letting him simmer.

"Good afternoon. Will you tell me now?"

"She agreed."

"Just like that?"

"Of course not. I had to tell her a sob story about how I need to get away from the tensions in Paris."

He suspected she wasn't telling him the entire truth. "Did you tell her about Reiner?"

"I thought it better not to."

"So what exactly did you tell her?" He couldn't fathom what had done the trick, since French people were normally unwilling to help out the Germans. But maybe Paulette was an exception.

Margarete smiled at him in that absolutely gorgeous way of hers. "She thinks I'm not really your sister."

"What?" He grabbed her arm and pulled her toward him, glaring into her eyes. "Did you tell her you're a Jew?"

She peeled his hand off her arm, even as she said, "Of course not! I'm not suicidal. But she has suspected something for a while now, so I simply went along with her insinuations without giving her any details."

He had to give her credit, she was a lot smarter than a Jew was supposed to be. Although… Hitler always insisted they were cunning, cutthroat criminals always out to deceive the good citizens, so maybe this cat-and-mouse-game ran in her blood. He shook his head at his own thoughts. Margarete was the least cunning or deceitful person he'd ever met. Somehow, despite the fact that she pretended to be someone else, she managed to stay true to herself with her day-to-day actions and behavior. He'd seen the kindness in her eyes, the way she treated shopkeepers, waiters, and even the annoying concierge.

"What's wrong?" Margarete asked.

"Nothing."

"Then, why are you so vigorously shaking your head?"

He hadn't noticed he was doing it and stopped the movement. A suspicion crept up on him. "Who exactly does she think you are?"

"Isn't it obvious? An unmarried girl living with you, pretending to be your sister."

"My…? *Herrschaftszeiten*! She can't be serious. There are enough gorgeous French girls, I really don't need to import a drab and boring one from Germany."

The words left his mouth even before he knew what he'd said, but when he saw the hurt on Margarete's face, he felt awful and apologized. "I'm sorry, I didn't mean to say that. Naturally you're different, you're not drab… you're not even vile and cunning like the rest of your kind…" By the expression on her face, he realized that he was talking himself deeper into trouble with every word he uttered. "Please disregard everything I just said. My nerves are getting the best of me, because I've spent every single minute since you left the apartment worried to death about you."

Margarete took off her hat, coat, gloves and shoes, before she said, "I need some water." Then she disappeared into the kitchen, clearly indicating she did not wish to talk to him right now.

Wilhelm was furious with himself. Why did he even care whether she was hurt? When had he started consulting a Jew for her opinion? Or consider her an actual human being? Worse still, how had he allowed himself to be enchanted by her? She was an enemy of the Reich. He wasn't supposed to like her, and yet these pesky emotions and… possibly compassion… kept getting in the way.

He sighed and walked into the kitchen, where Margarete was standing with her back to him. Her shoulders were shaking. He just couldn't do this any longer. It was so wrong, everything about her being here with him was treason. He should tell her to get the hell out of his life. All the money in the world wasn't worth betraying his country for.

But when he noticed she was crying, it hit him deep inside and he realized his feelings for her were much more than compassion. He actually loved her and would do anything to keep her safe.

To hell with both money and patriotic duties. He'd make sure Margarete would survive this war unharmed.

"Please don't cry, I didn't mean it."

She turned around and her beautiful hazel eyes locked with his. "I know, and that's part of the problem. There can never be anything between you and me. Not now, not after the war. Not ever. We're on opposite sides of a fight for the very existence of my people, and the trenches have been dug far too deep to be crossed during our lifetimes."

He sighed. "What I did… what I'm still doing. It's treason against my Führer, my Fatherland, my family, my friends, even my own convictions. When I first took you in, it was for Anne's money, but now…" He swallowed a few times, before he could finish his sentence. "Now all I want is to keep you safe."

He opened his arms and Margarete stepped into his embrace, leaning against him and letting her tears flow. His heart filled with so much emotion, he thought it would explode and he relished every single second of holding her in his arms. But after a while, she shook her head almost imperceptibly and stepped out of his embrace.

She dried her eyes, straightened her dress and said with a voice completely devoid of emotion, "Paulette agreed to take me to her parents' place for a while under the condition that I can't tell anyone about you, or about her relationship with Gerald. Otherwise, the villagers would surely kill her and me."

Her words were like a cold shower, washing away his warm feelings and replacing them with disbelief, and even disgust. He'd never understood why so many Frenchmen were so mean-spirited toward his people, when they had demonstrated nothing but kindness and respect toward the French. Didn't these hooligans understand how exceptionally graciously Hitler treated them? But instead of feeling kindly toward the superior Germans, the

French opposed them every step of the way. What an ungrateful bunch of *clochards*, behaving like little children who had to be slapped to learn discipline and reason.

"Her parents should be grateful that Paulette has found such a good man to take care of her, instead of vilifying him."

"Perhaps they should," Margarete agreed with him, although he sensed that she was just saying what he wanted to hear. "In fact, I told her that I need to get away from Paris, because… I'm a victim of violence."

"And who would be beating you up?" Wilhelm found the entire story ridiculous at best and would have told Margarete never to talk to Paulette again, if he weren't so desperate to get her out of Reiner's way, who was likely to show up in Paris any time.

"You."

"Me? Don't be ridiculous. I would never."

"Actually, you'll have to. I told her you're obsessively jealous and it has become so bad I fear for my life."

He looked at her aghast. While it was true that he'd become possessive of her, he would rather knock the sense out of any man who even gazed at her, but never raise a hand against the woman he loved. "I most certainly won't beat you."

"Then my ruse won't work and she has no reason to take me with her." Margarete said it in such a cool voice, it was as if she'd begged him to pummel his fists into the wall and not into her soft body.

He felt the blood drain from his head. How could she even entertain the idea of him hurting her? It was disgusting. Without a word he took his coat and left the apartment to walk off the disturbing emotions attacking him.

When he returned home, she was pressing his uniform shirt and seeing her petite figure bent over the ironing board tugged at his heartstrings. He walked over and waited until she put the iron aside, before he turned her around by her shoulders. "I'll do it. But only because I want you to be safe."

Her eyes became deep pools and he glimpsed right into her soul, saw the fear, the uncertainty, the wariness, but also the hope and the affection she had for him. It was too much. He leant down and pressed his lips on hers, warm tingles rushing all the way down to his toes. She opened her mouth for his tongue to explore and for the next exhilarating, breathless, and passionate minutes he experienced heaven on earth. But then reality sunk in again and he quickly broke the kiss. "We can't do that. It's not right."

"No," she sighed, looking excruciatingly beautiful with the rosy blush on her cheeks.

He couldn't resist and skimmed his lips over her cheeks and toward her neck. She tipped her head back, giving him more room to kiss down her throat, and when he found the sensitive spot behind her ear, she gasped.

Nibbling on her earlobe, he whispered, "I'm afraid I have fallen in love with you."

CHAPTER 30

A few days later, Margarete and Wilhelm returned from a shopping trip to the antiques market. He was carrying a package with a pair of exceptionally beautiful candleholders. They featured gild bronze mounts on a red marble base. The white central column looked like the columns in a Greek temple and was made of gilt porcelain, while the part holding the candles was bronze decorated with Champleve enamel in striking turquoise, royal blue and white.

As always, Madame Badeaux was waiting for them and assailed them with a million questions, the moment they stepped inside the foyer of the building.

Wilhelm answered a few of them and then cut the woman short, opening the elevator door for Margarete. Once they arrived in the apartment she said, "The candleholders are so beautiful."

"They are, and according to the salesman they have a turbulent history, although I very much doubt that, since they can't be older than late nineteenth century."

She was amazed how much he knew about antiques and smiled at his enthusiasm to tell her everything he knew about bronze candleholders. It was a topic he dearly loved and could talk for hours about.

"Wilm, where do you want to put them?" she interrupted him after a while.

"I thought…" He paused for a moment. "Why don't you decide?"

After their kiss, everything had changed. Although they had agreed that it could never happen again, they both felt the invisible bond between them.

"What about the windowsill in the sitting room?"

"That's a fantastic idea." He unwrapped the candleholders and placed them beside each other. "They look great, don't you think?"

She nodded. "Now we only need two candles." She hadn't even finished her words, when she became nostalgic, thinking about how she and Aunt Heidi had bought a candle for Hannukah. She'd written her aunt a postcard with the agreed code phrase to let her know she'd arrived well, but hadn't dared to put an address or even a name on the postcard for fear the censors might somehow make a connection to her. Instead she'd added, *I will continue my travels and hope to meet you again, soon.*

"What are you thinking?" Wilhelm had stepped beside her and took her chin in his hand.

"Just some memories. Yes, candles would be nice. I could get them at the haberdashery tomorrow."

"You do that."

The ringing of the telephone cut through the room and the two of them looked at each other. She shrugged. Nobody ever called her, not even Paulette, who preferred if the two of them met somewhere in the city.

Wilhelm answered the phone. "Wilhelm Huber."

By the way he knitted his brows together, she instantly knew it wasn't good news. Not wanting to eavesdrop, she disappeared into the kitchen and quietly closed the door behind her. Putting on her apron she busied herself preparing tonight's dinner.

It didn't take more than a few minutes, before Wilhelm came inside, a grave expression on his face. "That was Reiner."

"What did he say?"

"His plans have changed and he'll be in Paris by tomorrow night."

"I should leave for Paulette's this very instant." She wiped her hands on the apron and looked at him expectantly.

"What?"

"You need to hit me."

"I can't possibly do this…"

"You promised."

"Isn't there any other way to keep you safe?"

She traced her finger down his cheek. "We've been over this a thousand times. There isn't. And to make it look real, you have to hit me. Don't be shy." She'd said it with nonchalance, despite the fact that she was frozen with fear from inside. Wilhelm was a strong man and even if he didn't want to cause lasting harm, she was sure it would hurt. When he still hesitated she said, "It will hurt a lot more if the Gestapo does that to me, so do me a favor and make it fast."

He shook his head. "This is not funny. And I'm doing this only to protect you. Please forgive me."

Then he stepped back and hit her hard across her face with the back of his hand, his eyes torn open in horror when he watched the skin just above her eyebrow break at the contact with his signet ring. She stumbled and bumped against the wall, letting out a high-pitched scream. She'd begged him to do this, but the pain still caught her unawares.

Only moments later, he launched at her again and pummeled his fist into the soft flesh of her upper arm and her rib cage, where she knew it would leave an ugly black mark. When she sank onto the floor sobbing, he stopped and helped her up, his face hard as stone. But nonetheless, she recognized the shock in his eyes at seeing her bleeding at his own hands.

"I'm so sorry, darling. You better pack your things and go to Paulette for help now."

Then he turned around on his heels and left the apartment in a hurry, for which Margarete was thankful. It wouldn't do any good to get all sentimental or conscience-stricken for their plan to work.

*

Margarete was sitting opposite Paulette on a regional train, which was carrying them away from the city and toward the country. Since the compartment was filled with other people, they didn't talk and she had time to relive the events.

When Wilhelm had told her about Reiner's imminent visit, she'd been shocked at first, but after mulling it over she'd seen the occasion as her opportunity to escape, although their kiss had complicated things—a lot. Despite their agreement that she should return as soon as Reiner was gone, she had no intention of doing so, and she certainly wouldn't agree to a sham marriage anyway.

On the contrary, she planned to finally give Annegret Huber the funeral she deserved and take on another identity, although she hadn't worked out the exact details yet. But for the first time in years, she felt like she was calling the shots in her own life. At long last, her fate lay in her own hands and she was determined to use her new-found power in her own best interest.

So far, it hadn't been hard. After rushing to Paulette with the sob story of Wilhelm abusing her, she'd taken her sweet time to *confess* that he was blackmailing her to stay with him, or he would leave her penniless on the street if she didn't do his bidding. With a performance worthy of Marlene Dietrich, Margarete had bawled her heart out and wrenched the promise from Paulette that she could never tell anyone where she was, because Wilhelm would surely beat her to death for running away.

A twinge of guilt tugged at her. She shrugged it off. Wilhelm was no angel and deserved everything that came his way for no other reason than being part of the SS.

But then the memory of his kiss flooded her with sensations like she'd never experienced before. Even now, her entire body tingled as she relived the precious minutes in his arms. At first, it was a shock to feel his lips on hers, but before she could make him stop, her body began to act on its own account, her feet going on tiptoes to be closer to him and her lips opening up for his probing tongue.

Goosebumps broke out all over her skin, as his tongue entered her mouth, soft and warm, yet persistent as it explored every crevice. She sighed with delight.

"Are you alright?" Paulette asked from the seat next to her.

"Oh yes. I'm so happy that I finally got away from him." *You treacherous liar!*

"I can only imagine, what it must have been like." Paulette put a hand on Margarete's goose pimpled arm and whispered, "Don't worry, you're safe now."

Margarete gave her what she hoped was a timid-grateful look. "*Merci.*" Paulette had instructed her only to speak French and as little as possible, since her accent was still strong.

About an hour later, they disembarked from the train in a quaint little village.

"I'm afraid from here on we have to walk. It's about an hour," Paulette said apologizing.

"Don't worry, it'll be fine. As long as I'm safe." *Because contrary to what you believe, I'm not a spoiled brat.* Margarete had debated with herself whether to confide her true identity in Paulette, but since the other woman had been so eager to help her even pretending to be Annegret, she'd opted not to. What did they always say in the war posters? *Loose lips sink ships.* If needs be she could still come out with her real identity, but since many French seemed to be anti-Semites too, and were actively helping the Germans to rid their country of Jews, it felt better to stay silent.

"People around here…" Paulette glanced at her, before she quickly averted her gaze again. "People around here are not really fond of Germans, therefore I thought…" She stopped and looked straight into Margarete's eyes. "Telling them that you're running from an abusive relative won't cut it, unfortunately. Too many men still think it's their prerogative to chastise the women in their family, and they would find fault with you for not obeying your brother's or even your lover's orders."

"Will they send me back?" Margarete made her voice shriek almost without effort, for she was truly concerned.

"No. I won't let that happen. But we need a better cover story for you. I thought maybe you could pretend to be a German communist who's been working undercover, until you were found out. Only thanks to the intervention of your SS brother did you escape being sent to a concentration camp. But now you're living in his place like a prisoner."

"Me? A communist?" Margarete wanted to laugh out loud, since this was such a ludicrous idea. She thought the communists were almost as thuggish as the Nazis, although she had to give them credit for being Hitler's most fervent opponents. But on the other hand, it was frightening how close to the truth Paulette's suggestion was, except she was Jewish and not a communist. "I don't really know all that much about communism."

"But you know what they say in the newspapers, right?"

Margarete nodded. Since living in Paris she'd been reading all the German newspapers Wilhelm brought home, so she knew at least what the Nazis thought the communists were. "I don't think my superficial knowledge will hold up to scrutiny. What if other communists start asking me stuff?"

Paulette scrunched her nose. "Well, that could present a problem. Not that I know any, but that doesn't mean there aren't." She continued to walk in silence and after a while she exclaimed, "I've got it! If someone asks questions, you simply pretend your French isn't good enough and answer only in platitudes."

"Well, I can certainly do that." Margarete wasn't convinced her new cover story would pass a closer inspection, but for the moment she didn't care. She wouldn't stay in the village for long and once she acquired a new identity, she'd never see Paulette or anyone else again, because she'd find a way to escape to the free zone or even to neutral Spain.

They arrived at yet another charming little village called Envermeu. Paulette waved at everyone, but hurried along the main street until she came to a stop in front of a warped little house.

"This is my grandmother's place. It's safer here, because too many people mill about my parents' place. But Granny is a bit soft in the head, in addition to being almost deaf and blind, so virtually nobody ever visits her. And she certainly won't bother you while I'm gone. I will return for the weekend to look after you."

She had been right, and Margarete passed the next three days in a blissful state of feeling completely herself—and secure. Friday night, Paulette returned and, after putting her grandmother to bed, she opened up a bottle of wine. "Let's sit next to the chimney and have a drink."

Margarete didn't usually drink alcohol, despite Wilhelm's efforts to teach her the finer details of French wines, but she politely nodded. Sitting in front of the warming fire, Paulette regaled her with stories from her childhood in the French countryside.

The comfortable temperature and the effects of the wine made Margarete relax and soon enough she was on her third glass, talking like a waterfall. She warned herself to keep quiet, but didn't heed her own advice. After another glass and a few close calls with spilling the truth, she said, "I really should go to sleep."

"Let's just empty our glasses before we go. It would be a shame to waste this good wine."

"Why not?" Margarete readily agreed, since she dreaded leaving the warm fire and walking upstairs into the cold cubbyhole where she slept. She took her glass and swung the red liquid in circles, sniffing the scent the way she'd seen Wilhelm do so often. "Wilm always wanted me to learn how to appreciate wine. But I'm just not that fond of it."

"You still love him?"

"It might sound strange, but I do. Despite everything, he's the one who keeps me safe."

"Safe from what?"

There. She'd carelessly given a hint. The alcohol made her brain slow and she searched for the correct words. "From Reiner."

"Who's Reiner?"

"His brother. He…" Margarete shuddered at the memory and, wise or not, spilled out all the horrible things Reiner had done to her, while she worked in his parents' household. At least she had remembered to pretend she was a normal servant, and not a Jewish house slave.

"Dear God! What a monster! Why didn't Wilhelm or his parents intervene?"

"I never told them, since I was too scared. But when his parents died, I escaped from Berlin. Wilhelm has been hiding me."

"Out of the frying pan and into the fire, I'd say."

"Why's that?"

"Because he beats you?" Paulette seemed to look suspicious, but that could also be the alcohol talking.

Oh, damn. Why had she come up with that ruse? And why did she have to open up her big stupid mouth to talk about

Reiner. She swore never to drink so much again. Tracing the scab above her eyebrow, she shrugged. "Only when he gets really angry with me."

"Does he… you know? Do other things, too, when you don't let him have his way?"

"Oh no… he would never." Margarete shook her head, causing the world to spin around her. Judging by the way he'd kissed her, he probably would love nothing more, but he'd never force himself on her. "I miss you so much, Wilm!" Margarete blinked a few times and asked, "Did I just say that aloud?"

Paulette giggled. "You certainly did. So, what is it between you and Wilhelm?"

"What do you mean?"

"Come on, I've seen the way he watches you. He's clearly in love with you."

Margarete shook her head, but stopped the moment the world started swirling again. It was getting harder to keep all her lies straight and remember whom she'd told what about herself. It seemed safest to revert to the persona she'd been pretending to be. "You have too much imagination. He's my brother."

"I thought…" Paulette raised an eyebrow and out of nowhere produced another bottle of wine and poured her another glass.

"No… I'm drunk already… I can't."

"No time like the present to have fun, because who knows whether we'll still be alive tomorrow." Paulette raised her own glass to Margarete, who couldn't well decline. What harm would it do to get stinking drunk anyway?

"In the beginning he thought I was with child and that the Reichskriminaldirektor was the father. But this was not true. I never… I mean except for when Reiner forced me. But my monthlies have been coming regularly and I would show by now, wouldn't I?"

"Yes you would. There's no need to worry about that now. But tell me, did you know Reiner is about to visit Paris?"

"How do you know?"

"That's not important. Was his visit the reason for you wanting to disappear?"

"Hmm... I guess... I really, really don't want to see that monster ever again... he's awful. Even worse than his father. And their daughter, that cunning little bitch."

"Whose daughter?"

Margarete vaguely noticed that she was divulging things she shouldn't. "Herr Huber's."

"Which of the Hubers?"

"Their father. But he's dead. Died when the building collapsed on him. I was there. It was my chance to be free and live."

"What did their father do to you?"

"He made me work day and night and he wanted to send me away."

"Because of the baby?"

"What baby?"

"You said Wilhelm suspected you to be pregnant. Was this the reason Herr Huber wanted to send you away? Because it was in reality Reiner's baby?"

Margarete's head was hammering with every new question thrown at her. "I guess. I really don't know."

"So why are you here? You can trust me, I won't tell anyone," Paulette's voice was so smooth and comforting, and Margarete wanted so much to confide in someone. It would be so nice to have at least one person apart from Wilhelm to know who she really was.

A friend.

CHAPTER 31

Wilhelm had been on a turbulent roller coaster of emotions since the moment Margarete had left. On the one hand he was happy to know she'd be in a safe place during Reiner's upcoming visit, but on the other hand he missed her like crazy.

Despite fighting against his own feelings he had to accept that he'd fallen in love with her. Truly, deeply and irreversibly. He was doomed, because there could never be anything between him and her. Neither in her true identity as a Jew nor even less in her identity as his sister.

He picked up the phone and dialed Gerald's office number. It might not be prudent, but he needed to know whether Paulette and Margarete had arrived safely in Envermeu.

"Gerald Nadler."

"Hello, Gerald, this is Wilhelm."

"Oh, Wilhelm, you have good timing. Imagine who just arrived over here?"

Wilhelm suppressed a groan. "Our Führer?"

"Not quite that important. Your brother, and Heydrich is with him."

"Heydrich is here?" That was rather unusual, since he normally stayed in Prague, where he held the position of Reich Protector of Bohemia and Moravia.

"Yes, it seems he wants to personally make sure the deportation of Jews is done with the merited speed. Anyhow, if I were you, I'd swing my ass over here. They'll be starting with the first meetings in half an hour."

"*Herrschaftszeiten!*" Wilhelm cussed. "Why has nobody alerted me?"

"I just did."

"Thanks, man. I owe you." Wilhelm tossed the receiver onto the cradle and rushed from his office, putting on his greatcoat even as he flew down the stairs taking three steps at once. Apparently his new friend Karsten Bicke had forgotten that he'd assigned him to oversee the Drancy operations. Or was it a plot to set him up? But if he hurried, he could still arrive on time for the first meeting.

"It's about time you showed up. Are they allowing such tardiness in attendance here now?" Reiner greeted him, when he raced up the stairs, puffing like a locomotive.

"I had another important issue to attend to on the other side of town." Wilhelm gave him a salute and then gestured toward the doors. "Shall we?"

"Yes. There is much work to do and I am only here for a few days. You know Reinhard Heydrich, I assume?"

"Not in person."

"Well, let me present you to him, little brother."

Wilhelm fumed under Reiner's condescending tone, but he kept his voice neutral. "It would be a pleasure."

After the introductions were made, Heydrich excused himself to attend some other important business and left Reiner to explain the final solution to a room full of eagerly listening men.

"I won't have to tell you that everything spoken in here is top secret and cannot be divulged to anyone without the proper security clearance."

Everyone including Wilhelm nodded. He wasn't sure whether he was proud to be privy to such important issues or would rather bury his head in the sand.

"We all know, the World Jewry has been conspiring against humanity for centuries and our great Führer has decided to end this once and for all. We will eradicate every last member of this abominable species from the face of the earth."

The crowd broke out in cheers and Heil Hitler! shouts, and Wilhelm followed suit, although only half-heartedly. He had no idea what was wrong with him and why he couldn't be happy to rid the world of such an evil. Instead, his heart was breaking a little more with every sentence, because all he could see was Margarete's lovely face.

His lips were still tingling from their kiss and despite knowing how wrong and depraved it was, he could only see her as the pretty, kind and wonderful person she was. Maybe she wasn't really a Jew? Yes, there must be some mistake, perhaps she had accidentally been switched in the hospital at birth. Those things did happen, didn't they? In any case, he was glad Margarete was far away and safe.

"… our goal is to sweep Europe from west to east and have France and Germany free of this vermin by the end of 1942."

A murmur went through the room, since an estimated three hundred thousand Jews lived in France alone, and almost that amount in Germany. Wilhelm knew everyone was secretly asking themselves the same question he did. *Where shall all these people go?* Everyone in here knew about the existence of concentration camps and work camps, where people died like flies from overwork, malnutrition and diseases, but it was beyond his imagination to fathom how these camps could cope with an influx of half a million more inmates.

"To reach this goal, the decision has been taken to construct several camps in the General Governorate for the Occupied Polish Region with the main task to exterminate all non-able bodies upon arrival. Your task is to round up any and all undesirables in Occupied France, hold them at Drancy and then put them on trains toward the General Governorate as fast as you can. My organization will handle the rest. Any questions?"

Nobody dared say a word and Wilhelm sensed that everyone save for the most hardened men was feeling queasy at the implications. He'd known for a long time about the cruelties being perpetrated, had even participated in some of them, but this… what Reiner was talking about… murder on an industrial scale, was so inhumane it shocked Wilhelm to the core.

Since Reiner had not divulged any details, every man was free to think up ways they would murder vast amounts of men, women and children in the shortest time possible. There was nothing pretty or glorious about this imagination and he swallowed down the rising bile, while focusing his thoughts on Margarete. He had to make sure she'd never return to Paris, maybe he could convince her to leave France altogether and go someplace truly safe. South America. But for that plan to work, they needed money… and for the money she needed to marry…

After the meeting, Reiner came up to him and asked, "So, where is she?"

"Who?"

"Annegret. Where is she? I told you to arrange for the three of us to have dinner together. I wish to see her and let her know how worried she's kept everyone back home," Reiner told him in no uncertain terms. Wilhelm almost fainted as he realized he'd forgotten to come up with a viable excuse for Anne's absence, since he couldn't tell Reiner that she was hiding with a friend because he was allegedly beating her.

"I told you during our last phone conversation—" Wilhelm began, quickly thinking up something.

"No you didn't."

"Or, maybe I haven't. We were both so distracted with my promotion and your visit—"

"I already noticed your new badge, little brother. One more reason to celebrate, Herr Untersturmführer." Reiner slapped him on the back and for once Wilhelm believed his brother was actually proud of him. It was a nice sensation.

"Thank you."

"So, *when* is Anne joining us?"

"She told me to send you her deepest regrets, but she won't be able to make it."

Reiner furrowed his brow. "What does that mean? She's living with you, right?"

"She was, until a week or so ago. But she developed a bad cough. The doctor said she hadn't taken well to the air pollution in Paris and strongly urged her to stay at the countryside until the winter is over."

"Our Anne? The girl who never once caught a cold in Berlin?"

"I was as surprised as you are," Wilhelm lied. "The doctor thought it might even be TB."

"Tuberculosis? That's nuts! Our sister doesn't have that. It's a sickness of the poor and dirty. Jews get it, Gypsies too, vagrants, thieves and work-shy criminals, but not valuable Germans."

"That's exactly what I said. But the doctor is French and you know how they are…"

"I do not know how they are, but I know that you should have put this man in his place. Tell me his name and I will make sure he loses his license."

Wilhelm sensed his eyelid flutter. "He never said she had it, but he wanted to be extremely cautious. And honestly, can you blame her for enjoying a stay in the country?"

Reiner grumbled something incoherent, and Wilhelm suddenly had an idea, since Margarete had mastered the high-pitched voice of his sister to perfection.

"You know what? I'll arrange for a phone call between the two of you. That would quell your concern and you can ask her personally how she is."

"Hmm."

Wilhelm took this as a yes and changed the subject. "How are Erika and the new baby?"

"They're both fine. The doctor said to wait a few weeks, but I can't wait until we try for another one and this time it'll be a boy."

"I'm sure it will." Wilhelm was in no mood to argue.

"It is my duty to beget warriors for our Führer, and I'm more than willing to act upon it." Reiner smirked. "My mistress is with child, too."

"Are congratulations in order?"

"I guess. Although Erika doesn't seem to understand, so I'd rather you not mention it to her."

"Don't worry. I won't." After falling in love with Margarete, Wilhelm saw things differently and he'd begun pitying Erika for being stuck with insensitive Reiner, so he certainly wouldn't add to her heartbreak and tell her the unsavory news. Thankfully, he spotted Gerald. "Wait for a moment, I'll introduce you to a friend."

He walked over to Gerald and hissed, "If Reiner asks, Anne is in the country because of her bad cough."

Gerald raised a brow.

"I'll explain later." Then they had reached Reiner and Wilhelm made the introductions. He knew his friend was much too eager to get into both brothers' good graces to utter a wrong word. After Wilhelm made sure that Reiner would pay, they went out for dinner in Le Fouquet, the most expensive restaurant on the Champs-Elysees. Soon he wouldn't have this problem anymore.

With surprise he registered the stab to his heart at the thought of finding a husband for Margarete. It was beyond comprehension: he wanted her for himself, but he also wanted her to be safe. And for that reason they needed the money. Suddenly the idea of finding her a gay husband became very appealing.

Pushing thoughts of her far away, he leaned back in his chair, holding a glass of brandy in his hand. "To the success of our mission!"

Reiner jumped up and saluted at the surprised patrons in the restaurant, all of them German officers, some with a beautiful Frenchwoman on their arm. "I'm here to rid us of the Jewish conspirators and whoever else stands between Germany and greatness!" Reiner fell back onto his chair with a dreamy expression on his face. "I heard Paris has the most amazing women in Europe. I'd like to see for myself. Where do we go now?"

"So, now it's your duty to beget French bastards as well?" Wilhelm asked, half in jest.

Reiner laughed with him and lowered his voice. "Let the French tarts deal with our little presents! It'll keep them from getting involved with the Résistance."

Wilhelm nodded obediently and a few minutes later, he, Gerald and Reiner were headed to Pigalle, the quarter where the famous clubs and cabarets could be found. Perhaps a night of debauchery in the arms of a lusty Frenchwoman would distract him from his heartache for Margarete.

CHAPTER 32

Margarete woke with the distinct feeling that something bad had happened. When she got up, a headache reminded her of too much wine the evening before. How could she have been so careless? She remembered Paulette asking questions about Annegret's past and coaxing her into telling her about Reiner. But try as she might, she didn't remember anything past that point. Had she actually spilled the beans and told the other woman her darkest secrets?

Dear God, she sure hoped she hadn't. Perhaps it hadn't been such a good idea to come here after all. Her hand flew to her chest, needing the comfort of touching her amulet, but it wasn't there. She felt herself blanch with unspoken horror, when her gaze fell on the nightstand. On top lay the necklace with the Tree of Life.

She inhaled deeply. Just because it lay there in the open didn't have to mean anything. She could have taken it off last night and forgotten to put it back on. Or she could have shown it to Paulette. Her breathing became labored, and she jumped backwards when she heard steps on the stairs.

The door opened and Paulette came inside with a bright smile. "You're up. That's good."

Margarete stared at her, not knowing how to react. "Good morning. I feel a bit hungover."

"That's the wine. We had quite a lot." Paulette seemed different today, not her usual confident self. But before Margarete could ponder on that thought, Paulette stepped toward her and reached for the amulet, turning it to catch a ray of sunshine. "It's so beautiful, no wonder it gives you strength." She cocked her head. "You never told me what the inscription was though?"

"What inscription?" Margarete's heart was galloping with fear.

"The one you rasped off."

"Oh." She needed to come up with a believable excuse, and fast. "It was the name of my boyfriend."

"I thought your parents gave it to you?"

Shit. Shit. Shit. I must have blabbed all my secrets last night. "They did. But later, my boyfriend had the inscription done and when we broke up…" She didn't finish the sentence. The less she said, the less she could contradict herself.

"Come with me," Paulette told her right after breakfast. "There is someone I want you to meet."

"Who is it?" Margarete asked, running to keep up with Paulette's long stride.

"You'll see." Paulette led her across the village to the only bakery that double-served as a café. They went inside and sat down at one of the small tables. As soon as the woman buying bread left the shop, Paulette got up and took Margarete by the hand. Following the nod of the saleswoman, they walked through the door next to the counter.

Margarete felt queasy to her stomach, and not because she was nursing a hangover. As soon as they'd closed the door behind them, she heard the key being turned in the lock and an awful suspicion rampaged through her veins. Paulette must have betrayed her and she was being brought to the Gestapo.

She tugged at her hand to run away, but even as she was free from the other woman's grip, she didn't move, since it made no sense. The door back into the shop was locked and the storage room seemed to have no exit, except for a window too small to crawl through. She was doomed.

"Down there." Paulette opened a metal door and pointed at a staircase leading into the basement. On the landing were three more doors. Paulette chose the one to the right, knocked twice, waited a second, and then knocked once more. Almost immediately the door was opened and they were ushered inside. Two men stood there, guns at the ready.

"She's the Boche?" the one with dark curly hair and a five o'clock shadow asked. If it weren't for his threatening stance, Margarete would consider him quite handsome.

"She's a Jew, so she's on our side," Paulette answered.

Margarete felt the words like a punch to her guts, hurting more than the beating Wilhelm had given her. Apparently she'd spilled everything last night. And now she would pay for it. Although, these people most certainly weren't Gestapo. On the contrary, as she took in the scene, she knew without a doubt that the people in this basement were part of the Résistance Wilhelm always railed against. A flutter tingled in her stomach at the thought of him. Despite trying to lock away her feelings, she missed him like crazy.

"That's to be seen," the other one said. He looked the opposite of the first man: blond hair, a baby face with no trace of beard, and a small, lanky frame. Despite his proper appearance, she instantly disliked him.

"She asked me to help her escape, Armand."

"That could be a ruse, ratting us out. How do we know we can trust her?" Armand said. He seemed to be the leader, while the fair-haired one stood silently by, watching them.

"She hates the Nazis as much as we do."

Did I really say that? And does this mean Paulette is with the Résistance? Margarete cursed herself for drinking too much last night, because her brain was still slow in processing the facts. Of course, Paulette was with the Résistance. And Gerald? Was he, too? Probably not, but then… Paulette only pretended to like him… Margarete's hand flew to her mouth as she swallowed down the need to vomit.

When she looked up again, both men were directing their guns at her. She swallowed again. "I'm sorry, I'm still sick from too much wine."

The blond man smirked. "Is this how you got her to spill the information? Getting her drunk?"

"It works on men, why not on women?" Paulette said.

"Enough of that, Marcel," Armand scolded him, before he addressed the two women. "Why should we help her? She's nothing but a risk to our operation."

"She can pay."

Armand's face lit up. "Now that does make a difference. Fake papers, safe houses, escape routes, all of this is expensive, but if you can pay… How much money do you have?" He glared directly at Margarete, making her knees become wobbly.

"Nothing," she whispered.

He stepped forward and slapped her cheek, furious. "Don't you dare lie to me. How much can you pay for your escape?"

Margarete trembled, unable to utter a word, but Paulette came to her rescue. "Leave her alone, she's telling you the truth."

Armand's handsome face turned into a furious grimace and Margarete wondered why Paulette wasn't the least bit afraid of him, but received her answer only moments later, when he looked at Paulette with unabashed affection in his gaze. *The two of them are a couple!* The realization sent another surge of queasiness through her, since Paulette and Gerald were a couple, too. It was too much for her brain to process at the moment.

"She will inherit a quarter million Reichsmark on the day she gets married," Paulette explained, and Margarete wanted to disappear into a mousehole. What else had she told the other woman last night?

"And how does that help us?" Armand asked.

Paulette smiled smugly. "Because she's going to marry one of us. Then we get all the money, help her escape and keep the rest for our cause."

"Am I being asked about any of this?" Margarete asked in an outburst of courage.

"No," said the three of them in unison.

"She's a Boche. She can't marry a Frenchman."

"Marcel is half-German."

Marcel looked sincerely shocked. "You're not serious, are you? She's not only a German, she's also a Jew! I'm not going to shag a Jew."

"Nobody talked about having fun. You marry her, take possession of the money, and once we've secured a new identity for her, you can give your beloved wife a funeral," Paulette said.

"I'm not doing this," Margarete said.

"Your opinion is not relevant." Armand shot her a look that made her shiver inside. She could see why Paulette had fallen in love with him, since he was stunningly handsome, but he was also exceptionally cold-blooded and ruthless.

"How can it be legal to marry a Jew? And how can a Jew inherit that much money?" Marcel raised the objection. By his looks he'd already accepted the idea that he was the groom in this sick plan.

"Nobody knows, except me and the SS officer who's been presenting her as his sister Annegret, who actually died several months ago in a bombing."

Dear God, I did really tell her everything. Margarete swore never to drink a single drop of alcohol in her life again—should she survive this encounter and their crazy plan.

"An SS officer you say?" Armand put a finger to his lip.

"Yes. He's a friend of Nadler." Margarete noticed Armand's slight wince at the mention of Paulette's other boyfriend. So, even though he obviously knew about their relationship, might even have concocted it, he did not like it. "His name is SS-Untersturmführer Wilhelm Huber."

Armand's eyebrows shot up. "He's not, by chance, related to Heydrich's assistant?"

Paulette shrugged and three pairs of eyes expectantly turned toward Margarete. She saw no reason in lying, because they'd find out anyway. The Huber family connections were no secret and Paulette could always ask Gerald.

"Yes, Reiner Huber is my... I mean, Annegret's brother."

"Does Reiner know your real identity?" Armand's face was showing the excitement about this revelation.

"No."

"So that's the real reason why you had to come here? Because he arrived for a visit to Paris?" Paulette asked, looking pointedly at Margarete's black eye.

"Yes."

Armand stepped nearer. "Why does the other brother hide you?"

"For the same reason you want to help me. He's after Annegret's money," Margarete answered with defiance.

He grinned and turned toward Paulette. "I have an idea. I'll think about it and let you know. Meanwhile keep her safe, will you?"

Electric charges, strong enough for Margarete to sense, passed between the couple. She still couldn't fathom how either of them was alright with Paulette seducing another man for information.

On their way back, Margarete glared at the woman she'd considered a friend and accused her. "You betrayed me."

"You didn't tell me the truth either."

"That's not the same, since I'm the one threatened with death if someone finds out."

"Don't be so ungrateful or naïve. Everyone wants something in return for helping you. You marry Marcel. We get you out of the country alive. I don't see what the big deal is."

For a woman whoring herself out to the Nazis for the sake of gaining information it might not be something worth fretting over, but for Margarete it was.

CHAPTER 33

Wilhelm came awake with the stale stench of too much booze in his mouth. He stretched out to dispel the stiffness in his limbs, when he bumped against a soft and warm body next to his own. Soft breath blew across his naked chest. He forced his eyes open and looked down at the beautiful woman lying naked in his bed. For a moment he imagined it was Margarete, but it took only a second to remember it was a random dancer from the cabaret they'd gone to last night.

Guilt and self-loathing immediately ruined his morning. He glared at her, not even remembering her name and suddenly felt completely inadequate. Shoving her arm aside, he jumped from the bed and walked into the bathroom. When he returned sometime later, dressed and shaved, she was just waking up, rubbing her creamy white hand delicately over her face. He observed her stretching her elegant limbs just as he'd done not long ago, but couldn't find joy in her beautiful body. All he felt was disdain. For her, but mostly for himself.

"Why are you here?"

She looked at him with wide brown eyes, seemingly not comprehending his question. "*Alors,* you invited me for a nightcap after the show."

He knew that. It had been part of his plan to lose himself in the bosom of a willing woman to erase his inappropriate yearning for Margarete. But the opposite had been true and now he wanted her even more. All night, he'd wondered how it would feel to hold her in his arms instead of whoever this was.

"But why did you agree? We didn't even exchange names!"

She smiled coyly. "I figured you'd tell me your name if you wanted to." She rolled over and the sheet slipped completely off her, exposing flawless skin and long, slender legs. Legs that had been wound around his hips last night. But now he couldn't find any joy in appreciating her naked body.

"Cover up." He handed her the sheet and asked again. "Why me? Why not some other guy?"

"You're handsome and good-mannered." She was obviously distressed by his line of questioning, but didn't dare to move or even contradict him.

"Do you have a boyfriend?"

She sighed.

"The truth!" His lips pressed into a small line and he stepped closer to the bed, noticing how goosepimples showed up on her skin.

"My fiancé is a forced worker in the Reich." She trembled and Wilhelm felt a twinge of sympathy for her. It wasn't her fault that she slept with him for whatever benefits he could give her. He located his wallet and tossed a few Reichsmark bills in her direction. "Get out."

She hurried from the bed, gathering up her clothing on her way toward the door, only stopping long enough to pull her dress over her head, before she slammed out of the apartment.

Wilhelm picked up a pillow and tossed it at the door, giving a low groan of defeat. He couldn't even sleep with a whore without feeling guilty. Depression settled over him like a dark cloud. He had no friends. No wife. No nothing. Nobody truly liked him for his personality. Even his own brother hated him. Women might flock to him, but only because of his position in the SS and the benefits he could offer them.

He sank down onto the couch and buried his head in his hands, fond memories of Margarete and her sweet smile coming to him. She was different, she'd never been in awe of the uniform, she'd always seen the real him. *And that's precisely why she hates you as well.* He didn't delude himself about her motives to stay with him. While she couldn't care less about power, money or even extra rations, she had an even stronger reason to do his bidding. Survival.

Despite the most wonderful kiss they'd shared, he was now sure that she didn't love him, or why would she insist there could never be anything between them. No, she'd never return the affection he was developing for her. Affection he shouldn't even be feeling. As he wallowed in self-pity over his miserable life, the doorbell rang. Thinking the cabaret dancer might have forgotten something, he opened with a scathing remark on his lips, but stopped in his tracks when Reiner stood there. "It looks like my morning was much better than yours."

"My morning was fine," Wilhelm assured him.

Reiner strode through the room, before stopping in front of the huge wall mirror. "Fine piece."

"Art Nouveau giltwood, cost me a fortune," Wilhelm said with unconcealed pride.

"At least you're not squandering your money exclusively on booze and women."

Wilhelm fought the urge to land his fist on his brother's jaw and asked, "What brings you here this early?"

"Just stopping by." Reiner walked into the bedroom and sniffed the lingering scent of perfume mixed with sweat and other bodily substances. "Which one did you take home?"

"Brunette, lithe, busty."

Reiner chuckled. "Don't they all fit that description? Anyhow, I can extend my stay in Paris for two more days, and I came to suggested we drive up to the country this weekend and visit Anne in her sanatorium."

Wilhelm all but toppled over. "We can't. I mean, aren't you elbow deep in seeing that all of the Jews get to the transport trains?"

"I have underlings for those menial tasks."

"But it's not safe to drive to the countryside," Wilhelm protested meekly, feverishly searching for a way out of this situation.

"If it's safe for her, then it'll be certainly safe for me."

"We would need travel permits…"

Reiner shook his head. "Hello? This is me you're talking to. I can get any permits I want, I even have clearance for the Wolfsschanze." The Wolf's Lair was one of the top-secret high-security Führer Headquarters. He cocked his head. "Or… is there a reason you don't want me to see Anne?"

"Don't be ridiculous." Wilhelm was desperately racking his brain. "Actually, I just got off the phone with her. You know how impulsive she is, and when she heard you were here, she said the countryside was too boring anyway, and she'd rather return to Paris." Cold sweat was dripping down his back, as he sunk deeper and deeper into his own web of lies.

"Wonderful. Make reservations for Saturday at the best restaurant for the three of us, will you? Coordinate with my assistant, he knows my schedule."

"With pleasure," Wilhelm answered, using all his strength to keep the tremble out of his voice. He needed to get rid of Reiner—and fast, because he had to concoct a plan. "Maybe I should try and give Annegret a call? Just so that she's not caught unawares?"

"Never mind that. We'll surprise her. Come along, I want to introduce you to a few people. The car is waiting downstairs."

Naturally, Reiner had a car at his disposal, while Wilhelm normally had to walk. With no other option, he rode to the office with Reiner, hoping he might have a moment to slip away and find Gerald to ask him how he could contact Paulette. The consequences didn't bear contemplating should Reiner drive to the country to search for Annegret in a non-existing sanatorium.

After a never-ending slew of meetings, without the possibility of exchanging even a few words with Gerald, it was finally time for lunch.

"Come with me," Reiner said.

"Where are we going?" Wilhelm asked as they headed outside and got back into the vehicle being used to chauffeur Reiner around.

"Avenue Foch."

"Did you know the French call it Street of Horrors?"

Reiner laughed loud and heartily. "It's only a horror for those who oppose us. We should attend one of the tortures."

Wilhelm suppressed the urge to retch, but Reiner caught it anyway. "With your stomach you should have become a salesman, instead of joining the SS."

"You are right." Wilhelm would have liked nothing more than to become an arts dealer, or a curator for a museum, but his father had made it clear that none of his sons would take up a profession for faggots and wimps. Again, his thoughts drifted to Margarete and what she would have to endure if someone found out she was usurping Annegret's identity. A Jewish maid posing as a high-society Aryan—they would have a feast with her. His stomach felt as if it was tied into a huge knot, as he wondered what exactly they were supposed to be doing here.

"There's a traitor in the Paris SS," Reiner said, as they walked toward the Gestapo headquarters.

"What?"

"We don't know who it is yet, but he's in your department. I want you to give your opinion on all your work colleagues to the Gestapo."

Wilhelm's knees all but buckled, but he somehow managed to stay upright. Reiner wouldn't suspect him, or would he? Was this a ruse? Was he about to be interrogated by the Gestapo? Had the offhand remark of attending a torture indeed had a deeper meaning?

He schooled his features and answered as lightly as possible. "I can't imagine any of my comrades would do such a heinous thing, but I will certainly cooperate with the Gestapo to help them find the traitor."

"He's involved with a woman, who we have on good account works for the Résistance."

"For all that's holy! These people have no shame!" Hot and cold shivers ran down Wilhelm's spine. He'd given up all women, save the occasional tryst, since he'd lived with Margarete, but most of his comrades had a more or less steady French mistress. It didn't bear contemplating that one of those sluts might be a mole.

Much to his relief, his visit to the Avenue Foch turned out to be rather pleasant, with him telling the Gestapo every last detail about his comrades and their love interests. Reiner entered and left the interrogation room at his will and whenever he returned, he nodded, pleased about the wealth of information Wilhelm shared.

"I'm glad you cooperated so well," Reiner said on the way to a nearby restaurant.

"What did you expect? I hate the Résistance as much as everyone else and want the mole caught. Just last week those criminals shot a close friend of mine at point blank range, when he was walking home at night. It's beyond me to fathom how an SS officer could betray everything he believes in."

"Some men do foolish things for a woman."

"I wouldn't." But wouldn't he? Wasn't he, in fact, doing foolish things for a woman?

"And that's a good thing. Remember, we are the masters and women are there to please us and raise our children." Reiner chuckled. "If your comrades had been more eager spreading their gifts, all these Frenchwomen wouldn't have time to work against us, because they would be at home, raising their brats."

"As always, you aren't wrong." Wilhelm engaged only half-heartedly in the conversation, because he was still racking his brain for a way to warn Margarete, when an awful thought occurred to him. What if Gerald was the traitor and Paulette the one working for the Résistance? Then he'd have sent Margarete right into the lion's den? If anything happened to her, it would forever weigh on his conscience.

CHAPTER 34

In the afternoon, Armand showed up at the small house where Margarete was staying.

"Paulette is not here," she said, uncomfortable in his presence. Wilhelm had only ever talked with disdain about the Résistance, and Armand was the leader of some local group. Just knowing this made her pulse run faster.

"I came here for you." It sounded like a threat. "I want to propose a deal."

"A deal that doesn't have anything to do with marrying some man I've never met before?"

He grinned, exposing a chipped front tooth. It gave him a charming expression and she could see, why Paulette had fallen in love with him. "Since it seems so very important for you, yes."

Phew. A heavy burden fell from her shoulders and she mustered all her courage to give him a nonchalant answer. "Well, then I'm listening."

"I won't deny the allure of all that money to buy weapons for our cause, but despite everything you might have heard about the resistance fighters, we are actually the good ones. The Nazis—your supposed brothers, for example—came here to take our land and oppress our people."

She didn't answer, but Armand seemed intent on getting her to agree with him, because he continued explaining how he and his compatriots fought to preserve their identity and free their country from the Nazi suppression.

"Enough of this. I've been living under a Nazi identity to save my own life, but I'm not one of them. You don't have to convince me that they are the bad guys."

He chuckled. "Just making sure you and I are on the same page."

"What's the deal you're offering?" Since he apparently hadn't come to kidnap, force or kill her, she became more courageous.

"You're going to work for us and we will make sure nobody finds out about your true identity."

She looked at him closely. His offer was tempting. "What exactly would I have to do?"

"Nothing much. Share information with us."

"I'm not privy to any secret information." Sure, Wilhelm complained to her about the nuisance the Résistance presented, but he never once mentioned details, especially not on upcoming retaliations planned by the SS.

"That can be changed. We have someone working at the SS headquarters and this person could arrange for you to work there as a secretary. You won't have any problems with security clearance, because you're Obersturmführer Reiner Huber's sister."

She swallowed hard and then shook her head. "That will never work. If Reiner ever finds out…"

"He won't." A cruel expression crossed Armand's face while he delicately moved his hand from one side of his throat to the other one.

"You're going to kill him?"

"An unfortunate accident. It's all been planned since we learned about his visit to Paris. Your presence here is just the icing on the cake."

"Paulette," she whispered. The other woman had agreed so readily to take Margarete to her village, because this had been planned beforehand. But what had she wanted to do with Annegret?

Armand fixed her with his dark brown eyes, quietly waiting for her to process the discoveries.

"But how and when?"

"You'll find out soon enough."

Margarete's eyes became wide. "Are you planning to kill me as well?"

He padded her arm. "I was going to kill Annegret, but not Margarete. In fact, you'll be the one luring the Huber brothers and the Gestapo head of Drancy into the trap."

She shivered. She was just a young woman trying to survive, how could she entertain the thought of… killing people. "I can't."

"You know what happens in Drancy?" Everyone had heard of Drancy, the internment camp for Jews, so she nodded. He continued. "Heydrich and his right hand, Reiner Huber, have devised a despicable plan to rid France of her Jews and send them all to their deaths. Drancy is only the first station in their ordeal. As we speak, mass roundups are taking place and deportation trains to a camp in Poland are prepared."

"You must be wrong," she whispered, although nothing was too horrible for the Nazis to do. She'd heard it more times than she cared to remember when eavesdropping at the office door of Wilhelm's father.

"You could be on one of these transports." He looked her up and down. "After being tortured in the Avenue Foch, I should add. Your only way to stay safe is to get rid of the two Nazis in France who know that you're not Annegret."

"I could leave the country."

"Where would you go to? Nobody will take you, and fake papers cost a lot of money. Money you don't currently have."

She had known this all along, but now the certainty of his words trickled deep into her soul. As long as Reiner was alive, she'd be vulnerable and always on the run.

"But why Wilhelm? He's been protecting me." She simply couldn't bring herself to condemn him to death as well. Reiner was one thing, he deserved to be killed not only for his hand in the greater scheme of things, but also for what he'd done to her. But Wilhelm?

"I assume he hasn't told you that he's the newly appointed commandant of Drancy."

"No. He would never—" She violently shook her head, but by the sad and knowing expression in Armand's eyes, she knew he wasn't lying to her. She composed herself, drawing several deep breaths, and then said, "What do you need from me?"

"You're making the correct decision. You'll see," Armand said and then proceeded to explain to her exactly what she was supposed to do.

CHAPTER 35

Wilhelm arrived home after an exhausting day at the office. Now that he knew there was a traitor amongst them, he'd been furtively checking out all of his comrades, but try as he might, he couldn't imagine any one of them being the mole. They all seemed so loyal, so upright, so dedicated to Hitler's cause. Surely, Reiner must be wrong.

He took off his brightly polished black boots and placed them next to the door. On stockinged feet he entered the apartment, feeling its emptiness getting to him. As much as he wanted to deny it, he missed Margarete. Not even a glance at the newly acquired candleholders gave him joy, because without her, his entire life was dull.

The irony wasn't lost on him, though, that he was as much a traitor to the Reich as the mole the Gestapo was seeking. But hiding a Jew surely must be a less grave crime than giving information to the Résistance, so they could turn around and kill countless German soldiers.

Since he was expected to join some comrades for dinner, he entered the bathroom, turned on the water and began shaving. Although he wasn't in the mood to attend a raucous dinner filled with rich food, too much wine and beautiful women, it was still better than sitting alone at home and yearning for the one woman he could never have.

When he was setting the blade to his jaw, he heard the front door open, and startled. "Ouch!" Blood was running. He ignored it and grabbed the pistol he always carried with him. Then he tore the bathroom door open and charged into the bedroom. Through the open door he saw Margarete standing in the living room, her mouth open in a silent cry.

"You?" He returned the pistol into its holster and closed the distance to her. Despite his fright, he was overjoyed to see her and would have wrapped her into his embrace, if she hadn't stepped aside.

"You frightened me."

"I thought you were a burglar." He exhaled loudly. "You shouldn't be here, it's not safe."

"I know." She noticed the blood running down his jaw. "You're bleeding. Wait here or you'll smudge your shirt." She disappeared into the kitchen and returned moments later with a clean towel that she pressed onto the cut. Her hand applying pressure on his face felt so comforting, he forgot everything about the troubles of an exhausting day.

"Reiner is adamant about seeing you."

She ignored him and removed the towel from his cheek. "The bleeding has stopped. I'm sorry. I didn't mean to startle you." She spoke so tenderly, all of the feelings for her that he had been suppressing came rushing to the surface.

He took her hand, bringing it slowly down to where he could place a tender kiss in the palm. "I missed you."

The softness in her eyes vanished as she recoiled and hurled her question at him. "Is it true that you're the new commandant of Drancy?"

"How do you know?" He felt the blood drain from his face, because he knew she'd never forgive him for that.

"That doesn't matter." She glared at him ferociously.

"Please, Anne…"

"Don't call me Anne!"

"Margarete, please. It was as much a shock to me as it is to you, but I couldn't say no."

"You couldn't say no? You never wanted to! You're the same kind of monster your brother is, all you Nazis are!"

"Please, Margarete, I never wanted to cause you any harm. I—"

"Maybe you didn't want to cause me any harm. But millions of Jews across Europe—you have no qualms about causing them harm." Her shoulders were heaving with pure rage.

"I'm not proud of my part in this, but you have to understand—"

"Why do I have to understand? I'm the one who's been harassed all my life. I'm the one who's lost my entire family to deportations and—" She stopped talking, violently sobbing now. He closed the distance and wrapped her in his arms, stroking his hand across her back, murmuring soft words of comfort.

When she stopped crying, he took her chin between his fingers and held it up to search her eyes. "There's nothing I can do about your family, but I swear, I'll do everything to protect you."

"Why?" Her eyes shone with amazement.

"Isn't it obvious?"

"I missed you so much," she whispered, almost as if she was afraid to admit the truth.

"I know it's crazy and impossible, and wrong on so many levels, but I… I love you. I won't let anything bad happen to you."

"But Reiner—"

"Let me take care of him. For now let us forget about all the worries and the bad things happening in the world."

*

Wilhelm bent his head down to her and kissed her on the lips. Tenderly and soft at first, then with ever-growing passion when she opened her mouth for his tongue. Tingles of delight rushed through her entire being, body and soul, and she relished the feeling until the moment he swooped her up in his arms and carried her toward the bedroom.

"No. We can't. It's all wrong." She struggled to get out of his arms and looked into his face, that was almost comically contorted with disappointment, sadness and understanding.

"I know. I've been struggling with my emotions since the day you showed up here. I know it's wrong and I know we can't ever be together, but deep in my heart, there was some hope that we could escape reality somehow and be happy together." He hesitated for a moment, before he continued. "I love you the way I've never loved anyone before, but I guess that will never be enough."

It broke her heart to see him so defeated, and she couldn't help it. She got on her tiptoes and traced her finger across his jawline.

"It's complicated," she whispered. It would be so easy to give in to the emotions he provoked in her, sink into his arms, and let him take care of her. To forget reality for just a little while, but then? Would she be able to live with herself if she allowed him to make love to her and then betrayed him the next day? Or could the two of them escape all of this and lead a happy life somewhere far away where nobody knew who they were?

"Wilm, I…" She was tempted to tell him the real reason she'd returned to Paris was to lure him, Reiner and Kriminalkommisar Allgeier into a trap, so that Armand's people could kill them. But she bit her lip, since she simply couldn't overlook his role in the extermination of her race.

"Margarete?"

She shuddered. What she was doing was wrong. Maybe... if... if... he promised to help their cause? "Why did you really take the job at Drancy?"

He turned on his heel and walked toward the windowsill where the two candleholders stood and she noticed that he'd fitted them with beautiful white candles... just like Aunt Heidi had done. Aunt Heidi, too, was an Aryan and had never actively opposed the regime, hadn't done anything, not even to rescue her own husband. Did that make her a bad person? But Heidi was a civilian, whereas Wilhelm...

With his back still turned to her, he began to talk. "You must believe me. I never wanted this, I even tried to get out of the assignment. When Reiner told me about the plans for the final solution, I was sick to my stomach. Despite all the bad things the Jews have done to Germany, they don't deserve this."

She wanted to interrupt him, shout at him that the Jews had done nothing to Germany, that it all was vile and unfounded propaganda. Hitler had needed a scapegoat for the awful depression after the First World War and the Jews had been convenient victims to blame.

Had he forgotten that they, too, had served in the war? Had died, got maimed? Had returned home with honors and iron crosses? Of course he had, all of this had been purposefully blocked from the public awareness by possibly the vilest member of Hitler's cabinet: propaganda minister Goebbels. She shrugged, since it wouldn't do any good to try and make Wilhelm see how many lies he'd been fed throughout his life.

"... but I also realized that there's nothing I can do. If I refuse my job, they'll just shoot me and someone else will do it."

"That's your solution? Do nothing?"

He sighed with resignation. "I have thought a lot since taking up this job and I'm thoroughly fed up with the cruelties, but when I suggested to maybe not whip the inmates, Allgeier said in no uncertain terms that I would join them if he ever hears such subversive talk again."

"You could give information to the Résistance ?"

"And help them kill my compatriots? That's out of the question!"

She almost felt sorry for him, since deep down in his soul he was a good man, but he was too deluded, complacent, or even cowardly to act according to his conscience. He was caught in his role as a cog in the wheel, unable to break out and change the course of history.

CHAPTER 36

The next morning Wilhelm left for the office and she still had no idea what she should do. Her task was to lure Reiner, Wilhelm and Allgeier into the upper floor of a certain restaurant, wait for everyone to be seated, and then come up with an excuse to leave the room. She was supposed to bar the door behind her and get herself to safety before… she squeezed her eyes shut, unwilling to think about what would happen then.

As she pulled on her stockings, her gaze fell on the black apparatus on its table by the wall and she smiled. She might not look like Annegret, but she certainly sounded like her. For weeks she'd practiced using Anne's high-pitched tone, imitating both the modulation and the usage of words and even Wilhelm had congratulated her for her perfect imitation of his sister.

Before she lost her courage, she jumped from the chaise longue, picked up the phone receiver and dialed the number of the SS headquarters.

"SS headquarters," the receptionist answered.

"Good morning, my name is Annegret Huber and I would like to speak with my brother, Obersturmführer Reiner Huber."

"Let me see if I can locate him." The receptionist put her on mute, undoubtedly using the other line to call Reiner. It took only a minute, until it clicked and she spoke again. "I'm very sorry, the Obersturmführer is in an important meeting and cannot be disturbed."

"Well, would you please give him the message to urgently call his sister at this number." She gave Wilhelm's number, hoping Reiner wouldn't recognize it, or if he did, he wouldn't get the idea to stop by.

"Certainly. *Auf Wiederhören.*"

"*Auf Wiederhören.*" Margarete placed the receiver on the cradle, her hands trembling. She would feel relieved when all of this was over. Wilhelm came to her mind. Since he'd professed his love for her last night, the hammering guilt grew bigger with every passing minute. How could she betray him in such a vile manner and be responsible for his death? Was one person's life worth more than another one's? And who got to decide which person was allowed to live? Even if someone was evil, shouldn't only God be the one to take a life? Did human beings have the right to set themselves up as judges over life or death? Who was she to violate the sixth commandment 'Thou shalt not kill'? Wouldn't that put her on the same level as the Nazis?

She shook her head, trying to shove the doubts away. Just because he loved her, didn't make him a good person. Nobody who moved up the ladder in the SS was without blood on his hands. He might not agree with what the Nazis did, but he also didn't work against them. He wasn't an innocent.

The tick-tock of the mantle clock annoyed her and she stood up to walk into the bathroom to put on some makeup. She had to make a stunning first impression on the men, if she wanted her plan to work. Just as she finished putting black mascara to her eyelashes, the ringing of the telephone cut through the silence.

She started and rushed into the living room, where she came to a skidding halt in front of the apparatus. She took one deep breath in an attempt to calm herself and get into Annegret's head. Then she squared her shoulders, smiled, and grabbed the receiver. "Annegret Huber."

"Anne, it's me, Reiner. I thought I'd never get to talk to you."

In one instant, her nerves were gone and she actually became his sister. "Wilm phoned me to let me know you're in Paris, so I raced back here as fast as I could. I wouldn't want to miss the chance to meet up with you for anything in the world."

"That sounds strange coming from the woman who fled Berlin and didn't even bother to show up at our parents' funeral."

So, he's still furious. "I'm so sorry, I wasn't myself after the bombing." Margarete's memory returned to the day that had changed her life for good. "I was right next to them, but stumbled and got knocked out by a blow to my head. When I came to, I was lying in a small cave beneath the staircase that had folded into a triangle like a piece of paper. It was so awful. The staircase saved my life, but when I crawled out…" She sobbed for good measure. "Mother and Father were lying next to each other. Dead. I've never seen anyone dead before and I couldn't think clearly. I just wanted to get away." She sobbed some more.

Reiner sighed into the phone. "It was awful for all of us, but you really should have come to see Erika and me. We would have helped you to get over this."

"I realize that now. Look, are you free tonight? We could go to this wonderful little French restaurant I recently found. It's a hidden gem, and does have the best French cuisine in all of Paris."

"Good idea."

"Is eight o'clock suitable for you? And let me bring a lovely girlfriend of mine as a way of saying sorry?"

"Well, that sounds good. I have to return to my meeting now."

"I'll give the address to your secretary and will meet you there. Eight o'clock sharp." She hung up and shouted "Yes" into the empty room. She'd done it. One down, two to go.

Next, she called Wilhelm and asked him to meet her at seven in the apartment, because she had an idea how to deal with

Reiner without exposing herself. She also convinced him to invite his counterpart at Drancy, Kriminalkommisar Allgeier, to the restaurant. He wasn't happy at first and only agreed when she said they might need a neutral person present who had never met her as either Annegret or Margarete.

After that phone call, she flopped onto the chaise longue, more depleted than if she had been climbing the Eiffel Tower. Being a conspirator and resister was beyond exhausting and she had no idea how a glamorous woman like Paulette did it all the time.

She spent the rest of the day going over her plan, other than when she snuck out to meet a contact person to let her know that everything was set up for the night. After that, she returned to the apartment and changed into the evening gown Wilhelm had bought for her when she first arrived.

Tender feelings rushed through her as she caressed the silky-soft material of the bright red dress she'd worn for the New Year's party at Hotel Meurice. She turned in front of the mirror, trying to decide if this particular dress was too glamorous for the occasion, when the door behind her clicked open and Wilhelm came inside.

"Gorgeous!" He dropped his briefcase and kicked the door shut with his boot, before he came behind her and wrapped his arms around her shoulders, while pressing his cheek against hers and observing the two of them in the mirror.

As her gaze caught his, a delicious shiver ran through her veins and she relaxed into his arms. The dress had definitely been the correct choice. And the red color would make sure nobody overlooked her when everything was over. What a shame that dress would suffer.

"You must be the most beautiful woman in Paris." He took her by the shoulders and turned her around to press a passionate kiss on her lips. The sensations it evoked made her lightheaded and she had difficulty extricating herself from his embrace. This was not the time to delve into her overwhelming feelings for him. She had a job to do.

"You'll need to put on your dress uniform," she said matter-of-factly, hoping he wouldn't notice that she was just barely holding onto sanity and one single word by him would have her back in his arms, forgetting everything but the two of them existed in this world.

"Aye, aye, captain," he said, mocking her. "So what is the plan?"

She couldn't tell him the truth. "I phoned Reiner to make the dinner plans tonight, but you will present me as Anne's friend Lieselotte."

"What if he recognizes you?"

That was the one detail that might derail the entire plan, and she'd given it much thought. Reiner only knew her as his parents' maid in drab clothing, with lackluster and shock-headed hair, and the yellow star pinned to her chest. The red gown, the much-too-bright makeup, the elaborate hairdo, she'd put everything in place for him not to be reminded of her former self. But her biggest weapon was her voice, since she'd adopted a bored upper-class nasal tone for her role as Lieselotte.

"He might see the resemblance, but I don't think he'll guess."

Wilhelm frowned. "I still don't like it. It's much too dangerous."

"Wilm. Please, we must do this. It's the only way out. And you know your brother, he'll be too smitten by a pretty face to do anything but salivate."

"And… what happens when Anne doesn't appear?"

A solution occurred to her in that very instant. "Then you excuse yourself, pretending to go and fetch her."

"That will never work. How long do you think he'll wait, before he gets suspicious?"

"It will work, I promise." She couldn't do this any longer. It was if someone had lifted a veil and she could suddenly see clearly.

There was no doubting, no vacillating, it was clear as crystal glass; she loved Wilhelm with her entire being: body, heart and soul. She simply couldn't send the man she loved to his death. "Please, Wilm, I beg you. I need to string him along just for a while… Can you just say hello to Reiner and Allgeier, and then leave the restaurant to fetch Annegret? Please?"

He gave her a long and scrutinizing stare, and she felt as if he could see right through her.

"Please. I promise, everything will work out."

"Alright."

CHAPTER 37

Margarete and Wilhelm arrived in front of the restaurant at the same time as Reiner and Allgeier. She felt bold and courageous in her red gown as she stepped out of the taxi and her only worry was whether Wilhelm would adhere to the plan and save himself.

Reiner spotted them and came over, stepping a bit closer than was socially acceptable. "Wilhelm, who is this lovely young lady you've been hiding from me?"

"You must be Reiner." Margarete raised her hand for him to kiss. "I'm Lieselotte. Anne has told me so many things about you, I couldn't wait to finally meet you in person."

"I hope she said only good things." It took a load off her mind, when Reiner bent down to kiss her hand and she used the opportunity to shoot Wilhelm a warning glance.

"Only the best."

"Where is she, by the way?"

"She'll be here in a moment. She wasn't ready yet when we left," Wilhelm said.

"That sounds like our sister. Always late."

Margarete gave an amused giggle.

"May I introduce you to Kriminalkommisar Allgeier from the Gestapo?" Reiner said.

Despite the cold fear creeping up her spine, she managed a pleasant smile and said, "Nice to meet you, Herr Kriminalkommisar."

"Please, call me Hans." He bent down to kiss her hand.

"With the greatest pleasure."

"Shall we go inside?" Wilhelm asked, visibly distressed.

She sidled up to him and said, "Don't worry about Anne, she'll get here as soon as she can, and if not, you can go and fetch her."

Inside the restaurant, they were greeted by the owner and led to a table in the corner. That was not what had been agreed with Armand. He'd instructed to reserve the *separé* on the second floor so as to make sure none of the men could leave the room.

"Mademoiselle, may I take your coat?" the owner said and when he helped her out of it, he whispered, "There was a delay, you need to buy us some time."

She slightly bowed her head to show that she'd understood, while her insides were in turmoil. All she wanted, was to get this ghastly occasion behind her, but instead now she had to make conversation for who knew how long. Damn Armand!

She was seated between Reiner and Wilhelm, with Hans sitting opposite her, who was wearing the field gray uniform of the SD-Sicherheitsdienst and had his blond hair slicked back with Brylcreem in the fashionable way. Despite his good looks and pleasant manners, she shivered every time his gray eyes locked on hers, because she imagined the cold expression of those same eyes should they ever have the misfortune to meet in the Avenue Foch.

"Lieselotte, tell us, what are you doing in Paris?" Hans asked.

She forced herself to give a silly giggle. "So far, I have been very busy enjoying all this wonderful city has to offer, but I want to do my bit for the war effort and take on a job. You wouldn't have any suggestions for me?"

Wilhelm gave her a kick against her shin beneath the table.

"What are your talents, beautiful Fräulein?" Hans was in full flirting mode and she decided to take advantage of this to make conversation until the waiter gave her the agreed sign that the upstairs room was prepared.

"I'm afraid my typing isn't very good, but I could certainly be a switchboard operator," she suggested. Dodging further potentially dangerous questions about her past or her reason to be in Paris, she moved the conversation into safer waters and talked about the beauty of the city, including the Eiffel Tower and the Arc de Triomphe, while she was sweating blood on the inside.

Wilhelm came to her aid, extolling the virtues of the city of love, and together they kept Hans and Reiner entertained, until the waiter finally arrived with the information that the table upstairs was ready for them. She would have kissed him with relief if that wouldn't have destroyed her cover story.

As they got up, Reiner put his hand on her hip and whispered into her ear, "You remind me of someone, are you sure we haven't met before?"

Margarete had difficulties standing still under his unwelcome touch that brought back horrible memories, but she managed to whisper back, "I'm sure I would remember a handsome and powerful man like you."

"I have a spacious hotel room with a king size bed," he said and let his hand travel down her back to rest on her behind.

Closing her eyes for a split-second, she breathed in, telling herself that if she did her job well, he'd never be able to abuse her—or any other woman for that matter—again.

"Obersturmführer Huber!" someone called and when Margarete turned around to look at the man, she felt her knees go wobbly. Ludwig Greiner who'd flirted with her at the New Year's party in the Hotel Meurice approached their party. And of all things she had to wear the same dress tonight! There wasn't a chance in hell he wouldn't recognize her as Annegret Huber.

Frantically searching for a way out, she quickly said to Reiner, "I need to powder my nose, I'll be upstairs with you in a minute."

Then she escaped toward the bathroom and leaned over the sink, retching with fear. After waiting a few minutes, she slipped out of the restroom, hoping that Reiner was already upstairs with the other two men. But when she climbed the stairs, Wilhelm was waiting for her.

"You have to leave. This whole charade is too dangerous."

She shook her head. "I can't. But *you* need to leave. Once everyone is settled, I will ask about Annegret and you offer to go and fetch her."

"And what will I do then? We both know she's dead, Margarete." He was so close to her, she could smell the scent of his shaving cream. If only she could throw herself into his arms and ask him to take her somewhere safe. Unfortunately there was no safe place for her, not as long as Reiner lived.

"Please, you must trust me. Everything will work out. And we'll be safe."

Realization flashed in his eyes. "This is crazy."

"It's the only way."

"He's still my brother, I can't allow that to happen."

She already regretted warning him, but it was too late. "I hate that it comes to this, but it wasn't my choice. There are people who know and they forced my hand."

He leaned against the wall and shook his head in utter disbelief. When he looked at her again, he seemed to have aged at least a decade. "The Résistance. I should have known. Gerald is the traitor. And Paulette…" He shook his head. "They've planned this for a long time. I was so stupid. I have to stop this."

She shook her head. "You can't. Nobody can. They are watching from across the street and it will happen regardless of what you and I do, but you can still save yourself, if you disappear in time."

"How could you agree to this? Have people killed?"

"How could you agree to becoming commandant of Drancy? Aren't there many more people killed every day?" she spat at him, angry that he still wouldn't leave his ideology behind.

The despair was evident in his face. "You're right. I don't deserve to live. But you…" He looked at her with so much love and pride in his eyes, it touched her very soul. "Will you promise me that if you survive, you'll take the Huber fortune and do good with it?"

"I can't possibly."

"You must. Promise!"

She sighed, since she had wanted to leave Annegret Huber behind for good after this evening, but Wilhelm said exactly what Armand had mentioned too. She could do so much good with all that money, it would be outright irresponsible to renounce it. Perhaps it was time for her to do what Wilhelm never could: to stop thinking only about herself and play a role in the fight for good.

"I promise." She was about to press a kiss on his cheek, when Hans came to the landing and looked down. "Ah, there you are, Lieselotte. What took you so long?"

She didn't reply, but clutched her purse in her hand and climbed the stairs as elegantly as she could. Just when she thought it couldn't get worse, she entered the room and saw Reiner standing side by side with Ludwig Greiner. Only Wilhelm's hand on the small of her back prevented her from stumbling backwards down the staircase.

"I hope you don't mind that I took the liberty of inviting Ludwig to join us for dinner. He seems to be a great admirer of our sister."

Ludwig smiled his brightest smile and took a step toward her, saying, "Annegret, it's such a pleasure to meet you again. You have me enchanted."

Margarete watched the blood draining from Reiner's head and then returning to turn his face a dark shade of crimson as his gaze darted between her, Ludwig, and Wilhelm, who was still standing behind her with his hand on the small of her back.

Suddenly time passed in slow motion and she heard Reiner's voice in a peculiar drawn-out way shouting, "What are you talking about? This woman is not my sister."

"Please, Reiner, this is a misunderstanding…" Wilhelm's voice cut through the rushing blood in Margarete's ears.

"You!" Reiner seemed ready to punch his brother, but at the last moment stopped himself and turned toward Margarete, who stood frozen in shock, unable to prevent him from coming within inches of her and glaring into her eyes. "Why are you here and who are you really?"

Too frightened to control her voice, she said, "I'm Lieselotte von Andechs."

A cruel light passed through his eyes. "No, you're not. In fact, now I know why you seemed so familiar. You're that Jewish bitch who worked for my father."

She knew in this moment, that this was the end. Her end.

CHAPTER 38

Wilhelm was petrified. His worst nightmare had come true and he was caught between his brother and Margarete.

His own flesh and blood versus the woman he loved. Whatever he did, he would sentence one of them to death. It was an awful quagmire and he couldn't think of a way out. Moments later, his heart took over and he pushed Margarete aside, positioning himself between her and his brother, thus effectively shielding her with his own body. Without thinking, he drew his pistol, pointing it at Ludwig and said, "If anyone moves, he's dead."

The look of betrayal on Reiner's face was almost comical. "You can't be serious about this, Wilhelm."

"I am."

"Come on, I appreciate she's a looker and has evidently warmed your bed for many nights while pretending to be our sister, but there are plenty of beautiful women, especially in Paris."

"It's not like that. I love her."

"You're stupid. She's a Jewess, there's nothing lovable about her."

"She's one thousand times more valuable a human being than you are," Wilhelm shouted, his finger on the trigger.

"Wilhelm, I tell you what. You put that pistol away, and I'll make sure this woman disappears and nobody will ever talk about this little episode again. Right?" Reiner looked at Ludwig and

Hans, who both nodded their agreement. "It'll all stay between the four of us and won't even impact your career. What do you think?"

Wilhelm was sweating profusely. Despite having joined the SS many years ago, he'd never killed anyone and he certainly didn't want to start today, but he had only one single thought in his mind: protecting Margarete's life at all cost.

While he couldn't bring himself to kill his comrades, he could certainly wait for fate to take its course. Still holding the others at gunpoint, he said to Margarete, "You leave now and do what you must."

"No, please. I won't."

"There is no other way. Go. Now."

Seconds later he heard her slip out of the room and lock the door from the outside. His arm sank down and he let the pistol drop to the floor, where Hans caught it with a masterly full-length dive, while Ludwig jumped at him, turning Wilhelm's arm behind his back and holding it there with painful pressure.

"Little brother, what was that stupidity?" Reiner said and made to open the door to go after Margarete, but found it locked. "What the hell is going on? The bitch has locked the door!"

He turned around and raced to the windows, tearing open the thick blackout curtains, just to find the windows were nailed shut with wooden planks.

"This is a trap!" he yelled, just when the sound of a thousand guns and cannons burst upon them. Flashes of fire and explosions rocked the room, sending large pieces of the ceiling crashing down upon the occupants. Wilhelm met his brother's eyes for one brief moment before he felt himself sliding toward his doom. *Now she's free.*

*

Long after the dust settled and the Germans began to sift through the rubble, looking for survivors, a solitary figure stood at the edge of the street a block away, tears streaming down her face.

"We need to go now," a person cloaked in a dark shirt and pants called to her from the shadows.

Margarete nodded and then, with one last look at the building where her heart had just been shattered, much as the concrete and plaster had crumbled beneath the weight of the bomb, she turned and set off to begin her new life. She would never forget Wilhelm and how he'd sacrificed his life for her.

EPILOGUE

Margarete stood at the window in Wilhelm's apartment and looked down on the street. Madame Badeaux had been eager to tell her that since the main tenant for whom the apartment had been requisitioned was dead, Margarete couldn't stay there. Supposedly because she was a civilian—but in reality, because she was one of the hated Boche. Although the woman hadn't actually expressed the last part, it had been clearly written all over her face.

Margarete took out a match to light the two candles in the twin candleholders, her heart filled with grief. Despite all his flaws, she'd loved him and, in the end, he had redeemed himself by offering his life to save hers. It was a sacrifice she would never forget.

So many people had already died in this war, and many more were still suffering. After Reiner's visit, she knew with certainty that Hitler planned to extinguish the Jewish race and to eradicate every trace of its existence. Her heart grew weary at the realization that there was nothing she could do to stop his vile scheme... So why did she feel guilty?

The Résistance had urged her to work for them, relaying valuable information they could use to sabotage infrastructure and kill German soldiers. She shivered. As much as she hated the Nazis, she didn't want to assume God's role and decide who would live and who would die.

In her mind though, she knew it was the correct thing to do, something that might shorten the war and ultimately save thousands of lives. But her heart wouldn't comply. How could she cause further grief and sorrow? Leave widows and orphans behind? Tear families apart? On the other hand, how could she not help? How could she not do everything in her power to end the killing of her race?

I'm just one person. It won't make a difference anyway.

She gave a deep sigh, knowing she was lying to herself. Armand and Paulette had scolded her for being shortsighted, selfish and even downright stupid, but Margarete simply couldn't do what was expected of her. Now she stood at the window, her suitcase packed with the clothes and the beloved statue that Wilm had bought for her, the valuables—except for the two candleholders—sold, ready to leave Paris and live someplace far away where Hitler and his war wouldn't reach her.

Although… Wilhelm's words echoed in her ears *Will you promise me that if you survive, you'll take the Huber fortune and do good with it?*

"Is having other people killed really doing good?" she asked the empty room.

Her conscience answered. *You can't just run away and bury your head in the sand.*

Turning around to look at the empty place, thinking about the past months, she remembered all the people who'd lent her a helping hand, without whom she wouldn't be standing here today. The candles cast flickering shadows on the walls and a sudden loneliness engulfed her. No human being could exist on their own, and she was no different. Maybe it was time to repay the kindness and help others? To honor Wilhelm's last wish?

Her gaze fell on the telephone and she had an idea. It was crazy and even dangerous, but if it worked out, she'd inherit the entire Huber estate and would be a rich woman.

A woman who could truly make a difference. Not by getting the perpetrators killed, but by using her fortune to help those in need. As she knew from her own experience, getting to a safe place was costly. Fake papers, train tickets, clothing, accommodation, food... everything required money. And she'd be in a position to provide just that. Yes, she'd give money to Jews in need, enabling them to escape Nazi Germany.

How exactly this would happen, she didn't yet know, but she was determined to do good. Wilhelm's sacrifice and everything that came before and after would not be in vain. If she could save but one life, as Wilhelm selflessly had hers, then it would be worth it.

She turned toward the window again, the burning candles casting the room in a warm light. She grabbed her suitcase, leaned down and blew softly to extinguish the flames, before she left the apartment with a newfound mission in her heart.

A LETTER FROM MARION

Dear Reader,

Thank you so much for reading *A Light in the Window*. If you did enjoy it, and want to keep up to date with all my latest releases, just sign up at the following link. Your email address will never be shared and you can unsubscribe at any time.

www.bookouture.com/marion-kummerow

I first had the idea for Margarete's story when I was asked to contribute a short story to an anthology commemorating the seventy-fifth anniversary of Pearl Harbor. The short story is called *Turning Point* and tells in more detail about the bombing and Margarete's escape, taking on Annegret's identity. But ever since, she wouldn't let me go and I was intrigued what might have happened to her after arriving at Aunt Heidi's house. Would she be found out? What would happen if someone did? Would they betray her? Blackmail her? How is it to live under a different identity, repudiating your race, your family, even your core beliefs?

When I told my wonderful editor Isobel Akenhead at Bookouture about the idea, she instantly loved the premise and gave me the nudge needed to finally write a full book about Margarete's story.

As always the book is a mixture of historic events and fiction. All the characters including Margarete, Wilhelm, and Reiner are entirely fictional, but I have taken great care to make them as realistic as possible. I even visited Berlin and Leipzig several times to get a feeling for the cities, before travel restrictions were imposed in 2020.

This is also the reason why I couldn't travel to Paris (obviously exclusively for research, because who wants to visit Paris anyway ☺) and instead had to rely on my memories from previous visits. Thankfully, the wonderful Genevieve Montcombroux, who lived through the occupation in France as a child, graciously offered to check my manuscript for historical accuracy. She helped me to add some *couleur locale*, including restaurant names. The restaurants mentioned in the book all actually existed back then. Genevieve also alerted me to the fact that all Parisian apartment buildings had to have a concierge, so I introduced nosy Madame Badeaux to the story.

Since Margarete works in the university library in Leipzig (which is absolutely worth visiting alone for its stunning architectural beauty), I had to include the topic of banned books. You might already know that in May 1933 public book burnings took place. Initially they weren't ordered by the authorities, but organized mostly by students who wanted to promote the Nazi ideology.

Gradually this awful practice was institutionalized by making lists of so-called *verbrennungswürdige Bücher*, books to be burned, which had to be gathered and put on the stake. Later, all public libraries were tasked to revise their inventory and remove all banned books. The scientific libraries, mostly those at the universities, while included in the "book cleaning," didn't have to burn the books. Instead they were ordered to segregate "demoralizing or subversive" literature to be kept in a special room. These books could only be borrowed by academic personnel or otherwise trustworthy people for scientific purposes.

It may surprise you, but the Gestapo indeed had national headquarters in Leipzig's *Deutsche Bücherei*, the national library, where they oversaw the "banned book business" and kept a meticulous record of who had requested what book for which purpose—although it is improbable that librarians actually went there every week to hand over a list like Margarete does, which I introduced to have her ultimately meet Horst Richter.

Another thing where I took a little liberty is the date of the bombing in which the Huber family died, because I wanted it to happen just before the attack on Pearl Harbor. In reality, the last raid on Berlin by the RAF was done on November 7 1941. During this raid, 21 out of 160 bombers were shot down. After the November disaster, the RAF concentrated their efforts on easier targets, especially the heavily industrialized Ruhr area that was nearer and less well defended. It wasn't until January 1943, when the RAF received brand-new four-motor bombers like the Avro Lancaster, that they started another bombing campaign on Berlin.

One of the moral dilemmas Margarete has to deal with is the rather philosophical question whether one human is worth more than another one. Being the one who is oppressed, she obviously thinks that her life is as valuable as that of Annegret. But what if she's the one who gets to decide who dies and who lives? Can a human being ever have this right? And does condemning a person to death put her on the same level as the Nazis she hates so much?

My own grandfather fought over this issue when he planned to assassinate propaganda minister Goebbels, which I've written about in the trilogy, "Love and Resistance in WW2 Germany." As you know from history, his assassination attempt was never realized, but not for lack of planning.

Reading my grandfather's letters to his mother I got a glimpse into his mind and how he pondered this issue for a long time. While he wasn't a Christian, he still believed in the existence of a higher power and asked himself, whether one human has the right to kill another one, even if it possibly saves a thousand lives. Is guilt weighed in numbers? Does saving many erase your guilt for killing one? I believe he never came to a final conclusion on this question, but he decided that he would accept the responsibility for his actions, not only in this life, but also in the next one, which is exactly what Margarete does, too.

In the end she accepts that to end this war, sacrifices have to be made and her helping to kill others is one of them.

I hope you loved *A Light in the Window* and if you did I would be very grateful if you could write a review. I'd love to hear what you think, and it makes such a difference helping new readers to discover one of my books for the first time.

I love hearing from my readers—you can get in touch on my Facebook page, through Twitter, Goodreads or my website.

Thanks,
Marion

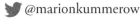 AutorinKummerow

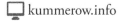 @marionkummerow

kummerow.info